CW00500419

ACKNOWLI

I am deeply indebted to a number of individuals who read early drafts of the novel. I will be forever grateful to Debi Alper for her acute insight into various aspects of the book. Linda Cook, Helen Dhillon, Margaret Jones and Susan Kent gave freely of their time and also helped to shape the book. Last but not least, my profound gratitude goes to Amy Durant at Sapere Books for her considerable editorial skills, and the grace and wisdom with which she helped to hone the final narrative. My heartfelt thanks to all of them.

'*History makes us who we are*'
Banner unfurled by fans at the Leicester City versus Swansea
football match, King Power Stadium, Leicester, 24 April 2016

'*There is such a thing as evil which can exist without causation. The
black heart which takes joy in being black. In almost every kind of herd
animal, there is the phenomenon of the rogue.*'
John D. MacDonald, *Cinnamon Skin*

PROLOGUE

The electric impulses in Geeta Mehta's brain weren't firing properly anymore. She squeezed her eyes shut till they hurt. Trying to dredge up a memory from the deepest part of her brain. Through the blackness. Of a place or a person she knew. Neurons flashed and sparkled, eventually linked with each other, and a warm, colourful fragment appeared behind each retina. Her mother's face smiling at her, lovingly pinching her cheek. Her father offering her his soft brown hand with long fingers as they walked to school when she was a little girl.

The image suddenly shattered into millions of pixels, like an erratic satellite signal scattering and bouncing the digital fragments within a television screen. The kaleidoscope of swirling colours, blue, yellow, red, orange and violet, slowly going round. And round. And round.

Geeta desperately willed her brain to drag the pixels together again. *Come on, come on. Please.* And the scene of her eighteenth birthday party came to life. When was it? Two months ago? Or was it three? An upmarket country hotel. A large reception room with a deep maroon carpet. Her friends smiling as she entered the room. The young men in dinner jackets and black ties. The young women in expensive dresses or skirts. All gathered around her. 'Happy birthday, Geeta,' 'You look wonderful,' as her father led her towards the top table where the cake stood with its pink and white icing sugar and yellow marzipan roses. She was dressed in a pink *shalwar kameez* with a long-flowing matching scarf. Blowing out the eighteen candles. The champagne. The mouth-watering food, mainly Indian and Chinese, with the occasional slices of pizza and roast chicken.

And then the dancing to the loud pop music played by the DJ her father had hired, bhangra, some popular Bollywood beats, Beyonce, Lady Gaga, Taylor Swift, Ariana Grande, the laughing, the hugging, and the endless love bathing her. Her friends asking her to play on her violin which had appeared from nowhere and she played the opening tune from *Fiddler on the Roof* and they clapped and they clapped and Geeta bowed and bowed and —

Zzzzzzzttt.

Nothing.

Blackness.

A short circuit in her brain. The colourful, vibrant, happy images shut down.

'No!' she croaked. Or did she? She wasn't sure.

The sparks flashed again, the colours swirled round and round and the neurons fused together again.

And the image appeared in the pale yellowish-orange cotton wool resting on her retina. She stared at the cream-coloured letter with black type on the thick A4 paper. The letter telling her she'd been offered a place to study for a degree in music at the Guildhall School of Music and Drama in London.

Dear Miss Mehta,

We are pleased to offer you a place on our four-year honours degree course in music…

She didn't even read the rest. *Yesss!* Punching the air with her clenched fist. Her mother and father beaming. Wide-eyed. Full of love. Arms outstretched. About to hug her. To say, 'Well — '

Zzzzzzzttt.

Another short circuit as the pixels flew off in all directions.

What was happening to her? She must be sitting on a chair because there was a hard wooden surface beneath her. She forced her eyes open and hot needle points burned behind each retina.

Geeta wanted to shield her eyes from the dull light but couldn't move her hands or arms. Her leaden, bowed head felt it would never lift up again. Her arms rested on the discoloured and chipped wooden supports of an old carving chair. She stared at them as if they belonged to somebody else. Tried moving them again but could not.

Geeta slowly squeezed her fingers and looked at them. Saw the thin plastic bands around her wrists, tied around the arms of the chair. Panic rose. The chest tighter. Her breathing faster. Heavier. She looked at her pale brown thighs. Oh God, she was wearing only her white knickers and nothing else. She wanted to scream but her throat felt as if she'd swallowed a hundred razor blades, her mouth dry as sandpaper, her tongue swollen.

It was so very cold. She shivered. Goose pimples formed on her arms. Her left leg was painful. She tried to stretch it. Could not. She bent down, stared at it. The ankle had a strip of plastic around it tied to the leg of the chair. She looked at her right thigh. Tried to raise the leg. Yes, it moved. She put her weight on the free leg and tried to stand up with the chair. Could not. The chair's legs were attached to metal plates screwed to the ground.

Geeta lifted her head and looked around. A trickle of cold sweat streaked down from her armpit. Bile reached the back of her throat and she wanted to retch. She swallowed, the pain reached down her throat. Wrenched the top of her stomach.

She tried to relax, to ease the pain by breathing slowly.

In… Out… In… Out… In…

It was quiet, apart from a slow, steady mechanical humming. There was a cool draught behind her.

She sensed she was in some sort of cellar or basement, with her chair towards the back wall. About three or four metres in front of her was a solid metal door with a narrow rectangular viewing hatch at the top and a wider hatch at the bottom. Big enough to pass a plate of food through. Like a prison. The brick walls were uneven, painted a dirty white. Mould grew between the ceiling and the walls. The basement was damp and dank. She breathed in the musty smell. Sweaty feet and old socks.

Trowel marks were gouged on the hard cement floor. A hint of jasmine and sandalwood mingled with the smell of the socks and sweat. She moved her throbbing head gently to the right. In the corner was half a potato. Stuck into it were two incense sticks. Like the fragrant scent of home as her mother lit a *diva*, a cotton wick dipped in cooking oil in a brass holder, at the small shrine in the lounge to pray to the Hindu gods. Her mother would light the incense sticks, waft the smoke over the portraits and statues of the gods, and place them in a small silver holder with tiny holes for each stick.

Diagonally opposite was her dark blue rucksack. Resting at an angle on the dirty, uneven floor. Covered with laminated photographs of Adele and Beyonce, Jacqueline Du Pré, the cellist, and Sarah Chang, the Korean-American violinist. And the Stars and Stripes. She'd always wanted to go to America. See the Grand Canyon, the Big Apple, San Francisco.

But it was not to be. Her books were strewn from the rucksack, books with her name, books with scribbles and doodles, her Samsung tablet, pens, sheets for composing music. And her mobile phone. It was either switched off, or the battery had run down.

She shivered, then whimpered as she saw the single bed against the wall. Trying to blank out the memories of what had occurred on it.

All four walls had mirrors stuck to them, almost to the ceiling. Through the hazy light and the cobwebs in her brain, through the pain behind her eyes and the painful and insistent hammering of a thousand hammers in her head, Geeta saw multiple images of herself and everything else in the cellar.

What was she doing here? The last thing she remembered was walking down the usual street on her way to college. The shops had not yet opened because it was only eight o'clock on a bright sunny morning in late November.

As she walked past a white transit van, its side door flew open. A hand grabbed her mouth. It held a piece of cloth. An acrid smell. She couldn't even scream, the rag smothering her as she was dragged into the van. Her whole world had changed for ever. In an instant. She'd woken up here.

Geeta was exhausted. And desperately thirsty. Her bottle of Highland Spring water nestled in the webbing at the side of her rucksack. Oh God, if only she could reach it.

She started weeping. Then sobbed, her stomach muscles cramping.

She must have fallen asleep because she was woken by the heavy thud of the metal door banging against the brick wall. A red light blinked above the small camera in the corner above the door. She stared at the threadbare, plaited black electric cable hanging from the roof beyond the door. A dimly lit bulb, swinging slowly. Like a pendulum. Throwing a ghostly orange light on the brick wall beyond. An urgent cold breeze blew a few strands of Geeta's hair onto her cheek.

Must get out, must get out. She forced herself up from the chair. Could stand up. The plastic ties, snipped from her wrists and leg, nestled on the uneven ground.

Her calf muscles cramped and throbbed. She looked again at the open door. *Must get out.* Her head hurt. Her eyes tried to focus. She breathed in deeply. Rushed towards the open door.

A black shape. Lurking in the dark corner to the right. Moving. Slowly.

Geeta hurtled towards freedom.

The shape lunged at her.

Geeta's left arm stretched out, longing to touch the daylight. To follow the flecks of dust as they glided towards the opening in the roof.

Longing for freedom.

CHAPTER 1

Saturday, early December. I had woken up in a cold sweat at about three in the morning and kept tossing and turning, staring at the ceiling, staring at the walls. My troubled sleep had disturbed Fernando (had I screamed?) and I could hear him pacing up and down in the room next door.

The shortest day of the year was a couple of weeks away so it didn't get light till way past seven o'clock. It was a bright day, some cirrus clouds high up in the sky, lots of blue for this time of year. *Be grateful for small mercies.* I swallowed another couple of paracetamols to ease my headache, grateful for a weekend off as a relatively new detective inspector. Inspector Rohan Sharma. *Look Ma, top of the world.* Yeah, well, pull the other one.

I had agreed to pick up the kids at nine in the morning. As I approached what was once *our* house in a well-to-do suburb in south-east Leicester, the sunlight poured in through the windscreen, pale and cold.

The kids were pleased to see me but Faye was, as ever, cool and distant. I stared into her eyes during the forced exchange of pleasantries and wondered how two people who had once been so much in love could be so far apart now.

Faye had graduated from Cambridge with a first in English, had then become a chartered accountant with a big firm and a big salary in the City of London but decided it wasn't for her. She wanted to mould young minds and characters and make a difference and so wanted to teach, especially in inner-city areas. Quite a life and quite an ambition for somebody from rural Lincolnshire. Her parents were happy to say to friends that they enjoyed working with foreigners but could not bear the thought of their daughter sleeping with one. Especially one from a working-class background in Leicester. My parents weren't exactly overjoyed about the situation either. But Faye and I had been inseparable and nothing was going to come between us.

I drove along the inner ring road heading west to the zoo. Not the first choice for a cold December day. Well, what else can a father do for a whole day with two kids? Yasmin, aged twelve, was sitting in the front seat wearing designer sunglasses, even though the sun was behind us.

'Do I look cool in these, Dad?' she asked.

'Yes, darling, you look cool, as always.'

'Just ignore her, Dad,' Karan, eight, called from the back seat. 'She's got a big head already. Any bigger and the glasses will fall off.'

Yasmin turned round and stuck out her tongue.

As we drove along the dual carriageway, slicing through the heavily built-up areas of offices, public buildings, bus station, indoor shopping centre and university buildings, the castle, museums and the Sikh temple, I reminded the kids of the historical importance of where we were.

Leicester's fame had gone through the stratosphere recently because of the unearthing of King Richard III's skeleton on the site of a council car park, plus the performance of the city's football team in the Premier League. The same stratosphere that the space rockets, meteors and moon rock went through that are now housed at the Leicester's National Space Centre, which attracts thousands of visitors every year.

Richard was killed at the Battle of Bosworth on 22 August 1485, having ridden out of Leicester the day before. We were driving over Bow Bridge with the River Soar flowing calmly and smoothly beneath us. Some believed that Richard's spur hit a large retaining block of stone on the bridge as he crossed it on his way to battle and an old woman prophesied that his head would hit the same stone on the way back. After he was killed in battle his body was placed across the back of a horse, feet hanging down one side, head hanging down the other and he was brought the few miles from Bosworth Field back to Leicester. His head may well have hit the stone in the bridge. Who knows? It was believed his body was buried at the nearby Grey Friars Friary and some thought that Henry VII ordered it to be thrown into the River Soar. Others thought that his tomb and bones were lost forever when the monasteries were ransacked and destroyed by Henry VIII while a Protestant nation was being created from the ashes.

Yasmin interrupted my flow. 'We're studying Richard at school, Dad. You don't have to go on about it.'

'Yeah, me too,' said Karan. 'But my teacher told us they didn't find the whole skeleton. He said the feet were missing.'

'Yeah, it's because he was de-*feeted* at the Battle of Bosworth.'

Yasmin roared with laughter at my joke, instinctively putting her hand to her mouth to hide the brace. Her dimples were becoming more pronounced. 'How's Fernando, Dad?' she eventually asked.

'He's fine,' I replied.

'Say hello to him from us,' she said.

Karan went back to playing his games on the PSP. The constant *ping, ping, ping* was irritating but I didn't say anything. He was becoming fascinated with technology but it was also making him reclusive and I wasn't sure how to handle it. *Must speak to Faye about it*, I thought, yet again.

The bright sunlight piercing the windscreen didn't help my headache. I wound the window down to breathe in some fresh air. We drove along the road bearing Richard III's name and I wondered what he would have made of the Leicester of today.

I parked the car and bought a guidebook. We strolled through the imposing entrance towards the compound for the two Himalayan snow leopards. We stared through the enormous wall of glass at the leopard, which had emerged from one of the specially constructed caves. It was magnificent, with a soft grey coat and a white belly, covered in brown blotches ringed with black, and a black streak along its back. It glided from rock to rock, sat down, licked its lips and then glared back at us. A long, long way from its home in Central Asia and the Himalayas.

'Dad, when you were growing up in Kenya, did you see wild animals?' asked Karan.

'I was only about five when we came here but I remember seeing some ostriches running along the road, racing Grandad's car. And I saw zebras, gazelles and giraffes.'

We approached the large wooden door of the reptile house but it was locked. A sign said, 'Due to circumstances beyond our control, the Reptile House is temporarily closed.' I looked through one of the square windows in the door. It was dark inside, with subdued lighting, and I could feel the heat and humidity through the gap between the doors.

My mobile rang. My heart sank when I saw the number.

'Inspector Sharma,' I answered.

'Sir, I know it's Saturday but we need you back here,' said the familiar voice from the admin section at headquarters. Major crimes and homicide division. 'A body's been found. Young woman, late teens. And the super wants you as the senior investigating officer, Sir.'

'Are you sure?' I said without thinking. There was a pause on the line. 'Sorry, forget that. Has the site been secured?'

'Being secured now, Sir. Uniforms and other support staff are already on their way. I'm sure Detective Sergeant Shepherd will have things under control.'

It was late morning and I needed to be at the scene. I cut the call and turned to face my children. 'Okay, kids, I'm really sorry. I promise I'll make it up to you but we've got to go back. I've been called into work, something really important. I'm really sorry. I'll get you whatever you want for Christmas.'

'But, Dad, we don't see enough of you as it is,' cried Yasmin. 'How can work be more important than us? It's Saturday. We were enjoying being with you.'

A fist tightened around my heart as her eyes welled up.

'Yasmin, Karan, I'm really sorry. I'll take you to Grandma and Grandad. Please ring Mum and ask her to pick you up from there. You haven't seen Grandma and Grandad for a long time now, have you?'

Karan stared at me from his big brown eyes with their long eyelashes. A look not of resignation, but of deep resentment.

CHAPTER 2

I arrived at a field near one of the main arterial roads south of Leicester. I parked in a layby for lorries, along with the official police cars, vans and other unmarked cars. The biting wind was picking up speed. Blowing in from the south-west. Thick cumulus clouds rolling in and chasing the cold sun away. The skies gradually darkening. I wondered whether it was going to thunder. I put on my thick designer coat and walked along the road, the collar pulled up, shielding my neck and cheeks.

The field, left fallow for the winter, was near the main road, separated from it with dry stone walling and a strip of grass about ten yards wide. At the far side, running perpendicular to the road, a row of mature oak trees lined the boundary, their branches waving with the strengthening wind. I could see a narrow country lane running behind them and onto the main road. Probably not wide enough for motorised vehicles. Furthest away from the road, the field was bordered by another drystone wall. There was a barn near the wall and, on the other side, larger farm buildings housing machinery, ploughs, harrows, tractors and the like. The farmhouse was near these buildings.

Blue and white crime scene tape cordoned off a large part of the land. A roadblock and diversion had already been set up. Much of the open land across the road had been secured. Good preservation of potential evidence across a wide enough area. We could always narrow it down later.

'Hello, Shep. How're you?' I asked Sergeant Jack Shepherd as I approached.

'I'm fine, thanks, Sir. Congratulations on becoming a detective.'

I thanked him, and for the work he had done at the scene so far. 'Where's the body?'

'Under one of the oak trees,' he said, pointing. 'Found by the farmer when he went to get hay from that barn. She's naked. At first, he thought she was a mannequin, thrown over the wall. Nobody's been to see her yet. I didn't want the site contaminated. Oh, by the way she's uh … she's Asian.'

I wasn't sure why he was uncomfortable with this information.

'I've already sent the uniforms out on house-to-house enquiries. But dwellings are isolated round here. I thought you'd want to speak to the farmer. He's in shock. Said the killer had done *strange things* to the body. The forensic investigators are working away. The pathologist is on her way.'

Right on cue, I saw a tall, slim South Asian woman running towards us. Her shoulder-length black hair was parted in the middle and blowing back in the cold breeze. A gold nose stud glinted in her left nostril. She panted a 'hello' and introduced herself as Dr Khan.

Sergeant Shepherd turned towards a young woman standing nearby. 'This is Detective Constable Joy Wheatley, assigned to us.'

I asked Constable Wheatley to liaise with the uniformed officers as they came back from their house-to-house enquiries and told Shep to accompany me to the support cars and vans from the forensic services. Ben Carter, the senior forensic investigator, was present and I nodded to him.

'Shep, Ben and Dr Khan, come with me to look at the body. I'm working on the assumption the perpetrator and victim came into the field from the side of the road. Or from the narrow country path next to the field. From now on, this is to be the only entry and exit point for the scene. Make sure everybody knows that. The crime may have been committed here or it could be a dumping site for the body.'

We zipped up in the white full-length forensic suits and approached the tree under which the body lay. The freezing wind pierced through the suits. My breath felt warm under the white mask and my breathing was laboured. We walked towards the tree, avoiding the pats of cow dung on the uneven ground.

The young woman lay on her back, spread-eagled on the coarse winter grass under the tree. Although naked, she was the only one out of the four of us who didn't have goose pimples.

We crouched in front of her, our knees resting on the square plastic stepping plates used for preserving evidence. The wind blew strands of her shoulder-length black hair across her right cheek and, for a moment, I expected her hand to come up and move them away. A dry oak leaf blew and settled on her right thigh.

Her right arm rested on the ground, hand near her head, palm pointing upward. Her right leg was bent at the knee and pushed up towards the body. Her left leg was similarly bent, the kneecap smashed. Her left arm was stretched out from the shoulder to the elbow and the arm bent back from the body, hand pointing down. There was a symmetry to the position of the arms. The positioning of her elbows and knees indicated the shape of a rectangle.

Her lips were slightly parted revealing even, white teeth. The tip of her tongue was visible. It was tinged red, a sign of trauma and stress before death. Black lipstick had been applied to her parted lips. A trail of dried saliva was visible on the side of her mouth. Flecks of talcum powder were dabbed on both cheeks, covering faint traces of blusher.

Her eyes were open, staring lifelessly at the thick, dark clouds tumbling across the sky above her. Her pupils were pinpricks, as if trying to hide the horror she had experienced. Her long eyelashes remained still in the cold wind. They were thick with mascara and her eyelids had pink eyeshadow with silver flecks. Black kohl painted the bottom and top edges of both her eyes, meeting in a V-shape at each temple like Elizabeth Taylor playing Cleopatra in the Hollywood blockbuster of the 1960s.

Her young skin, without any excess fat, was stretched tight across her middle and her slim hips. Never to bear any of her own children or to suffer and complain about flab and wrinkles.

A life stolen.

Her belly button was painted black, the pupil of a large eye, the iris painted blue. The outer rim of this eye had a thin line of black. If she had been alive, had been told to breathe in, and to pull up her stomach muscles, the eye would have blinked.

Below the mutilated breasts, a few inches down the middle, were four deep cuts, about five or six inches long, running parallel, left to right. Deep enough to expose white flesh. One of the cuts showed a rib. Some caked blood was visible around these cuts so she could still have been alive when this was done to her. There did not appear to be any other obvious cause of death.

As I stood up, I noticed letters carved deep into the bark of the tree trunk. 'A' and 'S' next to each other. And below the letter 'S' was 'H'. About four inches in height, a few millimetres in width and in depth, and freshly carved by the point of a knife or a chisel.

Daylight was rapidly fading and time was of the essence. I asked Dr Khan and Ben Carter to start their work, first by erecting a tent so that no outsiders could gawp and ogle at the body. God knows, there are enough weirdos in this world.

'What d'you think, Shep?' I asked as we stood by the drystone wall.

'Obviously staged,' he said. 'A signature killer and a nasty piece of work. Taunting us with what he's done to that poor young woman.'

'What about the word "ASH"? That's not an ash tree, is it? It's an oak.'

'Yes Sir, it is.'

'Mmmm… I'll go talk with the farmer. Ring HQ, tell them to set up an incident room. One of the medium-sized training rooms, with an interactive digital smartboard so that the whole team can watch video images, CCTV, and so on. We also need a media liaison officer. And get in touch with the missing persons' people. Ask them whether any young Asian women have been reported missing recently.'

I left him to get on with it and walked towards the farmhouse.

CHAPTER 3

The darkness was quickly shrouding the day as I told the officers and support staff at the scene to start winding down for the day. Ben and his team and Dr Khan would continue for as long as they could. Support vehicles powered arc lights for the night, more tents were hoisted up, windbreakers remained in place. A few officers volunteered to stay at the site for the night, helping the crime scene team and Dr Khan. One said he was volunteering so that the poor victim would have as much company as possible, wouldn't feel alone at night and wouldn't be scared. At times like these, even the most highly trained officers can lose a sense of reality. I didn't argue with the sentiment. There was a certain logic to it.

I gunned the car towards Leicester, the V8 Kompressor engine purring. The dipped headlights of my car picked up the cats' eyes in the middle of the road as they stretched into the black distance. High up in the western horizon, four bright stars, each forming the point of a rectangle standing on its side. The constellation Orion. Shimmering.

I was feeling melancholy. The day had promised so much, especially with my children, and had ended up so differently.

I drove across the city boundary, past the railway station, through the centre and stopped at a roundabout. Turning right, my breath was taken away by the thousands of decorative lights hanging from lamp posts along the central reservation and along both sides of the road. As far as the eye could see were lights of varying colours: gold, silver, red, blue, orange. They reflected off my car windows and on the inside of my windscreen as I drove along. The vibrant colours danced and glowed in my rear-view mirror. Diwali, the Hindu Festival of Lights, was almost upon us. And the Golden Mile, in all its glory, was getting ready to welcome the thousands of visitors from all over the country and from distant parts of the world.

I turned down one of the side roads. Late Victorian terraced houses lined both sides, the pavements brightly coloured with traditional *rangoli* patterns, inviting people into houses for Diwali sweetmeats. The aroma of Indian cooking, with a tinge of coriander, mustard seeds and fenugreek, hung heavily in the air, making my mouth water.

I parked and waited while a middle-aged Indian woman pushed a wheelchair past me on the pavement with an elderly man in it, head lolling to one side, mouth dribbling. I put both my palms together in greeting, said, 'Namaste'. The woman nodded and carried on pushing the wheelchair.

My house smelled dank. Through the door in the lounge was the dining room and beyond that the small kitchen. I heard a voice say, 'Welcome home, Rohan.' Then a wolf whistle. I went into the dining room and saw Fernando looking in the mirror. He always fancied himself.

I said, 'Hello Fernando, how're you? I'm sorry I've been gone so long and it's so late.'

He carried on looking in the small round mirror and gave another wolf whistle.

I walked up to him and stroked the top of his head, wondering whether he'd had enough to eat.

Fernando, my African grey parrot, my loyal friend. He has been with me all my life. My parents acquired him in Kenya a few years before I was born. He stood tall on his perch, short gossamer white feathers around his eyes and a long tail with splashes of red. He had enough seed in his tray, and I cut up an apple and gave him a few grapes.

'Thank you, Rohan. Thank you, Rohan,' he said.

'You're welcome, Fernando,' I said.

There was no way I could watch anything on the television. I took a sip of Sauvignon Blanc and tried not to think about what I'd seen in the field. The farmer, a Yorkshireman who had migrated south, could not add much to what Shep had already told me. The farmer had gone to the barn for some hay, saw the body, rushed to the farmhouse and had rung the police. Neither he nor his wife had heard anything the previous night or earlier that morning. I thought about the young woman's parents and how the family was going to be forever devastated.

I got up and selected a CD from the rack. Leonard Cohen. Listening to Leonard is uplifting, especially if I'm feeling down, because he reminds me there's always somebody else in a worse state than me.

I got up as he was singing a song about the rain falling on last year's man and heated up a ready-made lasagne meal in the microwave.

The landline rang. My heart lurched as I stared at the caller display window. I didn't want to pick up the phone.

'You can be a right bastard sometimes, Rohan. They were really looking forward to seeing you, spending time with you, and what d'you do? Dump them on your parents the minute something crops up. They're both feeling miserable now.'

'Look, Faye, I'm really sorry. Don't you think I want to see my kids?'

'Not the way you behaved today, no. I try so hard to make sure you've access to them. That the three of you have a good relationship. You're their father after all.'

'I know that, Faye.'

'Well, with what happened today, you bloody well need reminding.'

'Faye, what happened today was desperately sad for another set of parents. Their daughter was found murdered. Their lives have changed forever. I haven't even spoken with them yet. I'll need to do that, even though it'll be hard… My first homicide. D'you think I could turn that down?'

A momentary silence at the other end of the line. 'Why have they given the case to you? There are others with more experience who could've done it. Have you become their blue-eyed boy?'

I ignored the comment.

'Or is it because they need a whipping boy if things go wrong? Think about it, Rohan. I don't want you to get hurt, or worse.'

Faye was always good at reading situations and she was saying out loud what I'd been thinking. As this was my first homicide case, I should have been allocated a mentor. But this had not been mentioned by anybody.

'But Faye, what if I succeed?' I eventually said.

'Rohan,' she said. 'They're far more powerful than you. Just be careful —'

She was interrupted with: 'Come on darling, we need to go,' in the background. My heart did a somersault, feeling hollow, a part missing, the part that Faye had always caressed. Had always loved.

'Sorry, Rohan. Saturday night. We're going out. Perhaps we can chat and catch up some other time,' and with that she was gone.

I continued to hold the handset for a few moments. I wanted to smash it against the wall.

My heart thumped in my chest. My cheeks felt hot and my palms clammy. I tried to calm down by gulping another glass of Sauvignon Blanc.

Eventually, I got up from the settee, wished Fernando goodnight, covered his cage and went upstairs to my bedroom. The wine had sneaked up on me and made me light-headed, with a persistent buzzing in my ears. I lay awake in my king-size bed, staring at the ceiling, not wanting to close my eyes because I was frightened of what might creep in. As the wine slowly took hold, I went to sleep but it wasn't long before I started tossing and turning, waking up, dozing, waking up, dozing.

The murdered girl was floating deep down in the sea, coming towards me as I swam underwater, face grimacing, screaming, bubbles of water escaping from her nose, mouth pleading over and over again, 'Help me, please help me.' Her arms beckoned to me, her eyes wide and full of sorrow, pleading with me to rescue her. The eye painted on her belly button winked at me. Her body, arms and legs stiff and locked, turned slowly like a giant Ferris wheel and tumbled towards me. Round and round in the water, the current carrying her along. No, not a Ferris wheel. A giant circular space station, high above the earth, and was that the music of the Blue Danube waltz I could hear as the body rotated to the music? And then she became a giant windmill, blades at right angles to match the elbows and knee joints, turning round and round, round and round, arms above her head, legs below and then swinging legs above and then arms pointing below.

I woke up in a cold sweat before drifting off again.

My sister's face stared at me. My dear sister Maya. Not quite four years old. Round baby-fat cheeks, big and bright brown eyes, a ready smile, even with a bottom tooth missing. Short and wavy dark hair resting above the penny-sized birthmark on the side of her neck. Maya sitting on her bottom on the cold floor in the dark basement below the house. Feet bare and toes curled up. Stretching out her arms, begging me to help her. But I had betrayed her.

My heart pounded like a giant hammer reverberating through my chest.

I sat up. Wide awake.

I had chest pain and struggled to breathe properly. I might have screamed Maya's name.

A tear rolled down my cheek.

CHAPTER 4

I finally woke up at about six in the morning, under a duvet of pain from the wine and the state of my mind. I stepped under a hot shower and stood under its warm glow for a long five minutes. I swung the tap to the right to finish with a blast of freezing water.

It was dark, a silvery half-moon dangling in the black sky, as I crossed the city boundary and drove along the country lanes to the south. I parked the Mercedes in the same layby near the crime scene. As soon as I got out, I was blinded by powerful arc lights. A microphone was thrust in front of my face, a woman's voice saying, 'Inspector Sharma, is it true the victim is a young Asian woman? Is it true she was killed in a particularly hideous manner?'

I growled, 'Kill the bloody lights!' Apart from anything else, I didn't want my headache to return. My fists clenched tight.

As the TV lights dimmed, I looked at the reporter and recognised the face from the local news programme. Wendy Weaver. I wondered how she knew. Who the hell was the media liaison officer back at police HQ? Why had nobody contacted me?

I forced a smiled. 'I'm sorry, I can't comment at the moment. This is a crime scene; our investigations are continuing but I'll make a statement later.'

I walked towards Ben Carter and Dr Khan, who were waiting further up the road. They looked exhausted as they must have worked long into the night.

'Shep, how the hell did they find out? Mole?' I asked, gesturing towards the television crew.

'Your guess is as good as mine, Sir. Feels like a mole, either here on the team or back at HQ.'

I tried not to think about the implications of that as I exchanged pleasantries with Ben Carter and Dr Khan. The officers who had stayed the night were allowed to go home to get some rest. I confirmed with Ben that the uniforms would undertake a fingertip search of the ground in all directions from the crime scene.

'Anything from missing persons, Shep, about Asian women or girls?'

'Yeah, several have come to their attention. But one or two will be runaways, another couple may have overstayed their holidays to Pakistan or India or wherever. However, there's one, sad to say, who may well be our victim.'

A woman's voice carried across the field, shouting 'Inspector, Inspector.' I turned and saw the farmer's wife running towards me.

'Inspec — tor, it's — it's missing,' she said between breaths.

'What's missing, Mrs Morley?'

'My husband's cock.'

I stared at her.

The crimson moved up from her throat to her face. 'A cockerel. Called him Thumper. He ain't in his cage no more.'

'And when did you notice he was missing, Mrs Morley?'

'This morning, Inspector. After all that went on yesterday, forgot about him and the hens. Went to feed him, normal like, let him roam around the yard, but his cage were empty.'

'It couldn't have been opened accidentally, could it? Or maybe the cage wasn't properly secured?'

'Noways, Inspector Harmer. Jim and I lock the cages every night with thick wires and bolts. To keep foxes away, you see. No, Inspector. Somebody slid the bolts open an' grabbed him.

Strange, we didn't hear no cackling or crowing or any other noise. From Thumper or th'hens. Might be 'cos it was so windy other night.'

'Thank you, Mrs Morley. I'll get one of the team to check it out.'

She looked at me and said, 'Aint you…? Ain't…?' and stopped. 'Right, I'll be getting on with 'ousework then.'

She turned and walked back to the farmhouse.

I sensed that Shep was going to make a sarcastic comment about Thumper but my look stopped him.

'Mind where you jump,' I warned as I vaulted over a low wooden gate from one field into the next, looking at the cow pats in front of me.

'Oh shit,' Shep said.

'Precisely. Told you not to step in it.'

'Didn't. But wrenched my bloody ankle.'

The ground was cold and the earth uneven as we crossed the field. Shep hobbled slightly for a while. The cold wind stabbed my face and hands. I pulled on my black leather gloves and turned up the collar of my coat. Over to our left lay a half-eaten carcass of a dead hare, eyes wide open. The birds of prey had been gorging themselves.

'Didn't see Constable Wheatley at the scene, Shep,' I said as we walked.

'No, Sir, neither did I. I'm sure she'll have been around somewhere.'

'Shep, you don't have to call me *Sir* when we're alone.'

'You've earned it, Sir. Anyway, it'll stop me getting confused in public.'

'Fair enough, Shep. How's Molly, by the way?' I had met Shep's wife two or three times at social functions. I always thought how they made a good couple. Perfect for each other.

'She's fine, Sir.'

'No children yet? I remember Molly saying how much she wanted them.'

'No, Sir. Although we keep trying.'

We walked in silence.

'Seems the problem's with me,' Shep eventually said. 'Sperm count's low and what there is, isn't good enough to swim upstream, so to speak. Ironic, isn't it? Always wanted kids from when I was a teenager.'

'I'm sorry, Shep.'

'Might happen yet. Trying IVF treatment. Have had two attempts already. Maybe the third one will be successful.'

'Hope so, Shep. Will be worth it and I wish both of you well.'

'Thanks. Where exactly are we going, Sir?'

'We're here,' I replied.

We entered the woods and walked on thick layers of rotting leaves, dead branches covered in mildew, twigs and pieces of bark. Some snapped as we walked on them. Ferns, bracken and holly bushes covered the ground and visibility was poor as not much daylight penetrated this far down. It was bitterly cold, the damp air circling my hips and my knees. Shafts of pain pierced my ligaments and tendons.

The dark, dank ground had been disturbed at regular intervals. Somebody walking through. These signs led to a large tree in the middle of the woods. We approached it and I looked up. I leapt up, grabbed a branch and struggled to lift my whole body. My shoulder muscles ached and my knees seared with pain. I climbed up a few more branches and rested between the two enormous trunks where the tree split.

'Shep, the bastard might have been watching us from here,' I shouted. 'Highly organised killers monitor police investigations. Those footprints might be his.'

Shep looked up at me.

'Tell Ben and his team to give this place a good going over. Phone him now.'

CHAPTER 5

We carried on working at the scene for several hours. I had organised the teams and they were all undertaking different functions. Roadblocks had been set up and drivers interviewed to see whether they, especially those who used these roads regularly, had noticed anything or anybody out of the ordinary. The doors of remote farmhouses were being knocked upon. Lines of officers crouching on hands and knees, almost touching each other, reminding me of the devout praying to Mecca, carried out fingertip searches of every blade of grass and looked under every loose stone. Ben Carter and his team continued to search and to photograph near the site where the body had been found. They wore their paper suits, heads and feet covered in white, latex gloves sealing the cuffs. Some were kneeling on plastic stepping plates, brushing grass and other samples into evidence bags and glass bottles. All the time, the media vans lurked in the distance.

I put on my forensic suit and went to see Dr Khan who was still working near the body. She started covering the victim's arms and feet in plastic.

'Hello, Inspector Sharma,' she said.

'It's all right, Dr Khan, you can call me Rohan.'

'I prefer to keep professional relationships professional, Inspector. Hope you don't mind.'

This was the second time today I had been told that. I wondered whether Shep and Dr Khan had been on any team building courses. To build up trust, camaraderie, that sort of thing.

'Fair enough, I respect your wishes. D'you mind if I call you Nasreen?' I asked. 'I prefer it that way.'

I had found out her first name earlier from one of Ben's team.

'You can call me what you like.'

'Well, "What you like" what have we got here? What can you tell me so far?'

She laughed through the face mask. A girlish giggle. Her brown eyes flashed playfulness.

'Can't say anything too definite at this stage,' she said. 'Have to wait for the full post-mortem. The body seems to have been thoroughly washed, not a lot of trace evidence on it. Our killer must know water gets rid of DNA. The body was moved not long after death. See the congealed blood here and the purple discoloration of the skin?' she said, while carefully pushing the body on its side and pointing to the young woman's buttocks and lower back. 'Signs of livor mortis. The blood will have settled there after about eight to twelve hours. The blood will not now move within the body. Body temperature and the ambient air temperature are the same so she's been dead for at least forty-eight hours. Most probably longer than that. The muscles are now flexible again.' She prodded the victim's right thigh with her gloved hand. 'Rigor mortis would have set in within the first twelve hours making them rigid but after about another eighteen hours the muscles relax and become flexible again. A chemical reaction within the body, Inspector Sharma. Not a lot more to say at this stage but I hope to perform the post-mortem soon, after you've notified the coroner. I assume you'll be attending.'

'Of course,' I said. I would have to be present but wasn't looking forward to it.

'Any idea about the cause of death?' I asked.

'What d'you think I am? A miracle worker?' I could sense her smile behind the mask. 'No, Inspector. No obvious sign of death. The cuts in her chest aren't deep enough to have killed her. No other visible injuries on the body, apart from the right nipple being bitten off.' Nasreen shuddered. 'No sign of strangulation marks around the neck,' she continued, 'but these two puncture marks are interesting.' She pointed to two tiny puncture marks I could see near the big toe on the victim's right foot. 'There's some swelling and discoloration around each. Probably evidence of toxins.'

'What d'you mean? She's been injected with something? Poison?'

'Maybe. But why two marks, Inspector? And if she was injected, the skin wouldn't necessarily swell up. Why the foot? One of the most difficult places to insert a needle. Why not the arm or thigh? They look bigger than a puncture mark made by most syringes. Even the ones used for hepatitis vaccinations. We'll find out more after the post-mortem, Inspector. Now, I need to ensure the body's secure enough to be transported to the morgue.'

As I walked away, Ben beckoned to me from a distance. 'Look at this, Inspector Sharma,' he said, pointing to the ground as I approached the narrow country track near the farmhouse and the chicken coop. 'See this tyre mark?' He pointed to the right side of the track. Tufts of grass ran down the middle of the track rutted on both sides.

At first, I couldn't see anything but then I saw a faint outline of a narrow tread. The squiggles were not deep, suggesting a worn tyre.

'The interesting thing is there's no matching track on the other side. And there should be because the ground is just about soft enough and damp enough. There are no other tracks whatsoever, either further up or further down. Or sideways or wherever. I'll get the boys to make a cast of it. Could be relevant given the proximity to the farmhouse and to the body.'

Eventually, all the different teams indicated they had completed their work and I ordered them to clear up the scenes, to ensure all the evidence was properly transported and all the required paperwork duly filled in. I informed them of when to be in the briefing room the next day. Not too early. They needed a break too. Darkness was beginning to draw in quite early and I walked towards Wendy Weaver, the TV news journalist.

'Okay, Wendy. Let's roll,' I said, immediately regretting my words. 'I'll make a brief statement. No questions at this stage if you don't mind. Too early in the investigation. But before I do that, can you please tell me how you found out about this and the location of the body?'

Wendy Weaver looked at me and smiled a big, beguiling smile. 'I'm sorry, Inspector. I was told to get here with an outside broadcast crew by my superiors. Can't tell you anything more.'

I suppose I wasn't expecting anything else.

CHAPTER 6

The gentle sounds of the chorus of the Hebrew slaves from Verdi's opera *Nabucco* filled my car as I drove back home.

'Go thoughts on golden wings
Go settle upon the slopes and hills,
Where warm and soft and fragrant are
The breezes of our sweet native land…'

More *pardesi*, I thought. The displaced. A Hindi word referring to anybody who doesn't belong to a country, place or situation. Like the third person in a relationship. Were not most people in the world *pardesi*? I wondered, as I drove along the dark country lanes.

I thought of the murdered young woman and how quickly we had identified her. As Shep had said, her parents had reported her missing a number of days ago and had left a photograph and other details such as height, weight and so on at the police station. A face, like the Mona Lisa, immortalised for ever in the photograph, taken in a photographer's studio. She was sat at an angle, big brown eyes staring into the camera. A soft, dreamy look in her eyes, healthy round cheeks, well-shaped lips, the beginning of a smile. Hair parted in the middle, shoulder-length. The collarless pale blue blouse, short-sleeved. She was now beyond pain but Mr and Mrs Mehta's was only just beginning. And would never end. I tried not to think about that, or what I'd do if anybody ever told me something had happened to my children. My heart suddenly ached for them, feeling guilty for deserting them yesterday. I would ring them when I got home.

'Welcome home, Rohan. Welcome home,' came the familiar words as I entered the house.

'Hello, Fernando, you *pardesi*.'

'*Par — desi, par — desi*,' he replied. Then blew a wolf whistle.

'Okay, Fernando. That's enough. I'm glad to see you too.' I went up to his cage and stroked the top of his soft grey head.

After changing, I fed him bits of kiwi fruit, pineapple, pumpkin and melon seeds, then settled down with a tray on the settee, with a glass of Sauvignon and some chicken wrapped in bacon, boiled potatoes and sweetcorn. And gravy. Thank God for gravy granules. I switched on the television for background noise so the house didn't feel too quiet and thought about the team briefing tomorrow and what I'd say. I wondered who was leaking information about the investigation.

The sound of my mobile ringing interrupted my thoughts.

'Superintendent Breedon here. How's it going?'

'Hello, Sir. I was going to ring you but didn't want to disturb you on a Sunday.'

I briefed him on the investigation. He listened, not asking too many questions.

'Why me?' I eventually asked.

'Are you feeling victimised, Rohan? Or just paranoid?' I could picture him smiling at his own witticism. 'Look, Rohan, this is your chance. There are others who could have led the investigation. But orders came from on high you were to lead this. Somebody up there likes you.'

I knew he didn't mean the divine either.

'Rohan, do your best. This could be a really big case. If you need help, ask for it.'

It sounded comforting but I knew it wasn't. I knew what asking for help meant. After a few more pleasantries he hung up. The food was now cold but I ate it anyway. I got up to put the dirty crockery and cutlery in the dishwasher and, as I bent down, I did a double take at the sound of my own voice. I stood up and stared at the television screen.

'*The body of a young Asian woman was found in the field behind me early yesterday. We're carrying out a thorough investigation and examining all the evidence. At this stage, we don't know the identity of the victim or the cause of death. I'll make another statement to the media when the time is right and when we have more information. Thank you.*'

'*Can you tell us what kind of evidence —*'

'*Thank you. That'll be all for the moment.*'

I looked confident and in control on the news channel. A 'trust me I'm a detective' look.

The landline rang after a few moments.

'Hello, Mum. How're you and Dad?'

'We're fine, *Beta*. We were worried about you after you dropped off Yasmin and Karan yesterday. Now I see you on television. Have you eaten yet? You looked handsome, son. Very official. Could be a hard case. I suppose you can't tell me anything.'

I sensed her ears pricking up, desperate to know more.

'No, Mum, can't tell you anything and, yes, I've eaten and, yes, I'll be careful. What's Dad up to?'

'Oh, he's gone out to one of his clubs or pubs. Drinking and playing the gambling machines, no doubt. You be careful, *Beta*, won't you?'

There was an uneasy pause between me and my mother. The silence and the sadness stretching to a time and place far away. The anniversary of my sister Maya's disappearance almost upon us again.

'You can't keep blaming yourself, son, you know that. What happened to your sister Maya happened.'

The house was silent after I hung up, apart from the voices on the television. I turned round to Fernando. 'We'll always be together, won't we, Fernando?'

'I love you, Rohan. I love you, Rohan,' he replied.

Tears welled up in my eyes.

I picked up the mobile and tried Yasmin's number.

'Hello this is Yas —'

'Hello darling —'

'— min Sharma. If you're a friend, please leave a message and I'll ring you back.' She blew some kisses. 'If you're not, please go away.'

My heart sank. I scrolled down to Karan's number and got his voicemail message too. Were they ignoring me or had they gone out? If they'd seen me on television, surely they would have rung?

CHAPTER 7

It was six o'clock in the morning and the icy breeze of the night was receding, although I could feel its cold grip deep inside my lungs. It was still dark and the streetlights cast an eerie glow on the tarmac and the houses.

As I scraped the ice from my car windscreen, I worried about my kids. Why had I not heard from them? I wanted to ring but it was too early in the morning. As I scraped, I sensed somebody behind me.

They were walking slowly and quietly, their breathing shallow.

My body tensed, arm muscles taut. Body weight on my heels. I swivelled round. Fists tight.

'Rum weather, isn't it…? Rum weather.'

I relaxed. He was a white man, in his early fifties, unkempt, runny nose. He stared at me and then at my car.

'Yes, it's rum weather,' I replied.

He shuffled past me, repeating, 'Rum weather, isn't it…? Rum weather.'

As I drove, Handel's *Messiah* played on the radio, the soprano singing: *'Behold, thy King cometh unto thee; He is the righteous Saviour, and He shall Speak peace unto the heathen…'*

It felt good to be the heathen and to enjoy the music. I let it carry on.

It was still early but I couldn't wait any longer and punched in Yasmin's number. No reply. I tried Karan's number and, as it rang, I muttered, 'Come on, pick up, pick up, pick up.' No reply.

Should I try Faye's number?

'Rohan, why the hell're you ringing so early? It's not seven yet.'

'I'm sorry. I was worried about the kids. I haven't heard from them.'

'Rohan, get a grip, will you? Why should they ring you after you dumped them?'

'It's just that I thought they might have rung. After seeing me on TV… I was on the news.'

'I'm sorry, Rohan. We were all out last night. Went to see a film so the kids wouldn't be too disappointed about the weekend. Didn't know you'd been on the news. Not making it were you?'

'Please, Faye … don't. Any chance of speaking to them? Just briefly?'

'Will have to be brief 'cos they've got to get ready for school. Hang on, I can hear Yasmin having a shower. You might be able to speak to Karan.'

The tenor took over from the soprano: *'Thy rebuke had broken His heart; He is full of heaviness. He looked for some to have pity on Him, but there was no man, neither found He any to comfort him…'*

'How you doing, Dad?' Karan said, when he eventually picked up the phone.

'I'm fine, son. Just wanted to say again to you and Yasmin I'm really sorry. About the other day. And I got worried when I didn't hear from you yesterday. I was on the telly. I tried ringing you both many times.'

'Were you really on the telly, Dad? We didn't know. We went to the pictures with Mum and Pierre…'

The iron fist around my heart squeezed harder when I heard his name.

'Our phones were switched off. Was a really good film, Dad, in 3-D. A bit long, almost three hours. Have you heard of it? *The Fantastic Voyage.* 'Bout some scientists being mini…'

'Miniaturised?'

'… yeah, mini … choo … rised, and they go into a mini … choo submarine and are injected into a blood vessel, and they have to cure the body they're in and being in 3-D it felt you were right in the body, in the heart and in the lungs and in the brain…'

I hoped they didn't show the inside of some parts of the body I could think of.

'… and it felt the white cells were coming to get you … as if you were in the blood and floating with the red blood cells. Then there were all these scary parasites in the stomach and gut. It was just great, Dad. I wish you could've been there … 'cos … well, I miss you a lot sometimes. We both do.'

'I miss you too, Karan. And Yasmin. We'll get together and have a good time before long. I promise. Perhaps you and Yasmin can come and stay with me one weekend soon? I'll speak to your mother about it. It's been great chatting to you and now you must get ready for school. Okay?'

'Okay, Dad. Byeee…'

The 'Hallelujah' chorus from *The Messiah* boomed through the eight speakers in the car. The dashboard vibrated.

'Bye, Karan. I love you.'

But he'd already gone.

With Joy Wheatley in the passenger seat, I drove down a long tree-lined avenue in the southern suburbs at the edge of the city, towards the Mehtas' residence. I turned right onto the straight driveway and pulled up behind a new silver Audi A4 parked outside the garage.

As Joy and I got out of the car, a woman dressed in a cream cardigan and dark saree ran out the front door and screamed, 'You've found her, you've found her, haven't you?' She rushed towards Joy, sobbing, fists clenched. Her husband stood at the door, unshaved with flecks of white in his beard. He probably hadn't eaten properly for days.

'Please, can we come inside and talk?'

'Tell me my darling, my *Beti*, is all right,' pleaded Mrs Mehta. 'She's all right, isn't she? It wasn't her, was it? The one we heard about on the news? Please tell me it wasn't her.' She gasped for air. Her husband put his arm around her and walked her back to the house.

We went into the front lounge and the scent of jasmine invaded our lungs. The television was switched on, music from *Zee TV*, the volume low. In one corner, a polished silver shrine stood about two feet high. The interior housed pictures and statues of the main Hindu deities: Lord Krishna playing his flute; Lord Ganesh, the elephant-headed god; pictures of the goddess Laxmi, and of Rama and Sita. A bright flame from a *diva* spluttered in front of the statues. Next to it was a thin silver stand. It had five small holes with burning joss sticks, confirming where the scent of the jasmine came from.

My heart ached when I saw Geeta Mehta's photograph in the shrine. She was smiling at the camera. Standing in faded blue jeans and a white tee-shirt in this very room. Her right arm was outstretched, supporting a violin and her left hand was holding a letter from the Guildhall School of Music and Drama.

A long and happy life awaiting her in that moment frozen in time. The photograph was placed there as her mother and father pleaded with the gods to protect her until she was safely back home.

'It wasn't her, was it, Inspector Sharma?' Mrs Mehta's eyes were moist, begging, not enough tears left in them, her face gaunt and haunted.

'As you know, we did find the body of a young Asian woman about Geeta's age on Saturday. We can't be sure but it may be your daugh—'

'No! No! It can't be!' Mrs Mehta screamed.

We explained that they would need to identify the body and escorted the Mehtas to my car, both unsteady on their feet, in a state of shock. The full impact would hit them later.

As I drove along the ring road towards the city centre, I could see the couple in my rear-view mirror. Mrs Mehta turned around to her husband and said, 'Minesh, it might not be her. We can't be certain of that. She's still alive somewhere. I can hear her calling out for us.'

'I can hear her too. I can hear the echo of her voice…' He turned and stared out of the window. Is that all he would be left with? An echo of his daughter's voice?

There was an oppressive silence in the car as we drove along. The silence of the dead. And of the living, slowly dying.

The grey, unremarkable brick building at the local city hospital is the mortuary. It can be approached through a gate at one of the side roads next to the main car park. Not many people passing by would guess what it was, or what happened inside. It also houses the rooms for post-mortem examinations and has an anteroom where relatives can view the bodies of their loved ones. A place where hearts are cut into little pieces, both of the dead and of those who loved and cared for them. Neither would be whole again.

The body lay on a steel table, covered by a soft white cotton sheet. Nasreen Khan stood at the front of the table, while Joy

48

and I stood on either side of Mr and Mrs Mehta, opposite Dr Khan. The room was icy cold and the smell of disinfectant lingered in the air and in my nostrils.

At my question, 'Is this your daughter, Geeta?' Nasreen Khan drew back the sheet covering the head. Geeta's eyes and mouth were now closed. Mrs Mehta stared, eventually shook Geeta's shoulder and said, 'Come on, darling, wake up. Then we can go home. Please wake up, darling … let's go home. Come on, stop playing around…'

A tear slid down Mr Mehta's cheek.

Geeta's mother let out a piercing scream, hugging her daughter's lifeless body.

Joy and Nasreen Khan put their arms around Mrs Mehta. I gently took Mr Mehta's elbow and we went next door. Although the room was much warmer, Mrs Mehta was shivering, teeth chattering. We sat down on the comfortable settees and I explained that we didn't yet know how Geeta had died, we needed to find out. I did not use the word 'post-mortem'. Joy would be their family liaison officer and keep them in touch about the investigation and I would come to see them later. I'm not sure how much of this they took in. If they didn't remember anything of what I'd said, I wouldn't blame them.

CHAPTER 8

Nasreen Khan and I stood near the steel wash basins, having first changed into surgical gowns, caps and shoes. We scrupulously scrubbed our hands and arms. A scene you see a thousand times in televised hospital dramas. Just that this was not televised fiction and I was trying to usher out the sadness and gloom after Mr and Mrs Mehta had left. I was also nervous about watching yet another post-mortem but didn't want to admit it to myself, or to Nasreen. I never did get used to them. And didn't like the thought of this one in particular because the viewing screen had been damaged recently by building contractors and I had to be in close proximity to the mortuary table.

To hide my nervousness at what was about to happen, I told her a harmless joke or two, courtesy of my children. We were easing into each other's company. As she was washing her arms I noticed some bruising, fading in parts, on the underside of both arms. Tiny blood vessels broken under the skin made the area look like crazy paving. Or hundreds of thin, tiny tributaries flowing into a river.

'How did you do that?' I asked.

She looked embarrassed, quickly dried her arms and rolled down her sleeves. 'I have to take aspirin every day. It breaks the capillaries, plays havoc with my skin tone … the strawberry patches. Better than having a stroke.'

As we walked towards the mortuary table, she asked if I wanted some Vicks VapoRub to smear under my nose. I told her there was no need as I could breathe easily.

'It's not what you breathe in that matters but what it keeps out, Inspector. The menthol, camphor and eucalyptus smell will help enormously.'

'Some of us are made of sterner stuff,' I replied, trying to be brave.

'Have it your own way, Inspector,' she said, raising a finely plucked eyebrow.

Nasreen was assisted by an earnest woman called Tracey who was in her mid-thirties, chubby face, snub nose, strands of dark hair visible under her cap and a pale forehead. Both had piles of forms to fill in on clipboards. Steel equipment was laid out near the table, including single-edged surgical knives of varying lengths and thicknesses to rib-cutters, forceps, scissors, hammer and chisel, a circular electric saw, syringes, bottles of chemicals, and weighing scales. Two rubber hosepipes were attached to the hot and cold water taps in a washbasin along the wall and they hung down from steel hooks over the top edge of the mortuary table.

Ben joined us, all scrubbed up and in his surgical cap and gown. He nodded towards me and Nasreen. He had witnessed many post-mortems in his time and had an air of confidence about him.

Geeta Mehta's fragile, naked body lay on the gleaming steel table. Many of the preliminary observations such as weight, height, hair colour, eye colour, evidence of injuries and so on had been recorded on paper and on a digital recorder. Photographs of various parts of the body had been taken.

Nasreen said, 'Okay, let's go,' and took out a long surgical knife and made a Y-incision along Geeta's body. She was careful not to cut the wounds near the left breast. Air gushed out from the stomach area and the most overpowering stench I'd ever smelt flooded my nose and the room. I gulped down a tide of nausea. Nasreen looked at me and said I could leave the room if I wanted to. I said I'd remain. But the sight of the stomach and raw liver was too much and I rushed out of the room.

I retched in the washbasins next door. Bile and saliva mixed near the silver drain and gushed down as I sprayed a jet of cold water into the basin. I rushed to the lockers, quickly changed and ran outside to get some fresh air where I breathed in deeply. I wondered how people like Nasreen do their job day-in, day-out and go home to their husbands and wives and children and enjoy an evening meal with them. Talking about everyday things, school and shopping and the like, between mouthfuls. There's no way I could do that job. No way.

I was sitting in the anteroom where the Mehtas had seen their daughter when Nasreen and Ben came through. Ben said my reaction was normal and even after many occasions a post-mortem wasn't easy to get used to. He recommended that I use the Vicks next time. I wasn't sure whether I'd want to attend anymore but it was part of my job and was bound to happen again some time.

'It's obviously too early to say anything definitive, Inspector,' said Nasreen, 'but the heart and other muscles stopped working quite suddenly. The nervous system seems to have suffered a catastrophic failure. In addition to the bites to the right nipple, there's no doubt we have a necrophiliac on our hands. The most intriguing aspect is the two puncture wounds on the right foot...'

Her speech was grammatically correct, I noted. Precise attention to detail. Cold and clinical in imparting information.

'...I've examined these wounds in great detail, magnified their photographs and taken swabs from them.' She shook her head. 'You may think me crazy but I've only ever seen wounds like those once before. In Karnataka in Western India, when I was on a training placement there for six months. The distance between the two wounds, their depth, the clean puncture wounds and the swelling around them suggest the victim was still alive when it happened. The discoloration of the skin around them indicates it's a snake bite.'

'You're kidding,' said Ben.

'What d'you mean? An adder bit her?' I asked. 'I didn't think they were that big or that poisonous in this country?'

'Too big to be an adder bite. And yes, you're right, people in this country don't usually die from adder bites, apart from the rare case of somebody dying from anaphylactic shock. But, as I said, hardly heard of. No, this one's a tropical snake, I'd guess. A cobra or a krait or even a black mamba…'

Ben and I stared at each other. I thought about the black mamba. My father talked about it often. Not usually black, but a greenish-brown, grey or olive. Its name comes from the inky-black mouth which it stretches wide open when about to strike. It has dead dark eyes, big and round. Can be seven or eight feet long, or even longer, found mainly in the savannah and woodlands of Eastern and Southern Africa. The only snake in the world which chases human beings. It can run, if that's the right word, at five metres per second. Its bite is usually fatal, the dendrotoxins in its venom killing quickly unless there is immediate treatment with anti-venom. It kills hundreds in rural Africa every year.

'But I can't say anything for definite until the toxicology reports come back,' I heard Nasreen say, as I tuned back in. 'I've taken tissue samples from the vital organs and the right foot. I'll be sending them to the London School of Hygiene and Tropical Medicine for analysis. I'm not sure how long it'll take for the results to come back but I'll keep on their case.

Please don't say anything in public until we get a definitive diagnosis… Oh, and I also found this.' She held up a small transparent plastic bag. 'A leaf, dry and broken in parts but definitely a leaf, was shoved inside her. Not sure what sort of tree or plant it comes from. I'll send a sample to the experts at Kew Gardens near London for an analysis. Also, there is considerable blunt force trauma to the knees and elbow joints. We have one really sick perpetrator. Now, I need to go back and finish up. Any questions?'

Neither Ben nor I had any. We just sat there and stared at her. A cold and clinical explanation, as if she had delivered such messages hundreds of times. But the snake bite… If true, how the hell was I going to explain it to Geeta Mehta's parents and to the wider world that a poisonous snake had killed her in Britain? What on earth would Wendy Weaver have to say about it on television?

Despite the grim news, I couldn't help but marvel at Nasreen's efficiency and professionalism. She concluded our meeting by stating that she would either email me the relevant reports herself, or get her assistant, Tracey, to do so if she wasn't in the office.

'You know what, Inspector Sharma,' Ben said as we walked out, 'I've been to lots of tropical places on holiday, East Africa, India, the Caribbean, but I've never come across anything like this. How the hell can it happen in Leicester, of all places?'

I looked at him and didn't know what to say.

CHAPTER 9

The drone of low-level chatter, laughter and the sound of mugs of tea and coffee being placed on tables and window ledges filled my ears as I walked into the briefing room through the doors at the back. I was slightly late as I'd been to see Mr and Mrs Mehta before popping into my office to prepare for the briefing. It was now late in the day and the winter darkness had already painted the city black, while streetlights fought to paint it a ghostly white. The fluorescent lights in the room provided a stark contrast, throwing everybody's faces into sharp relief. Shep had managed to commandeer one of the bigger training rooms at HQ for our briefing because it had a digital smartboard, fixed laptop and overhead projector. However, he had been left in no doubt that this room could not be used as a regular incident room. Ah well, we'd cross that bridge when we come to it.

I stood next to the screen and looked at the team of officers sitting in front of me. There were about forty or fifty of them, a handful in uniform, some of whom had been attached to the case and others who had been drafted in to help out. The room was packed, a sea of white faces, with three British Asian men and one woman of African-Caribbean heritage. Ben and his senior staff were also present.

I felt nervous and uptight, not only because this was my first major case but also because there was somebody sitting in the room, or maybe more than one person, who was leaking information to the media. I started by thanking them all for their hard work and said I'd go through what was known of the case so far and what evidence we had. After showing them a few digital photographs on the screen of the farmhouse and fields and roads near the crime scene, I pressed the remote control for the next photograph.

They all stared at it, absolutely still. The silence of the dead. One or two looked away, gazing at the window blinds or staring at the floor. Someone cleared their throat. I could hear the humming in the fluorescent tube above my head.

A member of Ben's team had taken the photograph by climbing a branch on the tree near Geeta Mehta's body. About ten feet above her. The photograph showed her naked brown body, spread-eagled, broken arms and legs carefully positioned, deep cuts near the heart, the black lipstick, the talcum powder and rouge on her cheeks, silvery-pink eyeshadow and black kohl around the eyes, and the blue eye drawn around her navel. The shaved pubic hair.

'I know this is painful and really hard,' I said, 'but we're dealing with one sick bastard and we've got to catch him before he does this to anybody else. We're obviously dealing with a highly organised and highly sadistic killer. But we're going to get him, make no mistake about that.' I so hoped I was right.

We had a good discussion about the placement of the body. The general consensus was that the arms and legs had been positioned to look like a swastika. The team knew the undertones of this but nothing was said openly. I didn't mention the probable cause of death or the leaf inserted into her vagina. I didn't want that information in the public domain. I explained that Mr and Mrs Mehta were traumatised and could not really answer any of our questions yet, but I was hoping to see them again at some point before too long.

I organised the teams and asked one of them to be positioned at roadblocks near the body dumping site to interview motorists in the morning, and to do so for a few days to see whether anyone saw or heard anything out of the ordinary. Other officers would continue their door-to-door enquiries along the last known route Geeta took. Another team would interview motorists between Geeta's house and the college, speaking to regular commuters between seven thirty and eight thirty in the morning. We would also interview any people in the vicinity who were making their way to their place of work or coming back home from their night shifts. And, of course, we would speak to any students who regularly walked to the college from the area near Geeta's house.

I instructed smaller teams to collate and organise all the witness statements and any other evidence coming in, and to keep me routinely informed. The only ones who knew about the snake and the leaf were Nasreen, Tracey, Joy, Shep and Ben. One or two of Ben's team could, I suppose, have guessed the nature of the wounds to Geeta's foot but this seemed unlikely.

The investigation was now in full swing and I felt better about being in control. My nervousness was easing off.

I rounded off. 'Okay, team, any questions?'

I looked around the roomful of tired faces, many having had enough and wanting to go home for the day. Would they say anything to their partners about the photographs they had seen? Would they sleep well tonight?

A constable hesitantly raised her hand. I didn't know her but was aware she'd been seconded to the investigation from one of the other directorates. The name *Angie Deacon* was on her badge.

I smiled and nodded at her to speak.

'Oh, sorry, Sir. It's nothing. Just reminded me of… May not be that important.'

'Are you sure, Angie? If it seems important, please say so.'

'It's nothing, Sir. Sorry.'

I closed the meeting. Some of them said they were going to the local for a drink before going home and I reminded them not to talk about the case in a public place. I also stressed that nobody should talk about colour, race or swastikas.

I thought I'd join them for a quick drink and asked Ben, Shep and Joy to come along if they had the time. The local was an upmarket pub called *Raffles*, serving a wide range of drinks, from draught beers to cocktails to fine red and white wines. There was a separate dining area which served dishes from around the world. *Raffles* was busy, even at this time of night early in the week, and I bought my team a drink to acknowledge the hard work that had been put in.

When the opportunity arose, I took Shep to one side and quietly told him to identify and visit all local pet stores, especially those dealing in exotic animals, and to ask them whether they had lost any poisonous snakes. I wanted him and nobody else doing this, he was not to say anything to anybody, and I wanted it done first thing in the morning. Their inventory had to be checked, along with the paperwork, including import licences. He nodded, and after half an hour or so announced he had to go home as his wife Molly was expecting him for dinner. Not long after, I decided to leave too and left Joy, Ben and the others there, not forgetting to remind them of starting work early the next day and the dangers of drinking and driving.

As I stared at the late news on *Sky TV* and bit into my pizza slice, I stopped chewing. 'Christ, Fernando, why the hell didn't I think of that before? I'm an idiot! The zoo, Fernando, that's got to be it. The snake must've been taken from there.'

Fernando's beak was in his tray of water and he ignored me.

It seemed obvious now but events had been moving at a rapid rate. What with the post-mortem, speaking to Geeta's parents, planning the investigation, dealing with my children, dealing with Faye and so on, I'd forgotten to look at the evidence in front of me. Cardinal mistake.

I put down the plate, scampered off the settee, picked up my mobile and dialled Shep's number. No reply. Can't say I blamed him; it was getting late. Still, I wanted to speak to him, so I rang his landline.

'I'm really sorry for ringing this late, Molly, but it's Rohan Sharma and I need to speak to Shep urgently. Sorry to ring on the landline but his mobile's switched off.'

'Oh, Inspector … I thought he was with you. He's not back yet.'

I paused. 'Er … I'm sorry for disturbing you, Molly. Perhaps he's on his way. We did finish rather late. Might be caught up in traffic.'

'Shall I ask him to ring when he's back, Inspector?'

'No, no, Molly. It's okay. Thanks.'

The guy was entitled to time off, I thought, as I put the phone down and regretted ringing. But he should have arrived home a long time ago. I desperately wanted to ring the zoo and talk to some of the senior staff but there was no point. Nobody would be there.

As I finished eating, my mind was racing. I felt excited and apprehensive. If a snake had been stolen from the reptile house, then there might well be some evidence, maybe even DNA evidence, of the person who had taken it. And how many people know how to handle highly venomous snakes?

The keepers at the zoo might be a good place to start. If not them, then somebody who knew the layout of the zoo really well. Say the admin staff, regular visitors, trustees, vets, volunteers…

The enormity of the task of interviewing everybody and tracing visitors to the zoo began to deflate me. But this was a lead. And it felt good.

Fernando let out a long whistle. 'Rohan's a bad boy. Rohan's a bad boy.'

'No, I'm not, Fernando. It's warm in the house and you've had some good things to eat, so I'm not a bad boy. Time to go to bed, Fernando.'

I put the cover over his cage and trudged upstairs. I wouldn't mind being a bad boy now and again. The way I used to be.

CHAPTER 10

The darkness of the night was slowly brushed away by the dull light sweeping over the horizon. Thick grey clouds drifted across the sky, covering the fading light of the stars. A cold wind cut across my face and tousled my hair. My finger joints and knees hurt as I stood outside the reptile house at the zoo. I had decided to come straight here in the morning knowing that the staff would be feeding the animals. A keeper eventually let me in after I'd flashed the headlights of my Mercedes outside the main glass doors for a few minutes. Having introduced myself, he took me to Mr Beauchamp, the man in charge of the reptile house.

Keith Beauchamp was in his mid-forties with thick curly dark hair, greying at the temples, dressed in a blue boiler suit, black wellingtons and thick brown leather gloves, which stretched all the way up and fanned out at the elbows. He carried two green plastic buckets, a closed lid on each.

'Are you absolutely sure nothing's missing, Mr Beauchamp?'

'Yes, Inspector, nothing's missing. We did the inventory. All accounted for.'

My heart sank. I was so convinced I'd found a good lead. I wasn't ready to give up yet. 'But the reptile house was closed on Saturday due to an incident of some sort. The notice said so. I know, I was here.'

'Yes, it was closed on Saturday, Inspector… You'll appreciate we have a lot of people on placement here. From vets to zoology students, volunteers, foreign animal rangers… A student forgot to close the glass door properly to one of the snake houses. A black mamba crawled out and we found it under a pile of wooden logs nearby. Found it fairly quickly, I might add.'

'Why close the whole reptile house, Mr Beauchamp?'

'The snake had only given birth a few days before. A clutch of seventeen eggs, which is a fair number for a snake. Unfortunately, three of the eggs didn't hatch. The veterinary student had been studying the birth, was writing a dissertation on it, and had also been feeding the mother so she wouldn't eat her young. She said her boyfriend rang her mobile, she became distracted and forgot about securing the glass case. We had to trap the black mamba. The buggers are incredibly fast. We had to wear protective gear and have anti-venom ready in case anything happened. This one's almost nine feet long. We also had to check all the other glass houses in case any of them had been left unsecured. The one housing the spectacled cobra was slightly loose but we dealt with it. A bit of a pain, all in all, but no harm done, Inspector.'

'What other kinds of snakes do you have, Mr Beauchamp?'

'All the usual suspects, Inspector. We're a breeding zoo and sell our products, so to speak, to other zoos around the world. That's how we've built such an international reputation. The black mamba hatchlings will be going to zoos in France, Germany, Japan and Australia once they're big enough. We've also got adders, pythons, boa constrictors, copperheads, coral snakes — though they are in the aquarium — cape cobras and so on. Got most of the deadly variety.' He stared at me with his deep brown eyes. 'We would love to have a king cobra. But they're too big. Grow to about fourteen or fifteen feet. You should see them when they raise their bodies to full height, hood stretched out, ready to strike. Mesmerising. No wonder they're so important in some Eastern religions. Source of supernatural power and all that.'

Behind me I could hear the piercing cries of the gibbons in their wooden house. Too cold for them to be outside. Snorting noises came from the elephant house. A door opened and a keeper came out, pushing a wheelbarrow full of steaming elephant dung.

'And the baby snakes?'

'All accounted for, Inspector.'

'D'you mind if I see the spectacled cobra, Mr Beauchamp?'

We went into the reptile house. It was much warmer than outside, and I must have stared at the glass cage with the spectacled cobra for at least five minutes, mesmerised by the dark, poisonous snake. I was drawn towards its black glossy eyes and its shiny flickering tongue. I wanted to squeeze the concentric muscles as they rippled along the length of its cold, six-feet-long body. Gently gliding along the thick and leafy branches of a lush tropical bush. Tongue flickering. I thought of the terror Geeta Mehta must have endured before she died. Nothing could prepare you for being attacked by something like this.

'Do you want to feed it, Inspector? You could wear my gloves, I'll get some goggles for your eyes. I'll supervise you. The food's in here.'

He smiled, stretched out his arms and held out the plastic buckets towards me.

High-pitched squealing and frightened sounds came from within.

CHAPTER 11

Joy and I stood in the main reception area of the college, waiting to meet with Charlie Garland, Geeta's teacher and the Vice Principal. A brightly coloured poster pinned to the wall facing the main door had the word *welcome* written in about twenty languages, including Russian, Polish, French, German, Mandarin, Hindi, Gujarati and Swahili. The receptionist behind the glass panel was asking a middle-aged man to sign the visitors' book. As we waited, a woman in her mid-thirties dressed in a blue tracksuit and white trainers walked over. She had a red lanyard around her neck with the word 'staff' printed in black but I couldn't see her name badge because it hung the wrong way round.

A student walked past her and said, 'Good afternoon, Miss Garland.'

I stared at Joy, she stared back at me and said, 'I'm sorry. We assumed Charlie Garland was male.'

Charlie Garland smiled. 'Not surprising given the name. And you are?'

'I'm Inspector Sharma. This is Detective Constable Wheatley. We've come to talk to you about Geeta Mehta. Can we go somewhere private please?'

'Certainly. Oh, by the way, it's "Mrs"… Mrs Garland.'

Mrs Garland fetched Miss Palmer, the head of Geeta's year group, and led us to her office. We were sitting in Mrs Garland's office, which was cramped and I tried hard not to brush my knees against the knees of the two women sitting opposite me. Joy sat to my right.

Miss Palmer cleared her throat. 'As you can imagine, Inspector Sharma, all of us at the college have been traumatised by what happened to Geeta. Both the staff and the students. They've been offered counselling and trained therapists are on site. Some of the students are too upset to attend at the moment. The Christmas decorations are being taken down and the pantomime's been cancelled. It's eerily quiet in the building even though there are more than six hundred people in it.'

To my left was Mrs Garland's desk and on top was the usual array of paperwork. A coffee mug was next to this pile with *The world's greatest teacher* written on it. At the far edge of the desk a thick silver frame held a photograph of Mrs Garland with a tall, slim, handsome man. They were laughing, arms around each other's waists and looking at each other. A couple very much in love.

I stared at the photograph a bit too long.

I thought I could smell cigarette smoke in the office and wondered whether Mrs Garland was a secret smoker, blowing smoke out of the window once the students had gone home.

'What sort of friends did Geeta have?' asked Joy.

'She was a popular student,' replied Miss Palmer. 'She was friendly, quick to help others. Bright and well-liked by all, both students and staff. She would've been successful as a professional musician in an orchestra. Or even as a famous violinist in her own right.'

'What about her use of the internet? Any ideas about that?' I asked.

'Can I ask what you're driving at, Inspector Sharma?' asked Mrs Garland.

'I'm wondering why the killer picked on her. Could it have been somebody she met online? Like a social networking site?

Did Geeta say anything to her friends about meeting somebody new online?'

Miss Palmer looked at Mrs Garland and then turned to me and said, 'I've no idea, Inspector Sharma. Our systems don't allow access to social networking sites. She could've used her mobile phone but none of her friends have said anything to me or anybody else that I know of. I'm sure Geeta would've been aware of the dangers.'

'Did Geeta's photograph appear in the local press recently? Say in a performance or on an extra-curricular trip?' I asked.

Both staff said no.

'Have there been any reports of strange men loitering outside the gates, Mrs Garland?' asked Joy.

'We've had no reports of anything out of the ordinary, Constable Wheatley.'

Miss Palmer replied, 'I'm so sorry we can't help. I've been trying desperately hard to think of why Geeta might have been targeted. Who could have harmed her? But I just can't think of anything. I wish to God I could help you.' A tear fell down her right cheek and Mrs Garland put a comforting arm around her shoulder.

CHAPTER 12

I pressed the accelerator gingerly as the car crawled along the snow-covered tarmac. I maintained at least ten yards between me and the car in front but the idiot behind me was too close and had left no braking distance. The windscreen wipers moved left and right, thick snow clinging to the edges of the blades.

Although only late afternoon, it was dark. The roads were busy and commuters were trying to get home before the weather became too bad. The road I was on hadn't been gritted. The snow fell steadily. Cars skidded as drivers drove in the wrong gear. Others drove too fast. One or two cars had already broken down by the side of the road, and some were blinding others with their fog lights. The endless stream of cars came towards me on the right, bonnets, roofs, boots and windows covered in snow, smoke spewing out of exhaust pipes. All snaking home for warmth and comfort. Some would make it on time and in one piece, others would not.

I had dropped off Joy earlier at her flat and tried not to think too much of her. I found her attractive and could easily imagine being with her. I was sure we could have had some good times. She was bright, vivacious and well-read. We seemed to have a lot in common. I think she found me attractive too. However, she was junior in rank, a work colleague and any notion of a relationship with her at the moment was a definite no-no. In the future, who knows?

My mobile interrupted my thoughts.

'No joy.'

'No Shep, I've just dropped Joy off at her flat.'

'No, sorry Sir, I meant no joy with the pet shops. All the —
shall we say stock — is accounted for. Also ties up with the
paperwork. I checked all of it personally with each owner.
Nothing missing.'

'Okay Shep. Thanks. Make sure you get off home. Don't get
caught up in the bad weather.'

'Thanks, Sir. On my way.'

My mind wandered back to Joy and what it'd be like to be in
a relationship with another woman. Now definitely was not the
right time. I needed to sort out a permanent house to live in,
build a good relationship with my children, move on after Faye
and…

And what? Life after Faye. Days after Faye. Or was it daze
after Faye?

I know it's a cliché but when you are young and in love you
think it will last forever. You do everything together. You
laugh, you sleep, you make love, you shop, you work, you
make love, you go out to eat, you go out for a drink, you make
love. And you think that life will never end. You and me. Me
and you. Make love. Make babies. And we'll live happily ever
after. Or not…

How had life gone so wrong for me, for Yasmin, for Karan
and, yes, for Faye too? I wondered yet again if I could have
done anything to stop Faye from doing what she did. There
were numerous clues I could have picked up on. But maybe
there was nothing I could've done which would have made
things any different.

Karma, kismet, fate and all that.

'And when we moved to Leicester, d'you know what she said?'

'I love you, Rohan.'

'Yes, she said that, Fernando.'

'Rohan's been a bad boy.'

'That too. She said that the first evening in our new house. Hugged me, squeezed my bum hard and said, "Let's make babies now."'

I chopped the onions, put them with the cardamoms, cloves, turmeric and other spices, some chopped tomatoes and stirred the ingredients. I put in the minced lamb and let it cook gently for half an hour. The smell was making my mouth water. The radio played in the background.

'And y'know what, Fernando?' I said as I put another mouthful of spaghetti and minced lamb in my mouth, 'I didn't notice the little things that had changed. They should have sent alarm bells ringing but the only alarms I heard were the sound of the sirens, often made by the car I was in.'

Fernando stood on his perch, grabbed a piece of banana, put it in his dark beak and stared at me. A pumpkin seed fell from the piece of banana. His eyes remained intense. Both of us stopped a while and listened to Simon and Garfunkel singing 'Bridge Over Troubled Water' on the radio.

I thought of how Faye had started coming home at irregular times, often later than expected, there seemed to be more evening meetings, she started taking an evening course at the university, talked a lot about one of the other people on the course, Pierre Thiebault, a twenty-five-year-old teacher from another school, a Black Frenchman from Martinique who wanted to be the headteacher of a secondary school by the time he was thirty-four — why that age, I never worked out — and then she stopped talking about him. 'That should have concerned me, shouldn't it, Fernando?' But it didn't. I didn't think anything of it.

One evening, when Karan was five years old, Faye said she had to attend an after-school meeting. I had come home early from work, picked up the kids from their school, watched some television and then we had a chicken casserole which Faye had left in the fridge. I don't think it was connected but Karan became ill, throwing up, a high temperature one moment, shivering the next and wanting his mum. Faye's mobile was switched off. I rang the school reception and one of the caretaking staff answered, saying that there was no meeting for staff anywhere in the school.

I felt sick to my stomach. And wanted to throw up. Just like Karan.

She came home and maintained the lie. I explained what I'd done and she couldn't hold the lie anymore. She admitted to being with Pierre, had been seeing him for more than a year, told me he made her happy, how life wasn't boring with him, that I'd become a killjoy, she and Pierre wanted to live together and she wanted a divorce.

Just like that.

Except this wasn't a Tommy Cooper joke.

I tried hard to make her stay and it was a good year for the roses. But eventually it was me who ended up leaving the marital home. Back to a rented two-bedroom Victorian terrace. Life had come full circle.

'And y'know what Fernando? You're lucky. Nobody's ever rejected you. When it happens, especially by somebody you care for, it tears you apart. And here we are, just you and me.'

Fernando looked at me, his neck danced to the left and then to the right. He then flipped around on his perch, his back to me, lifted his tail and pooped on the newspaper I'd placed at the bottom of his cage. Sometimes I think he understands more than he lets on.

'Gee, thanks a lot Fernando. You too, eh? Or is that *et tu* Fernando?'

Marlene Dietrich's face in black and white stared back at me from the wall opposite. Cigarette in hand. I thought of the words to the song 'Lili Marlene'.

But then Fernando started with

'*Vasco da Gama*,
Went to Ghana…'

'Not now please, Fernando. I don't want to hear it.'

He stopped and stared at me. He knew from the sound of my voice that I'd put the cover over his cage if he continued.

As I finished the food and was drinking the last of the Sauvignon in the glass my mobile rang.

'Hello, Inspector Sharma.' It was Angie Deacon. 'I'm sorry to disturb you in the evening but something's been really bothering me for a while. I wasn't sure whether to come clean and say anything to you. Even at this stage I'm not absolutely sure.'

My heart started racing.

My pulse quickening.

CHAPTER 13

I pressed the phone hard against my ear and listened attentively. My heart thumped hard against my breastbone. I couldn't believe what Angie Deacon was telling me.

'The body of a Black girl, about seventeen or eighteen years old, was found last August, sixteen months ago. Her family were refugees or asylum seekers — I'm not sure what the difference is. I can't remember where she was from. Yemen or Somalia or Sudan, one of these countries where they're always fighting and killing each other. Anyway, her body was found under an ash tree. Behind the perimeter walls of a big, detached house in the east of the city. The house is a retreat for the Hare Rama Hare Krishna types. You know the ones, loin cloths and saffron and the men have shaved heads and they play hand drums and jingle their brass bells and chant.'

'Angie, can you please get to the point. This is really important.'

'Sorry, Sir. Anyway, the body, you know the hands and arms were placed in a peculiar shape, unnatural angles. And the poor young woman was naked and there were marks on the tree and so on. The case we're working on is very similar. Sorry Sir, I thought somebody would've drawn it to your attention, the super or somebody.'

I vaguely remembered the case of the naked body of a young Black female being found towards the end of last summer but I was a detective sergeant at the time and not involved in the case. It was the height of the holiday season, Faye and I had recently split up and I'd gone to Morocco for three weeks. It was good therapy to escape the pain and the work. I didn't come back until mid-September so didn't know much about the case. I certainly didn't know any of the details and I couldn't even remember who was leading the investigation. Angie told me and I asked whether she remembered the name of the girl.

'I think the name was Solomon. And her Christian name sounded like "Iron".'

'What? Iron Solomon?' I asked.

'Something like that, Sir. You know what these foreign names are like. Difficult to remember and sometimes difficult to pronounce.'

I was silent.

'Sorry, Sir. I didn't mean yours.'

I said it was all right, we exchanged a few pleasantries and I broke the connection.

This case might give me a breakthrough. My mind started churning away at the endless possibilities. I wanted to rush to HQ, look at the evidence and speak to the senior investigating officer. He had a good reputation and was well liked by other officers. I didn't know him, apart from to nod to in the corridors and the canteen. But it was late at night, far too late.

'*Vasco da Gama,*
Went to Ghana,
Without his pyjamas…'

'Fernando! I don't want to hear it!'

The house fell silent. I sipped the glass of wine and thought late into the night.

CHAPTER 14

I shuffled the ten-by-eight glossy colour photographs and stared at the broken and twisted arms and legs of a slim, naked, young Black woman. The incident forms told me her name was Ayan Suleiman and she had arrived from Somalia almost three years ago, her family claiming asylum from the violence in that lawless state. Her contorted face and the grotesque posturing of her body, elbows and knee joints smashed with a heavy blunt instrument, hid her beauty. And her agonising death. The arms and legs were similarly positioned to that of Geeta and aerial shots taken from the ash tree showed the body in the shape of a swastika. I could see three black ants crawling on her bottom lip and into her lifeless open mouth.

I took the orange memory stick from the evidence box, inserted it into the USB port of my desktop computer and looked at all the photographs on the disc. I magnified many of the images, focused on each part of the body inch by inch. There were four deep cuts, parallel and running from right to left, just above her shaved pudenda. At the top of her left thigh was a dirty grey and white blob, with shades of brown. It had spread like an amoeba and stood out starkly against her skin. On her forehead the killer had drawn a big eye in white. The iris, however, was an iridescent blue, the colour of lapis lazuli. The pupil had been left black, the black of her skin. I scanned the photographs on the screen and focused on her feet and ankles. I couldn't see anything on the feet. But just above the webbing between the thumb and forefinger of her right hand I could see the tell-tale signs in the skin. Two small round puncture marks about an inch or so apart.

I put the hard copies of the photographs back in the box and picked up the forensic report marked *Preliminary* on the front cover. The report had been written by a locum Home Office pathologist, based with the regional team, who was covering long-term vacancies and holidays, long before Nasreen Khan appeared on the scene.

The report stated that Ayan was eighteen years and one month old, was relatively tall, and apart from a few other details it confirmed that the dirty grey, white and brown blob was the dropping of a large bird, like a crow or magpie or even a hawk or kite. Parts of an unidentified leaf were found deep inside her, past the stitching to the top half of the labia. Both knee joints had been smashed by a blunt instrument and the cause of death was thought to be a sudden heart attack brought on by the sheer terror of experiencing the other injuries. The two puncture marks on the right hand were noted but nothing more was said about them. Organs and tissue samples had been taken from the body but toxicology reports on them had not been requested.

The report commented that the time of death was difficult to establish because the body showed signs of having been frozen, probably in a deep freezer, and it had also been thoroughly washed. It was signed and dated by a Dr Rupert Bryce-Jones.

I then looked through the various statements. The first one was headed *The background of the victim* and it informed me that Ayan Suleiman was almost sixteen when she arrived in the UK with her family. Her father was killed by Al-Shabab fighters for being an informer for the British SAS and Kenyan troops fighting on the Kenya–Somalia border. Her thirty-seven-year-old mother, Filad, feared for her life and that of her three children, Ayan and her two brothers, Fahmi, aged eleven, and

Sooyan, aged thirteen. Filad had been given seven hundred pounds by the British army as compensation for her husband's death through an intermediary in the town of Kismaayo, not far from the Kenya–Somalia border. She and her three children travelled on foot to Addis Ababa, applied for political asylum at the Swedish embassy, stayed in Stockholm for a few months, travelled to Brussels and then to London where they applied again for asylum.

They came to Leicester, where there was a growing number of Somali refugees, and were allocated a local authority flat which had been condemned as unfit for human habitation. Various support workers helped them settle in and they seemed to have integrated well into the community on the large council estate.

Ayan was a friendly and sociable girl and she quickly adapted to her new secondary school. After intensive English language sessions, her teachers realised she was highly intelligent and she started doing well academically. Her mother, whose spoken English was still limited and who needed an interpreter, described her as happy and a hard worker, with friends from all backgrounds. She helped her mother with the housework and went shopping with her to the city centre and Indian shops on the other side of the city which sold fruit and vegetables they were familiar with. Her mother stated that Ayan wanted to be a model and be famous and earn lots of money. All the teachers and support workers interviewed confirmed the mother's view of her daughter.

I inserted the silver memory stick into the USB port and looked at the video footage of the crime scene. The house was set back from the main road. The camera focused on the wrought iron gates which were opened by a uniformed officer and led down a tarmac drive for about fifty yards. The large house was late Victorian or early Edwardian, stone with a slate roof, and as the camera panned from left to right it looked as if it had at least eight rooms, possibly ten. There were white sash windows and the large, white wooden door had a brass knocker in the shape of a lion's head.

The lawns on either side of the drive were well tended, bordered by flowerbeds of yellow, white and red roses, tiger lilies and chrysanthemums. To the right of the house was a cluster of plane trees, silver birch and elm. To the left was an ash tree in full foliage, and Ayan's body could be seen under it. The camera panned around but there didn't seem to be anything of consequence. The camera turned and the person walked backwards up the drive and through the gate. It was then that I saw the mahogany plaque to the left of the gate. Across the plaque, chiselled in letters painted in glossy white, was the word *Ashram*.

'Ashram', the Hindi word meaning 'retreat'. But there were four deep cuts running in parallel lines across the suffix 'ram'. The prefix 'ash' had not been touched.

No mention had been made of this in any of the reports so far.

I turned back to a pile of papers marked *Witness Statements*. There were seven statements taken from the residents of the house. All were male, ranging in age from twenty-two to sixty-one. Most were white, two were Indian, and all were devotees of the Hindu god Krishna. The statements said more or less the same thing and were unremarkable. The occupants of the house finished evening prayers at about nine thirty and each undertook his domestic chores: ensuring that the dishwasher was switched on, that the black stray cat that had taken refuge with them three weeks previously had been let out for the night, that all candles and *divas* had been extinguished, all electric lights were switched off and all curtains drawn. The two wall-lights at the front of the house had been left on, as was customary.

All went to bed at about ten o'clock and woke up at four-thirty the next morning, ready for prayers to welcome the bright sunrise and a new dawn. As the early pale sun rose over the eastern horizon, and the chorus of blackbirds and starlings ushered in yet another day, ablutions were undertaken and curtains were drawn. It was when one of them, a yogi named Brother Morarji, drew the curtains from his first-floor bedroom that he noticed what looked like a black mannequin on the grass under the ash tree. And two of them went out to investigate…

A folder marked *Miscellaneous* contained a few press cuttings, some photocopies of online reporting of the case, some handwritten notes taken by various officers. Nothing of significance.

I had arrived at the office early, was feeling tired and rubbed my eyes. I thought of the desperately sad life of Ayan and her family. To go through all that in Somalia, her father killed, then travelling thousands of miles through freezing rain and snow, overcoming so many hardships, only to end up dead in a cold corner of some foreign land.

My thoughts were interrupted by a knock on my door.

'Sir, I'm not sure I had the authority to let you have that box,' said the constable who was in charge of the basement where the evidence boxes were kept. 'Isn't your case after all, is it, Sir?'

I stared at him for a moment. 'You can take it away. Thank you.'

I sat opposite Inspector Frank Genner who was reclining in a black leather chair. 'Do you think our lads will win the next test match at Nagpur, Rohan?'

'I don't really know. Haven't had much time to follow the cricket.'

'Oh, that's a shame. Our lads have a great chance of beating the Indians at home. The Indians are stronger when they're home. Usually crap abroad, even with all their so-called mystery spinners who rub sugary saliva into the leather. Who d'you support? Our lads or the Indians? D'you fail the Norman Tebbit test when they come here to play?'

'Sorry, Frank, haven't been following it much, as I said. Haven't had much time.'

'A good diplomatic answer. Now if you ever fancy some golf, do let me know. A few of us belong to an exclusive golf club, if y'know what I mean. Would be good if you joined us when the weather improves. I'll be happy to introduce you and nominate you for membership. Could take you far. Knowing the right people, socialising with them.'

'Thanks. I'll bear it in mind.'

'Now, you said you wanted help with the case you're working on. You did well to get that one. Not many would've been given a complicated case like that. Not so early in their career.'

'I don't need help with the case, Frank. Thanks. Just wanted to ask about a case you were investigating last year. The Ayan Suleiman murder.'

'Oh, the Black girl. From Somalia. Badly beaten and also the victim of female genital mutilation. Never can understand the practices of some people. There was a wall of silence. Nobody'd seen or heard anything. Asylum seekers don't want to get involved with the police. After a couple of months, the inquiry was wound down. But the case is still open.'

He smiled, drew back his lips and showed uneven teeth. I noticed there was a stain on his dark tie. His shirt looked like cheap twill.

'Frank, the FGM, was it recent?'

'How'd I know? The pathologist didn't say and I didn't think it was relevant to how she died. I assumed it was old. I didn't personally look.'

'What about the two puncture marks between her right thumb and forefinger? Did the pathologist say how they could've been caused?'

'No, he didn't. He was fairly new. Probably didn't think they were important.'

'Any CCTV images of the victim on her route?'

'Some. Walking past shops with security cameras. Getting on and off the bus. Nothing more after that. We think she was abducted near some disused industrial units, so no cameras there.'

'How about toxicology reports? Were any organs or tissue samples sent for further tests?'

He jumped up from his chair, slammed his fist on the desk and glared at me. A vein throbbing on his left temple. 'Who the fuck d'you think you are? How dare you question my methods? I became a copper long before you could wipe your fucking arse. Or wash it, or whatever it is you people do. How dare you tell me what I should and shouldn't be doing! Now get the fuck out of here!' His red face was full of rage. His hands shaking. 'And don't ever fucking look at any evidence box of mine without first getting my permission. D'you understand? Now fuck off!'

I stood up, walked to the door and looked back at him.

I slammed it shut as I went out.

CHAPTER 15

'I'm sorry Superintendent Breedon's busy,' said the PA, who shared the communal office with other personal assistants. 'He's Skyping with a senior police officer in Australia. Would you like to sit and wait, Sir?'

I sat down, then stood up and paced.

Eventually, the door opened and Superintendent Breedon walked out. 'Ah, Rohan, good to see you. How're you?' He smiled broadly and I was momentarily distracted by his distinctive salt and pepper moustache. I shook his hand and he placed his arm around my shoulder as we walked into his office. 'Sorry about keeping you waiting but I had to talk to a senior officer in Melbourne about policing in a multiracial and culturally diverse city. Might get an invitation to go out there if I play my cards right.'

'Why the hell didn't anybody tell me about Ayan Suleiman?' I said.

'Now, now. Calm down. Come and sit down. Who?'

'Ayan Suleiman. The Somali girl who was murdered in August last year.'

He paused for a moment. The wrinkles on his forehead appeared as he frowned and looked at me with his penetrating blue eyes, a stark contrast to his dark hair. 'Oh, her. Oh, yes. I wasn't here when it happened. I was tutoring at the national college. The case is still open and one of our most experienced inspectors is in charge of it. You've met Frank, haven't you? Could learn a lot from him. The team made some good headway but the Somali community clammed up and we can't get any further.'

I noticed faint wrinkles on the back of his hands. Old age and a hefty retirement pension were gradually creeping up on him.

'Sir, you've seen my reports on the Geeta Mehta case. The manner of the death, the injuries, the killer's signature. I've looked at the evidence box for Ayan Suleiman, such as it is. The deaths are similar, though I'm waiting for toxicology reports for Geeta Mehta so can't say anything for certain yet. Ayan's death doesn't seem to have been properly investigated —'

'Be careful what you're saying, Rohan —'

'There're too many unanswered questions. If I'm not mistaken, we could have a serial killer on our hands. One who has killed two young women — one Black and one Indian.'

'Now, now. You've been watching too many episodes of *CSI* and *NCIS*. Been reading too much about Hannibal Lecter and Ted Bundy and the Night Stalker. And anyway, it's only two — '

I could tell he immediately regretted the comment. He paused, smiled and then adopted an academic tone.

'The FBI definition is that we need at least three victims before a serial killer is identified as such. That sort of thing doesn't happen in a nice city like Leicester.'

'I suppose it didn't happen in nice cities like Bradford and Leeds when the Yorkshire Ripper was running amok,' I countered, 'or in Ipswich when Steve Wright was on the rampage killing vulnerable young women? Or when Dennis Nilsen was flushing body parts of seventeen gay men down the toilet in north London? Sir, there're two victims we know about. There may well be others.'

He looked at me and tapped his thick fingers on the edge of his desk. His fingernails looked manicured. The scent of expensive aftershave floated in the air between us.

He eventually said, 'Okay, take me through what you know.'

I went through both cases with him, explained the similarities, the possible cause of death, the need for proper toxicology tests, the possibility there may be other victims already or that the killer or killers would strike again. I suggested that the team may need to be expanded, that all the evidence and possible lines of enquiry contained within HOLMES, the Home Office Large Major Enquiry System, be looked at again in fine detail. This would pick up cases with any similar features across the country.

I could see that part of him was interested but another part was wishing this problem would go away. He did not want to believe in snakes. The only snake he was interested in was a Cobra beer.

'Apart from the tragedy for their families,' I said, 'and the need to catch the killer, what about the political ramifications if the crimes are racially motivated? Sir, as you know, he's staging the bodies in the shape of a swastika.'

He looked at me and I could sense the cogs in his brain whirring away. He didn't say anything for a while. I let him do all the computations in his head.

'Or the killer may be Black or Asian,' he said. 'Like the case in Atlanta where the killer of Black kids was a Black guy. This one may have a thing about symmetry and geometrical shapes. Got to think of all angles, Rohan. No pun intended.'

'Sir,' I implored him, ignoring his last comment, 'two young women have already been murdered. There could be others.'

After a long silence, he said, 'Okay, I'll go with you for a while but … er … if this … er … don't forget to keep an eye on the costs and staffing involved. Keep me posted at all times. Oh, by the way, don't write anything about Frank's investigation in any of the reports. I want our approach to be whiter than white at all times...' He paused, looked at me and shuffled uneasily in his chair. 'If you see what I mean,' he finished.

CHAPTER 16

The Suleimans lived in a two-bedroom flat in a tower block in the north-west of the city. Joy and I travelled up in the lift, which smelt of urine and disinfectant. The lift walls were covered in graffiti and so-called artwork done by spray cans. One of the lightbulbs had been smashed. The corners had black and grey mould. The gears of the lift ground, crunched and stuttered as we made our way to the eleventh floor.

The first thing that struck me when Mrs Suleiman opened her front door were the four deep parallel scars running across each cheek. Made by a sharp knife. A result of the body art and the cultural traditions which were common to the Somali and other Black ethnic groups in East and Central Africa. The second thing that struck me was the aromatic smell of fried fish and plantain coming from the kitchen. My mouth watered. She had probably prepared the evening meal for her family even though it was only mid-afternoon. I hadn't had time for any lunch.

Mrs Suleiman invited us in after we introduced ourselves. She was tall, in her late thirties but looked ten years older, with a face etched by poverty, heartache and a hard life. She said she was alone in the flat as her two sons were at school.

As we entered the lounge, through the cold uncarpeted hallway with fading and torn wallpaper, she pointed at the corner.

'There are some really kind people in this world, *Bwana*. They gave that to me for my children to use, to help them with their schoolwork. They gave it to the charity that helps us. *Na siklia, Bwana?*'

'Yes, I understand, *Mama*,' I replied.

The gift was an old black computer monitor, accompanied by a grey tower and keyboard, all sitting on a small wooden table. A cheap white plastic garden chair stood in front of the monitor. The flat was clean and tidy but the room screamed poverty and human degradation. It was cold in there despite the portable gas fire with two of its four bars lit.

The lounge was sparsely furnished. Some cushions and beanbags lay on the floor. On one of the walls was a print of a deserted white sandy tropical beach with palm trees leaning down, azure ocean and clear blue sky, a scene which could have been from any tropical country but I suspected was the coast of East Africa. The print, framed in white plastic, was mocking the cold and dampness in the flat. A cold breeze blew in through the gaps between the window frames and the walls.

On a shelf stood framed photographs of the three children, Ayan, Sooyan and Fahmi. Ayan, luminescent black skin, perfect white teeth and big eyes smiled at the camera, trying to suppress an embarrassed giggle. She hid the pain and the suffering they had already endured. She had no idea, of course, of the horrors to come. I noticed there was no photograph of Mr Suleiman.

'Beautiful, wasn't she, *Bwana*? We named her Ayan, meaning lucky. Only my poor daughter wasn't very lucky, was she? Why did Allah, who is merciful, do that to her and to us?'

I had no answer for her.

I didn't understand much Swahili, the common language binding different groups of people in much of Eastern Africa, but I could get by with a few words and sentences. It was still widely spoken in some bastardised form by the first generation of Kenyan and Ugandan Asians in Leicester and some of their children. The younger generation, British born and bred, didn't spend too much time wondering about this lost Black world and this dying Black language.

I felt uneasy about the term *Bwana* being used by Mrs Suleiman. It reminded me of old Tarzan films, with white men in khaki shorts and shirts and a brown pith helmet ordering the Black natives around.

'Yes, she was beautiful, Mrs Suleiman. *Pole sana, Mama.* I'm really sorry about what happened to her.'

'*Asante sana, Bwana,*' she replied. She sat down on the cushions on the floor. Joy and I were offered the chairs.

'Can you please tell me what sort of girl Ayan was? What she did in her last few days,' I continued.

Mrs Suleiman wore a tightly-wrapped light green niqab and baggy black cotton trousers. An old brown blanket was wrapped around her shoulders. I could see where Ayan's striking features came from.

She said that Ayan was happy and had been looking forward to the long summer holidays. She had recently started going to a youth club in the early evening, where she played pool, listened to music and socialised with the other girls. All the usual things for a young woman that age.

Ayan attended two extra-curricular school clubs run by the staff. Twice a week, one for science and the other for computing. She was a good daughter, Mrs Suleiman continued, and wouldn't have hurt a fly. Always came back on time and would ring on her pre-paid mobile if she was going to be late. Or she used a friend's if she didn't have enough credit.

'I'm sorry to ask you these questions, *Mama*, but what about the last day? What was she doing then?'

She told us it was a bright sunny Saturday afternoon and she asked Ayan to go to one of the Indian greengrocers at about three o'clock. The boys had gone out to play football. Mrs

Suleiman had a heavy summer cold. She gave Ayan ten pounds for the *mboga*, the fresh vegetables, the okra, mooli, yams, sweet potatoes, aubergines and fresh chillies. If you went late in the afternoon, she explained, things were cheaper as the shopkeeper would rather sell his produce than leave it till Monday to go bad. Ayan had to take a bus into town and then another one out to the shops and back again. Four bus journeys in all. She had done this often and the shopkeepers knew her, liked her, and would sometimes throw in a few items for free.

'*Bwana*, after that last time when she kissed me goodbye, she went down and waved to me from the road below. I was looking at her from that window,' she said pointing, 'and never saw her alive again.' Her chest heaved and she started sobbing. Joy sat down next to her on the cushions and put an arm around her.

'How could any man do that to my poor child? My beautiful daughter. Who had so much to live for,' she said between the sobs.

A few moments later I said, 'We know Ayan didn't attend the sixth form for three weeks before the start of the summer holidays. Why was that?'

'*Bwana*, it's because I was not feeling well. I keep getting coughs and colds. *Ulaya iko baridi mingi*. Europe is too cold. And the doctor also says that I am … what do you call it, when your mind is not working properly … feeling … feeling depressed … because all that has happened. My husband dying, escaping from Somalia, coming here. I have to take a lot of medicines. And I cannot find any work.'

'*Mama*, could she have gone to meet somebody that day? A boyfriend?'

'No, not my Ayan. Why you say that about my sweet, innocent child?'

'I'm sorry but I have to ask these questions. So we can find out what happened to your beautiful daughter. I was wondering whether she might have met anybody by using that computer.'

'Not my daughter. Anyway, I answer all these questions before. Ayan was going to the *mahindi* shops to get some *mboga* for us. That is all. She never came back to us.'

'Did she ever say that somebody was following her? Say, to and from the youth club?'

'No,' she replied, staring at me with those big brown eyes. 'We have nowhere to go. How can we carry on living like this? How will my children survive? Would you and your wife and children like to live like this? And then Allah called Ayan, my only daughter. Oh, Allah the Merciful, what did I do to deserve this? Who could've done this to me and to my beloved Ayan?' She uttered a deep wailing cry.

'*Mama, iko shauri ya mungu.* It was the will of God. Were you given a family liaison officer by the other police officer who spoke to you? When they found Ayan? To keep you informed of the case?'

'I'm sorry, nobody has explained much to me about what is going on. Or what has happened since we buried our beloved Ayan.'

I felt a bit edgy about the next question but had to ask her. 'I'm really sorry to ask you this but did Ayan have an operation down below. You know, between her legs?'

'*Bwana!* I would never allow that. I cannot even afford it. I had it done and I know how painful it is. And all the other problems which happen. For the rest of your life. I would never allow a daughter of mine to go through that.'

'So, she wasn't having that done when she was absent from the sixth form? Not even by a *mganga*, a traditional doctor?'

I immediately regretted saying that.

Mrs Suleiman just stared at me, eyes wide open, tears rolling down her cheeks. I wasn't sure whether she hated me at that point. I wouldn't have blamed her.

After a while, I got out my wallet, took out a twenty-pound note, offered it to her and said, '*Mama, chukua poundi ishirini. For mboga.*' She said she couldn't take the money but I was persistent and she eventually accepted it.

'*Asante sana.*'

I said *kwaheri* to her. Joy and I closed the door on her sadness and her grief and walked away.

We could do that. She could not.

'Her spoken English wasn't too bad, was it?' I said as we went down in the lift. 'I don't think she could've told us anymore, really.'

'No, but it's been more than a year since her daughter's murder,' said Joy. 'Maybe her English has improved since then. What about the scars on her cheeks?'

'It's common for certain Black tribes in East and Central Africa to have those. Both men and women. Deeply held religious and cultural traditions going back hundreds, if not thousands, of years,' I replied.

'D'you think the killer could be a Somali man then? The four cuts we've seen in both homicides. Maybe that's his signature.'

'No idea. I don't feel sure about anything anymore. All guesswork until we get toxicology and forensic reports.' I paused. 'I feel really bad asking about the FGM,' I said. 'Clumsy. May've been better coming from you. Woman to woman. She sounded defensive though. The pathologist's report stated the stitches were expertly done. Maybe there's a traditional doctor who does these sorts of things, like a back street abortionist from the past. She comes from a tradition where these things are practised. Maybe she borrowed the money to pay for it.'

'I'm not really sure what to think,' said Joy. 'There's no easy way to approach the subject. What's done's done. By the way, I didn't know you were such a polyglot.'

'Oh, don't be fooled. Just a word or phrase of Swahili here and there. That's all.'

'Well, I'm impressed. It was very touching to give her the money.'

We were both silent for a while as the winding mechanism crunched and groaned and the lift rattled. I was thinking of how badly Mrs Suleiman had been treated by the constabulary but given my recent experience it didn't surprise me. She was a vulnerable woman in a foreign land and would have no idea what to expect from the state. After all she'd been through, we owed her at least a proper investigation into her daughter's murder. She didn't even get that. I was determined to put that right.

'When this is all over,' Joy said, breaking the silence, 'can we go out for a drink to celebrate? Just you and me. Would be nice.'

She caught me by surprise.

'Joy, as you know, it's not the done thing for superiors to fraternise with the lower ranks.'

She looked hurt and stared down at the dirty floor.

I registered how smart and attractive she looked. Her blonde hair had been carefully combed back, held in place by an amber butterfly clip. Her pale-yellow blouse stood out against the dark and expensive navy jacket. A subtle but inviting scent of perfume rose above the other smells in the lift.

I smiled at her.

She looked up.

'Of course I will, Joy. I was only joking. Be really nice to do that.'

CHAPTER 17

It was just past seven thirty in the evening. My house was warming up, the old boiler and pump pushing hot water through the creaking and rumbling central heating system. I could hear the faint sound of the television from next door. They were watching the Bollywood film *Bodyguard* and the title song, *Teri Meri*, about unrequited love came through the brick walls. I didn't object to it. I was watching live cricket from a sunny Jamaica where Pakistan were playing the West Indies.

Once I had eaten my meat samosas and chicken tikka, I rang around. Nasreen was the first port of call.

'No, I don't know Dr Bryce-Jones personally,' she replied, 'though I've heard of him. I do remember the girl's name, Ayan Suleiman, because I went through all the outstanding cases when I was appointed. I know her tissue and organ samples were stored.'

'Nasreen, could you please do the full range of tests on them? Whatever you think necessary. I'm not sure how thorough your predecessor was. Have the other results come through yet?'

'Should be here any day now,' she said. 'I'll chase them up again.'

I heard a male voice in the background. 'Nasreen, who th'hell are you talking to this time of night?'

'Sorry, Inspector, I've got to go. My husband.'

'But doesn't he appreciate you're a professional involved in a murder investigation? That you need to speak to people at unsocial hours sometimes?'

'Goodbye, Inspector.'

I was irritated at the abrupt end of our conversation but, hey, I suppose they were entitled to a private life. I looked at Fernando whose head and beak were plunged deep down in the water tray, taking a long drink. 'Just you and me tonight, Fernando. Shall we go clubbing later? See whether we can pull a couple of birds?' His white and grey face stared back at me. And then he squawked. I'm not sure whether that meant he approved of my miserable attempt to be funny.

As I looked at the table, I noticed something strange. 'Fernando, have you been coming out of your cage when I'm not here? Moving things?' The two coasters weren't where I had left them in the morning. The trunks of the elephants normally pointed to the left, not to the right.

I stared at the two bright red coasters with the dancing Indian elephants and the paisley patterns. They had faint round traces where mugs of tea had been placed. Perhaps I was mistaken about them being moved. Fernando scratched the right side of his head with his claw and looked as if he couldn't care less.

My mobile rang.

'Are you all right, Rohan?'

I immediately felt defensive. 'Yes, I'm fine, Faye,' I said. 'Busy, y'know. How're the children? What can I do for you?'

'Yasmin and Karan are fine, Rohan. They're the reason I'm ringing.'

I knew it wasn't to enquire about my health. That's why I didn't enquire about hers.

'On Thursday evening, Pierre and I have to attend an important social event at his school. We won't be back till quite late. Yasmin's having a sleepover at one of her friends that night. Is it possible for you to look after Karan, please? He can stay the night with you, if you like.'

'Or if you like, Faye.'

She didn't say anything.

It would be good to spend some time with my son so I agreed.

'Bite me, Rohan! Bite me!'

There was silence.

And then the loud sound of Faye laughing down the phone.

'Is that Fernando?' she asked, laughing. 'Christ, he must've picked that up when we were … y'know? Shouldn't have had him in the bedroom with us.'

I didn't respond, wished her well and switched off the phone.

CHAPTER 18

Ben, Shep, Nasreen, Joy and I were in the incident room. Ben held up a transparent plastic evidence bag and said, 'Guess what the killer left behind? Hid this under Geeta Mehta's right buttock.'

We stared at some shrivelled and crumpled dirty white crepe paper. It was about six inches long and three inches wide at the top and tapered into a dark green base.

'Not much to look at in its current state, is it?' replied Ben. 'I've got a photograph of what it's supposed to look like. Here, let me show you.'

Ben walked over to the laptop and the large interactive screen flickered to life. The room was silent. The warm air on my face told me I ought to be in a warm tropical paradise, sunning myself on the beach under a pale blue sky and bright sun. Not living in this nightmare.

'Datura, or to give it one of its common names, jimsonweed. Some call it the devil's trumpet because of the shape of the flower,' Ben said as we stared at the photograph of a flower with a white corolla in the form of a trumpet, tinged with lavender, with a bright green base. Its stalk had broad leaves with a walnut-shaped fruit, about two to three inches in diameter and covered in thorns. I thought it looked like a drooping testicle but I didn't like the idea of small thorns hanging from it.

'It's also known as thorn apple or moon flower or moon lily because the flowers open after dusk and close by mid-morning the following day. For the romantics among us, some people refer to it as belladonna or beautiful lady. But absolutely deadly. One of the most poisonous plants known, with an intoxicating bittersweet scent. The dried seeds from the pod or its dried leaves, when ingested in a drink or inhaled with a mixture of tobacco and hash, can kill or lead to severe mental disorders such as schizophrenia. The seeds contain hallucinogenic alkaloids.'

'Is this native to Britain, Ben?' asked Shep.

'Can grow in the wild here, especially during hot summers. Ingesting the leaves and seeds will lead to severe bouts of delirium where the individual won't be able to differentiate fantasy from reality. They can become violent and suffer from hypothermia, convulsions, a rapid heartbeat and death.'

I swivelled my chair away from the screen and asked Nasreen, 'There were no traces of this in Geeta's system were there? Blood, lungs, other vital organs?'

Nasreen sat opposite me. I tried not to think about how my last conversation had ended with her.

'No, we did the full range of toxicology tests, and Ben alerted me to this. Nothing. The cause of death was definitely cobra venom and this was confirmed by the experts at the London School of Hygiene and Tropical Medicine. The only other thing we found were faint traces of sandstone dust mixed with coal in her lungs. Also, under the big toenail of her right foot. Other than that, nothing.'

'But why this flower under her buttock?' Shep asked of nobody in particular.

Joy said, 'It's obvious, isn't it? Another signature, along with the leaf in the vagina.'

Shep sat to my right and I felt his body tense. His right hand clenched into a fist. His annoyance at being put down all too evident.

'Well, yes, we all know it's a signature,' I said, as a way of defusing the situation. 'The leaf in the vagina was identified by the people at Kew Gardens. It's from a wood apple tree, which grows throughout Asia. All parts of the tree are widely used for medicinal purposes and Hindus consider it sacred.'

'So, the killer leaves us with a flower that can kill and one that can heal,' said Nasreen. 'What about the other evidence, Ben? Any idea of the chemical and mineral composition of the lipstick, talcum powder, eye liner, eye shadow and so on? Whether we can narrow down their origins?'

Ben walked back to the table and sat down. 'All are common items made by large companies specialising in beauty products, except the black kohl used on Geeta's eyes. That can only be bought online or from unscrupulous Indian shop owners. It contains dangerously high levels of mercury and lead which can cause cancer. Unfortunately, Customs and Excise and Trading Standards can't keep track of every shipment that comes into the country. It's still popular among Indian mothers who think using it around the baby's eyes wards off evil.'

'Didn't help Geeta much, did it?' said Shep, rather unhelpfully.

'The other thing bothering me is the tyre tread in the soft mud. We did a cast of it, compared it with known brands here, in Europe and America. Couldn't find a match. Then we contacted manufacturers in other parts of the world. And, bingo, we found a match with a tyre that's produced in India. But why just the one tread, not two? And why's the image relatively faint?'

We had no answer to Ben's questions.

'Anybody with any thoughts on the letters "A" "S" and "H" carved into the tree trunk?' I asked. 'Obviously spells "ash" but it's an oak tree and not an ash. And why four cuts? Why not three or two or five?'

They stared at me.

'And the most obvious question of all,' I continued, 'is do we have a racist killer, considering the way the body was positioned? Or is that too simple an interpretation? Is the killer from one of the many minority groups we have here? Before you think of an answer to that, have a look at this.' I pointed the remote at the laptop and pressed the play button.

They were stunned into silence as the overhead photograph of Ayan's broken and twisted body lying on the ground under the tree appeared.

It was getting late as I summed up the case to the team.

'The first thing is we can't say we have a serial killer on our hands. What we have is the brutal murder of two young women. The problem is there may be more. We just don't know. The level of violence has increased. He degraded Geeta, not just through the sheer brutality of the attack but also through necrophilia. There's no mention of it in the pathologist's report for Ayan, such as it is. So, we have a highly sadistic and organised killer who knows how *not* to leave DNA. Both the bodies were thoroughly washed before being dumped.'

'You're right, Inspector,' said Nasreen. 'There wasn't even a pubic hair left on Geeta's body.'

'Thanks, Dr Khan. We also know he can handle deadly snakes,' I continued, 'and has very good knowledge of highly poisonous plants. Ayan's mother said her daughter didn't undergo FGM. I think it's a fair assumption at this stage the killer did it and he has some sort of medical knowledge. If he's the one who did the stitches.'

Joy crossed her legs and shuddered.

'I think our killer is probably aged twenty-five to forty-five — most multiple killers and rapists are — that he's well-educated and well-read. He's physically strong because he can carry bodies weighing several stones. He may be well-travelled, because of his knowledge of tropical plants and snakes. He knows the city well because he can move about unnoticed at will. We can assume he either lives here or he visits regularly, for work or to see relatives. Both the bodies were left in the south or south-east of the city with easy access on the outer ring road. The level of violence used is becoming more intense and we could well have another victim soon. A psychological profiler might say he could be involved in a relationship and the woman knows about his bouts of violence. She may have experienced some of it herself.'

Nasreen said, 'Isn't it unusual for killers — multiple killers, serial killers, call them what you like — to target ethnic groups other than their own? Because here we have two different ethnicities, one Indian and one African.'

'There're plenty of killers who pick victims from different ethnic groups. They go for a *type* rather than a race. The Green River Killer in America's Northwest in the 1990s killed women of all nationalities. They were mainly sex workers hooked on drugs. Charles Sobhraj, a killer of Indian origin, killed young whites in Thailand in the 1970s. John Wayne Gacy and Jeffrey Dahmer, both white Americans, killed young gay men from the Far East. We do have the famous case of the Atlanta murders in America between 1980 and 1982 where Wayne Williams, a Black man, was jailed for killing black children and young adults. But there's plenty of doubt about whether he killed them all or whether somebody else was involved too. In this country, serial killers tend to be white. Harold Shipman, Steven

Wright the Suffolk Strangler, Ian Brady and Myra Hindley, the Yorkshire Ripper and so on. A Black or Asian one could be just around the corner.'

'A swastika is a Hindu religious symbol, isn't it?' asked Joy.

'The swastika's not exclusively Indian. It was an important symbol for the Greeks, the Chinese, the ancient Romans, and it's been found in old churches in Armenia, Israel and Ethiopia. It was also an important symbol for the ancient Celts. Believe it or not, at the northern edge of Ilkley Moor in West Yorkshire there's a stone with a pattern of the swastika on it, and it's known as the Swastika Stone. It was the Nazis who made the swastika infamous. Maybe the killer is Indian. But the bodies were positioned in the opposite way to how Hindus draw the swastika. The limbs of the young women were positioned clockwise. In addition, the Hindu symbol has four dots in each of the squares.'

Ben interjected, 'Maybe he's not *au fait* with such subtle nuances about Hinduism. Or about the other cultures and traditions associated with the symbol, Inspector. The killer could be a young Hindu male fitting your profile. The cobra *is* important in Hinduism.'

'Or he could be a widely travelled white supremacist,' said Shep, 'who doesn't like Black people and Asians. The snake was an important symbol on the shields of the ancient Romans. It was also widely used by the Nazis.'

I nodded in agreement. 'I'm not discounting anything,' I said. 'Anybody any thoughts about the letters or the word "ash"?'

'Maybe, he's alluding to his name. Ash. Could be short for Ashok,' said Joy.

'Or maybe it's Ashley. And his first name is Laura,' said Shep. He was still smarting from Joy's earlier comment.

'Now, now…' I said. 'The first time with Ayan, at least that's the first time we know of, he crossed out the letters "ram" from "Ashram" with four deep cuts. I'm fairly certain it was him, though the original reports don't refer to it. Not only that but he left her body under an ash tree. The second time, with Geeta, he carved the letters on the trunk of the oak tree under which she was found.'

Joy piped up to explain that 'ash' is significant in Norse and Germanic mythology, not to mention in some computer games. Apparently, the Norse god, Odin, is associated with war, victory and death but is also involved with shamanism, magic and prophecy. He had many sons, the most famous being Thor, god of thunder. He is credited with discovering the runes which are used in magic and divination to predict the future.

We all looked at Joy in amazement as she astounded us with her knowledge. 'There're twenty-four ancient alphabetic symbols which are usually carved on small stone tablets, or in wood or glass. The symbols represent aspects such as brute strength, journey, bliss or glory, beacon or torch, destructive forces, the negatives of human needs and so on. There are symbols for a yew tree, a birch, an oak and an ash.'

According to Joy, in Norse mythology, ash was referred to as 'The Tree of Life' because it was believed to have medicinal and mystical properties, and its wood was burned to keep evil spirits at bay. The symbol for ash is called 'ansuz' and it refers to Odin. If this symbol appears when your future's being told then you must listen to the advice of others and think carefully about your future actions. If the symbol is reversed you are supposed to watch out for trickery.

'There's also a symbol for a serpent, which ties in with the Nazi angle,' she said. 'Like all important gods, Odin is supposed to be all-seeing so that could explain the eye drawn on both bodies.'

'You mentioned computer games, Joy,' said Nasreen. 'What's the relevance there?'

'There's a game called *Dragonborn* where players can use the ash rune or be extremely wary of it. The ash rune explodes when enemies come near and immobilizes them in ash for thirty seconds. They can't attack or be attacked until the spell wears off.'

We all stared at her. None of us had seen this coming.

Joy looked uneasy. 'The product of a misspent youth and a mother who was into magic and the occult.'

'But going back to the Hindu angle,' Ben said, 'isn't one of the gods Ram and wasn't he responsible for rescuing his wife Sita from Ravan, the evil one, and destroying the monster? Ram won the fight of good over evil and that's why Hindus celebrate Diwali, the festival of lights. Couldn't our killer be indicating by crossing out the word "ram" that he'll win?'

'Interesting theory, though a bit far-fetched,' said Nasreen. Her response was a bit harsh. 'Could be for a battering ram or it could be Random Access Memory, as in computer terminology. Could be an anagram of "arm" or "mar". Could stand for anything.'

'Just trying to be helpful,' said Ben, slightly annoyed.

The room was silent. The heating vents rattled and grumbled. The fluorescent lights flickered. I had exhausted my knowledge of Hinduism, even though I was born one. I knew more about the Bible than I knew the *Bhagavad Gita*, a book I hadn't read, much to my shame.

I didn't know about the others but my mind was beginning to reel from the endless possibilities. It seemed the more we discussed, the less certain we became. The less we all knew.

'Has HOLMES identified anything of interest, Sir?' Ben eventually said, breaking the silence and the growing gloom.

'I went through the system again earlier this morning,' I replied. 'With a couple of officers who are highly skilled in its use —'

'Inspector,' interrupted Nasreen. 'There's a rather odd case in Liverpool which may or may not be relevant to us. The pathologist in Merseyside, she and I trained together. She rang me to have a catch-up and she mentioned she's working on a peculiar case. The body of an unidentified middle-aged man was found in a car park, dead through an apparent heart attack. But there was a lot of bruising to various parts of the body, especially around the eyes, burst capillaries, severely discoloured tissue. Also, respiratory problems and evidence of paralysis. She sent tissue samples to the path lab. They couldn't accurately identify the highly unusual toxins they found, especially around the eyes, and decided to involve the Liverpool School of Tropical Medicine. The LSTM's only just come back with the result. Was cobra venom, believe it or not.'

'Really? That's *really* interesting.' I paused, thinking this through. 'The victim profile obviously doesn't fit our cases but the MO is more than a coincidence. I'll contact Merseyside when I get a chance. In the meantime, Nasreen, please keep in touch with your friend in case she has more up-to-date information. Thanks for that.

'Okay, we'll wrap up for today. It's getting late. Shep, the sandstone and coal dust in the lining of the windpipeand lungs might well indicate the killer's got a den in one of the disused coal mines in the north or west of the county. Speak to the university's geology department tomorrow. Ask them for any coalmines which may have significant amounts of sandstone. Organise the uniforms in pairs and tell them to go round as many mines as possible. There must be miles and miles of tunnels leading to the coal seams but we've got to make a start somewhere.

'Nasreen, can you please get toxicology results on Ayan's tissue samples as a matter of urgency. Ben, chase the leaf found in Ayan's body, the pathologist makes reference to it so I'm assuming it's stored in your department somewhere, and ask the people at Kew to confirm if it's from the wood apple tree, like the one found in Geeta. Try to look at any other evidence the CSIs might've picked up, please, though I'm not holding out much hope of that. It was a badly managed inquiry. If anybody asks any questions about why you're digging into the Ayan case, please refer them to me. And Joy, first thing tomorrow morning, I want you here. You and I have work to do. Thanks to all of you. Let's call it a day.'

CHAPTER 19

'D'you know why Santa's so brainy, Dad?' My daughter Yasmin was on the phone.

'No, darling. I don't know why Santa's so brainy.'

'Because he's elf-taught! Or how about this one? Where's the best place to find mistle-toe? At the end of mistle-feet!'

Yasmin was twelve but still had a childish sense of humour. She giggled down the phone as she read from her joke book. It was about nine o'clock in the evening and I was sitting on the settee in front of the television with a tray on my lap. A slice of ham and mushroom pizza on a plate stared back at me. I wondered whether to refill my wine glass but decided against it. Instead, I put the glass to my lips and let the last drop settle onto my tongue and licked my bottom lip.

'What did you learn in school today?'

'In geography we're still learning about the Maasai in East Africa, who value cattle and recycle everything — even their shoes are made from old tyres. We've just started reading bits of Wordsworth in English — "a host of golden daffodils" and all that — and in maths we're learning how to solve equations, as if I care.'

'Now, now, Yasmin. Maths is important.'

'It may be important, Dad, but I don't know how solving equations is going to help me in life.'

'You need to study all the subjects, get good grades, go to university.' I paused. 'Have you forgiven me for the other day? I'm really sorry about that. I tried ringing you but your phone was switched off. I know you missed seeing me on the news.'

'Dad, have you forgotten iPlayer? When Mum told us, Karan and I watched your interview. You were good, Dad, and, yes, I suppose I've forgiven you. But it was hard. I know work's really important to you. But so are we, aren't we? Me and Karan?'

'Of course, darling. You're the most important people in my life.'

The television screen flickered and the film *It's a Wonderful Life* was reaching its end. James Stewart rushed into the house, hugged his children and his wife, tearful at being happily reunited.

'Why can't we all be together, Dad?'

'Sorry, darling, what did you say?'

'Why can't we all live together as one big happy family, Dad? Me, Karan, you and Mum. Why are we broken, Dad? What did Karan and I ever do to you and Mum?'

A tear ran down my cheek. 'I'm so sorry, darling. It's just that your mother ... well she ... she doesn't want me anymore.' I was glad Yasmin couldn't see me. 'I would do anything to make us whole again. Listen, what do you want for Christmas?' I asked, trying to be more cheerful.

'Oh, Dad, I just told you what I want.'

'Darling, when something's broken, like a glass vase and then it's glued together, it may look right but it'll never be the same again. The cracks will always show. I don't think your mum and I will ever be together again.'

There was a long silence at the other end. I thought I heard a stifled sob.

'Oh, Yasmin, please don't...'

But comforting across the digital airwaves could never replace a warm, reassuring hug.

The next morning Joy and I were standing in the middle of the lounge of the Mehtas' house, having left our shoes on the stone step outside the front door.

Mr Mehta raised his voice. 'How the hell can that be? We don't live in the jungle. This is England. There're no bloody poisonous snakes here.'

I didn't blame Mr Mehta for being angry. He stood before us, the tears welling up in his haunted eyes. His face was gaunt, the cheeks sunken, noticeable even beneath the beard. What the grief was doing to his heart was much more permanent. He could probably have done with a drop of whiskey or brandy but alcohol wasn't allowed at this time of bereavement.

As is customary when there is a death in a Hindu family, he had not shaved. Mrs Mehta stood next to him, dressed in a white cotton saree, white the colour of mourning. The burgundy three-piece suite and television set had been removed and the paintings and batiks of African and Indian scenes had been taken down from the walls. A cream cotton sheet covered the carpet and mourners were expected to sit cross-legged on the floor. The silver shrine stood in the corner.

Next to the fireplace, on a marble base on the floor, Geeta smiled in the photograph, holding a violin and the letter from the Guildhall School of Music and Drama. Her happiness filled the room, ready to welcome the sad and desolate visitors. A garland of jasmine flowers hung from each corner of the frame, a *diva* in a brass holder lit in a silver plate at the bottom, shining on Geeta's face.

'I'm so sorry, Mr Mehta. Even though Geeta had other injuries…' I paused, not wanting to go into the terrible details, cleared my throat and then continued. 'The pathology and toxicology results confirm she died from a snake bite. A cobra.

We've no idea where the snake came from. None have been reported missing.'

'No! Not my *Beti*!' Mrs Mehta wept uncontrollably. 'You must be … wrong. Mistaken… A snake can't kill her … not here … not in Leicester.'

'I'm so very sorry, Mrs Mehta,' Joy responded. 'I wish we were wrong. We promise you, we'll get the man who did this to your daughter.'

Mr Mehta hugged his wife, her chest heaving in involuntary spasms. It was clear they didn't want us in their house anymore.

'Mr Mehta … Mrs Mehta, we'll keep you informed of developments,' I said. 'I appreciate this is a harrowing time for you but, as DC Wheatley said, we'll catch whoever did this. Please don't say anything to anybody about what happened to Geeta. I'm sure the coroner's office will give you permission soon to arrange the funeral.'

There was a long silence.

'We would like our darling's soul to find peace soon,' Mrs Mehta eventually said, composing herself. 'At the moment, her *atma* is restless and we need to give it peace. It needs to be reincarnated as soon as possible.'

I asked whether they had any questions. They shook their heads. I put my palms together in farewell, Joy did the same, we turned and walked to the front door. As we bent down to put our shoes on, the first mourners arrived, a middle-aged Indian couple. The house would have an endless stream of mourners throughout the day and well into the evening. A community supporting its own.

The men would sit on the floor in the lounge for an hour or so, make small talk about what a lovely girl Geeta was, talk about the cold weather and various programmes on Indian satellite channels, and then slip away. The women would sit on the floor in the empty dining room with Mrs Mehta, say little, and some would weep to console and empathise with her, even if they barely knew Geeta or her mother.

As we walked down the drive, I heard footsteps and turned around. Mr Mehta approached, tears streaming down his cheeks, falling freely onto his unkempt beard.

'I'm sorry, Inspector Sharma, but thank you for what you're doing. This is so very hard for us, hard for any parent to bear. You don't have children so you can arrange their funerals. It should be the other way round.'

I put my hand on his shoulder. I didn't know what to say to him.

He stared past me into the distance. 'When I was a young boy at school, I liked reading ancient Greek myths and legends,' he said. 'I've been thinking about the story of Orpheus and Eurydice.'

Orpheus, the talented musician falling in love with Eurydice, the wood nymph, who was killed by a snake bite while running through the forest. He went into the underworld to get her back and was only allowed to do so if he didn't look at his beloved until they were both above ground and in sunlight, or he would never see her again. But Orpheus turned around and looked at her. Just as they were about to make it into the sunlight. And lost her.

Forever.

Mr Mehta gazed at me. 'If I had the same chance as Orpheus, I'd never look back until it was time to do so. Anything to keep my beloved Geeta with me. To bring her back to me. To us.'

110

We drove west along the ring road, away from the Mehtas' house. 'You can understand death from a knife wound, a car accident, a gunshot, or even a broken neck. Or from being strangled,' I said to Joy. 'But how on earth can you comprehend your daughter being killed by a poisonous snake in the middle of England?'

'You can't,' said Joy, shaking her head.

The dual carriageway was busy as we headed back towards police headquarters. The sun streamed through the windscreen and I pulled down the shade. I thought of how it would be very difficult for me to listen to the opera *Orfeo ed Euridice* by Gluck again. Through the car radio, Andy Williams sang about it being the most wonderful time of the year.

My mobile rang.

'Sir,' Shep said, 'I've organised ten teams of two uniforms each to go to all the main collieries in the north and west of the county. And into south Derbyshire as well. Many are obviously disused and we're trying to identify people through local records and through geologists to find out how we can get into the mine shafts. Oh, by the way, there're also drift mines, dug from the side of the hill and going down at an angle. Nothing so far but I thought I'd let you know. There's something more interesting though. I remembered you saying you spoke to Geeta's teacher, Miss Palmer. The killer obviously knew a fair bit about Geeta. I got to thinking about her and wondered whether the teacher had a boyfriend or husband or brother that was worth looking into. Anyway, I went to the college to speak to Mrs Garland but she was adamant there was nobody in Miss Palmer's life who was suspicious. Her boyfriend's a curate for the Church of England, apparently.

'Then I got to thinking about the staff where Ayan studied. I went there and spoke to the Principal. She informed me that

Ayan's pastoral manager has a boyfriend, an Indian guy born and brought up in Derby, who travels a lot around the world for his job. He's a research scientist with a pharmaceutical company. Goes to places like Thailand, Indonesia, Brazil and Costa Rica regularly to study tropical plants and trees for potential medicinal properties. And get this, he's also fond of reptiles. Apparently, their house is full of glass cases with scorpions, iguanas, rock snakes and the like. This pastoral manager is always talking about them in the staff room.'

'Sounds really interesting, Shep. We'll have to interview him. Or both of them.'

'Would be good, Sir, but he left yesterday to research in the forests of Karnataka in Western India. Don't know when he'll be back but I'll get in touch with the company he works for.'

CHAPTER 20

It was late Friday afternoon, daylight rapidly fading. I parked my car outside my house, remembered I had little food in the house and walked towards the shops.

Nothing significant seemed to be happening at the moment. The hours spent on the case were merging into days and the days into weeks. My team and I had gone through all the evidence and witness statements again, earlier in the day. The Merseyside car park connection seemed strong and unusual and I waited to hear back from the lead investigator there. There was also the research scientist who was somewhere in Western India. The pressure was getting heavier and heavier on me to find the killer or killers but we weren't getting any major breakthroughs.

My professional life was dominated by the case and my personal life remained a mess. Had been for some time. Karan stayed with me last night as I had promised Faye. She dropped him off but didn't come into the house. He was quiet and uncommunicative, watched a lot of television and played games on his iPad. We had pizzas and soft drinks delivered. He slept in the spare bedroom. Not a lot more was said in the morning and I dropped him off to school. *Great life with your son, isn't it?* I thought.

I wondered whether things would ever improve.

My footsteps sounded loud as I walked along the icy pavement, envying the families behind the living room curtains of the terraced houses I was hurrying past. I could smell exotic cooking. The pungent smell of asafoetida roasting in hot olive oil, mixed with mustard seeds and peppercorns. The enticing smell of cardamom with cinnamon and cloves, a sure sign that somebody was brewing strong tea with plenty of sugar. I tried to ignore the lingering aroma of turmeric and fenugreek in the air, which was making me hungry, and hurried towards the corner shop at the top of the road, striding past wooden stalls erected along the pavements, fruit and vegetables still in their boxes, packed in places like India, Pakistan, Brazil, Costa Rica, Florida, Louisiana, Kenya and South Africa.

Suddenly, I wondered, could a sedated cobra have been transported in one of these boxes, hidden by spinach leaves or bananas or oranges? The cardboard boxes had holes for air in their tops and sides, there was thick brown paper lining them, which could have kept an animal or reptile alive, even in the hold of a cargo plane. Particularly a snake with its low body temperature. I'd read about poisonous spiders coming out alive from bunches of bananas in supermarkets. Why couldn't a snake survive?

I stared into the brightly lit shop. More boxes were stacked near the front doors and behind the windows. The shelves were lined with bottles and cans of cooking oil, mango, lime and aubergine pickles. On the radio, playing one of the popular Asian stations in the shop, I could hear Mukesh, the long-dead playback singer, singing one of his last songs from a long-forgotten Bollywood film. A song about a poet and a singer moving from village to village in rural India, town to town, singing his happy songs and reciting his happy poems with a happy face for all who came to listen to him. But deep down his heart was breaking because of the pain and sadness caused by a lack of love. The perennial human condition.

The traffic behind me was getting heavier, the sound of tyres swishing, the grating of a car horn, and the occasional shout in Gujarati and Punjabi from car windows. Commuters heading to the northern suburbs out of the offices, banks, shops and warehouses in the city, getting ready for the weekend.

'Of all the gin joints in all the towns in all the world, she walks into mine.'

Humphrey Bogart, playing Rick the saloon owner, was saying these immortal words in the film *Casablanca*. It was about nine in the evening and I was stretched out on my settee, bare feet dangling, watching the TV in the corner. I stared at Ingrid Bergman.

'Vasco da Gama,
Went to Ghana,
Without his pyjamas,
Showing his long brown banana!'

The flying cushion, which a few seconds before had been supporting my head, crashed into Fernando's cage. The cage swung about and he squawked loudly. A fine grey feather fluttered down onto the newspaper lining the bottom of the cage.

'Serves you right. Not tonight, Fernando.'

He replied with a prolonged wolf whistle and a 'Bite me, Rohan, bite me' when he had settled down again on his perch.

My mobile rang. It wasn't a number I recognised.

I muted the sound of the television.

'Hi Rohan, Martin Donovan here. Sorry to bother you so late, especially on a Friday evening. Your voicemail sounded urgent.'

Martin Donovan was the senior investigating officer from the Merseyside police service.

'No problems, Martin. Thanks for ringing. What you got?'

'Our stiff's called Brian Flannery. The PM report's interesting. Flannery had a reasonable amount of fatty tissue round his heart. Also, two of his valves and main arteries to the heart were furred and almost blocked. He could've dropped dead at any time. But what killed him was cobra venom. May not have killed a fit and healthy twenty-five-year-old, but enough to cause cardiac arrest in a middle-aged man who had a dodgy ticker anyway. Seems it entered the bloodstream, most probably through the burst blood vessels in the eyes. That's where the venom was most concentrated.'

'What you got on Flannery?'

'Took a while to ID him. Dyed hair, false number plates on the van. We circulated photographs to informants across Merseyside and the north of England. Given the large Irish population in this area, we also contacted the Police Service in Northern Ireland and the Garda in Eire. Finally nailed him. Nasty piece of work from the loyalist side. Couldn't pin anything on him. Believed to have killed Republican sympathisers. More recently, he started smuggling anything illegal or dodgy into the country.'

'Including poisonous snakes?' I asked, thinking about the cardboard boxes full of fruit and vegetables I had seen not long ago outside the shops.

'If you wanted it, he could get it for you. If the price was right. Had contacts all over the world. But there's evidence he double-crossed people, especially on deals involving heroin and cocaine. So, his days were numbered.'

'You think he was killed by drug barons?'

'No idea at the moment. All lines of enquiry are open.'

We agreed to keep each other informed of any developments in our respective cases.

As Sam was playing it again for Humphrey Bogart and Ingrid Bergman, I sat and thought. It seemed possible that Brian Flannery had imported the snake into Liverpool docks, the killer had killed him, and then used the cobra to kill Geeta Mehta. But that didn't explain Ayan Suleiman's death, which I was convinced was through cobra venom as well. Were there two snakes? Then there was the time lapse. Ayan had been killed more than a year ago and then suddenly, in a space of three weeks or so, we have two deaths. Why a middle-aged white Irishman and a young British Asian woman? The victim profiles didn't fit. But did they need to? Brian Flannery might have been killed because he knew the killer's identity. Were there other victims I didn't know about? Was he going to kill again soon? What about the signatures he'd left, the leaf and the positioning of the bodies? The single tyre tread?

A thought occurred to me. I picked up my phone.

'I wanted to talk to you about your geography lesson, Yasmin. You said something about the Maasai recycling everything. Including tyres. Making soles for shoes. That's what you said, isn't it?'

'Yes, Dad. The teacher showed us snippets of it from YouTube. They cut the tyres to fit the size of the feet. Then cover the top with strips of leather made from cow hide or from goatskin. These shoes last forever.'

'Thanks, darling. That's really useful.'

'Why Dad, d'you want a pair? Aren't they paying you enough?'

'Very funny.'

We said our goodbyes.

I rang Ben.

'I'm really sorry to bother you on a Friday night but I needed to talk to you,' I said. 'Something's been bothering me. You know the single tyre tread left at the scene of Geeta Mehta's death? Could it have been made by a shoe with soles made from old tyres?'

'It's perfectly possible, Inspector. Just wait a minute and I'll bring up the prints of the tread on my laptop.'

I heard Ben start up his laptop.

A few moments later: 'I'm looking at the prints now. Not deep in the slightly wet mud, so definitely not made by a car. Could've been made by the weight of ten or twelve stones pressing on the tread, quite possibly the weight of a man. Also only one tread. The other foot could have been on the firmer ground with grass. That could be why we couldn't get a print.'

CHAPTER 21

It was Saturday, just getting light at about eight o'clock in the morning. My lounge curtains were still drawn, the central heating pipes clunking and the radiators gurgling as the boiler powered the hot water around the damp, cold house. The television and ceiling light were switched on as I sat on the settee unwrapping the parcels which the postwoman had delivered a few minutes earlier. They contained the presents I'd bought for Yasmin and Karan, including an upgraded eReader for Yasmin and various computer games for Karan. I also bought a pair of dangling silver earrings with blue topaz for Faye. Well, it was Christmas after all and we usually exchanged gifts. I didn't buy anything for Pierre.

I munched my mixture of Cornflakes and Rice Krispies and stared mindlessly at the television set. Wendy Weaver, the reporter I'd met near the field where Geeta Mehta's body was found, was reading the early morning news:

'*Mr Sandhu, a local businessman from Leicester, has donated fifty thousand pounds to charity. The millionaire businessman said his donation was a gesture of goodwill for the festive season and that the money would be split between two charities dear to his heart. One for people with diabetes and the other for people with muscular dystrophy.*'

I stared at the middle-aged man in a dinner jacket and black bowtie walking confidently on the red carpet into a high-class hotel. He was accompanied by a strikingly attractive Indian woman, dressed in a pale pink saree and blouse. They walked closely together, although not holding hands.

'*Mr Sandhu is well-known for his generosity and has donated many thousands of pounds to charities over the years. Close friends say he'd like*

to get involved more in national politics but he has always denied this,
stating that his business interests and family life do not allow him the time
to do anything else.'

My mobile rang.

Joy Wheatley informed me that Geeta Mehta's parents would be holding the funeral on Christmas Eve. Jesus Christ! What a day to hold a funeral. Joy must have thought the same as she added they were adamant it couldn't be delayed.

It was still early but I decided to ring Shep anyway, to catch up about the search teams at the coal mines.

'Not a lot to report, Sir. The teams are still working their way through the mines. It's very time-consuming. Some have tunnels stretching for miles. Most've drawn a blank but there're a few where the composition of the dust is similar to that found in Geeta's lungs. Could be she was kept in a coal mine in the north, or north-west of the county. The team at the university is working as fast as it can. But separating and analysing dust particles is laborious. Can take days to perform the tests on the soil and dust from one site.'

'Nothing further from the pet stores, I assume?'

'No, Sir.'

'Okay, Shep. Perhaps we're going to have a quiet weekend. I don't think anything dramatic is going to happen. Doing anything special?'

'Molly and I are going out for a meal. And how about you?'

'Oh, the usual,' I said, deflecting the question.

Mid-afternoon found me sitting in a cafe on the main road, not far from where I lived. I'd bought wrapping paper, silver and gold string, gift cards and Sellotape. I sat next to the main window, sipping Diet Coke from a bottle and munching *aloo chat*, savouring the mixture of potatoes and chickpeas in a tangy sauce. Outside, men and women wrapped in coats and scarves were hurrying along the freezing pavement, plastic bags bumping into each other, speaking in Gujarati, Punjabi, Urdu and Polish.

My phone rang. It was my mother and I wondered whether to answer the call. I didn't feel like talking to her. I told myself not to be churlish and hit the green button. After the usual pleasantries, she asked me whether I was going to them for Christmas dinner. I hesitated but said I would. How sad my life had become. What man in his mid-thirties, and a father of two children, goes by himself to his parents for Christmas dinner?

My life just had to get better.

As I turned the pages of *The Guardian*, my mobile vibrated again. The message that appeared on the screen took my breath away.

If you stray into Gayle's tonight
You'll see a sight to savour,
Behold and linger
On a lover's
Betrayal,
When a poisonous kiss
Like a snake's hiss
Will not go amiss.
Watch the two eager lovers,
One with a tail — to tell —
And one without.

It wasn't signed and the sender had withheld their number.

I read it over and over again.

Only a handful of people knew about the cobra and they were on my team. Who the hell were these two people in

Gayle's wine bar I was being urged to see? And why the spelling mistake? Surely, it had to be 'tale' and not 'tail'? Just an error, or was it? But then it didn't make sense. Why was it followed by 'to tell'? Or was it all just bad poetry? A frustrated Ted Hughes wannabe? I was getting more and more confused.

I read it again but that didn't help my confusion at all.

Was I being led to the mole who'd been leaking information about the investigation? Apart from Joy, Shep, Nasreen, Ben, Martin Donovan in Liverpool and Geeta's parents, nobody else knew about the cobra. I had written reports for Superintendent Breedon and he may well have passed them to his superiors. It wouldn't have been in their interests to leak anything.

I thought of *Gayle's* and its two owners. When they bought the derelict building about twenty years ago, they wanted to create an upmarket wine bar for the rapidly growing gay and lesbian population in Leicester and the surrounding areas. At first, they wanted to name it *Gayles*, without the apostrophe, but an elderly Muslim councillor on the committee that granted licences for such premises objected to the name. Saying it was too obvious who the clientele would be and it would corrupt the morals of the young as it would be a place of sin.

All it took was a punctuation mark to keep him happy.

If only I could say the same for me.

It was the last Saturday before Christmas and *Gayle's* would be heaving with people. Most would not arrive till fairly late. I would need to leave at least six hours before making my way there. I finished my Diet Coke, rolled up my newspaper, picked up my shopping bag from the floor and hurried back home. I needed time to think. And I needed room to pace.

CHAPTER 22

At five past nine in the evening I stood in the middle of the wine bar at *Gayle's*. There were at least a hundred people around me, and the round marble tables along the walls were all occupied. It took twenty minutes or so to get served as the bar area was heaving with people, three deep, flashing their twenty-pound notes or contactless credit cards, and waving empty bottles of wine and champagne. There was raucous laughter, people jostling, mouths next to ears trying to make themselves heard. Noddy Holder was singing at the top of his voice about Merry Christmas and everybody having fun.

I fought through the crowd, looking this way and that. I pushed some people as I made my way, one or two saying, 'Hey watch it,' while others gave me dirty looks. A woman with a bowler hat, short dark hair and long black eyelashes, trailing a long red feather boa, a spitting image of Liza Minelli from *Cabaret*, turned around and spilled some of her red wine on the sleeve of my jacket. The colour of the wine matched the colour of her lips. She stared at me, smiled, pouted her sensual lips and blew me a kiss.

I carried on pushing through the crowd. At one stage, I felt my bottom being squeezed. I didn't see who it was.

I stopped.

In a darkly lit corner, I saw a couple, a man and woman. The woman with shoulder length blonde hair had her back to me and she was passionately kissing a dark-haired man whose cheeks she held lovingly with both hands.

'Joy?' I called out.

She stopped, turned around and looked at me.

The man raised his head.

I stared at them both then rushed through the door to the men's toilet which was to my right and thought, '*Shit, shit, shit.*' The irony of this comment in the room I was in escaped me.

I paced up and down the black and grey tiled floor and looked into the mirror mounted above the washbasins. The door opened and I saw Shep staring back at me. His fists clenching and unclenching.

'Have you taken to spying on people you work with now?' he asked.

'Look, I'm really sorry. I didn't mean to barge in on you like this.'

The heavy door to the toilet swung open and the handle hit the inside wall.

'Jack, what's going on?' she asked.

'Chris, meet Inspector Sharma, a snoop and my ... my ... boss. This is Christine Dover ... Sir. *Not* Joy Wheatley.'

I offered my right hand. She took it and shook it vigorously. Her feminine hand and wrist belying her strength.

'Look Shep, I'm really sorry, I didn't expect you here. In the dim light it looked just like the back of Joy's head,' I continued. 'You said you were going out for a meal with Molly tonight.'

'You said what, Jack?' Christine asked.

'Yes, darling, I did say that. Because it's none of his business what I was doing tonight.'

An attractive man in his late thirties, dressed in a dark three-piece suit and with well-groomed brown hair, staggered in. He walked unsteadily towards the urinal, stopped, looked at the three of us and said, 'Is this a threesome or can others join in?'

I thought of the absurdity of the situation. Shep, Christine and me in a gents' toilet.

'Fuck off,' said Shep. Turning to Christine, he said, 'Please wait for us outside, darling. I'll be back when I've had a word with Inspector Sharma.'

The man looked at me, then at Shep, heard the words 'Inspector Sharma', quickly went to the urinal, was soon done and out of the room.

Shep walked towards the cubicles, checked there was nobody else around and then said, 'Yes, Christine is trans. I've been with her a fair while and I love her.'

'But Shep, what about Molly? She'll be desperately hurt.'

'You just don't get it, do you?' he said.

'No, Shep, I don't. Please explain it to me. And yes, it may not be my business. But then again it could be.'

He looked me straight in the eyes and said, 'Molly's a lesbian.'

'What?' I said, completely confused now.

'Molly and I met when we were both constables on the beat. One evening we bumped into each other here. She was with her lover and I was having a fling with a young guy. A bank clerk. Both Molly and I pretended not to notice each other. Anyway, next time we met at HQ there was no getting away from it. We talked at length about our sexuality, how impossible it was to come out given the rampant homophobia within the force. We decided we wouldn't say anything to anybody. Over time, we became good friends and both of us realised how much we wanted to have a child. We thought it'd be perfect to get married. We could continue seeing other people and also try to have a child. Had to be IVF.'

'Oh, Shep...' I said.

'I'm just explaining things as they are and I don't expect them to go any further. As you know, we started with IVF about a year ago. Molly decided it'd be best if she didn't see any other woman. Anyway, we were getting along fine but Molly wasn't becoming pregnant. Then Christine comes along and I fell deeply in love with her. And she with me. She's a research assistant at the local office of the regional television studio.'

My heart missed a beat. Wendy Weaver also sprang to mind.

'Shep,' I said, 'have you been discussing the case with Christine at all? Please be honest with me.'

'Yes, I have.'

My heart wobbled even further.

'But only parts of it. Not all. There's no way Christine would have said anything to anybody.'

I stared at him, feeling betrayed.

There was no proof Shep and Christine were the moles. But then, who else?

The music thumped through the walls of the toilet. A middle-aged Asian man walked in, looked at me and walked straight out again. In a close-knit community he didn't want word of his presence in a gay wine bar to get back to his wife.

Shep stared at me, waiting for a reaction. I pulled out my mobile and showed him the text message I'd received.

He read it. His sticking-out ears were bright red. 'I don't know who the hell's sent you that but I know Christine wouldn't have said anything. She loves me and I love her. She wouldn't do that to us.'

I turned around and walked away.

I wondered whether to ask for Shep to be taken off the case. How had the killer known? Was he here? Or was the message from somebody else?

CHAPTER 23

It was eight o'clock in the morning on Christmas Eve. At the Mehtas' home, a strong scent of jasmine and sandalwood clung to the walls and mantelpiece of the lounge. The smoke from half a dozen joss sticks curled upwards from the shrine sitting in the corner on the floor. A brightly lit *diva*, dipped in purified butter and sitting in a brass holder, shone a comforting light on Geeta Mehta's smiling face. Her photograph had a garland of white jasmine flowers. Next to the *diva*, resting in front of the photograph, were a handful of single flowers, pink carnations, white chrysanthemums and yellow marigolds. They were joined by small silver and brass statues of Hindu gods.

The lounge was still devoid of furniture, but the cream cotton sheet on the floor had been replaced by a white one. The mourners standing barefoot pressed themselves against each wall, stretched out into the hallway and towards the front door. Some lined the corridor at the back as it stretched into the kitchen. Others waited in the adjoining dining room, while some children sat quietly on the stairs. Middle-aged women wore white sarees, the colour of mourning, while the younger ones wore plain pink or maroon or dark green. The men were mostly in suits, nodding to each other, or staring at the floor. People talked in hushed tones.

I stood with Mr and Mrs Mehta in their lounge, looking out of the window, sometimes glancing back at the couple, not knowing whether to smile at them or not. Mr Mehta's beard was thicker and longer than the last time I'd seen him when he had narrated the story of Orpheus and Eurydice. He had lost weight and his cheeks were sunken beneath the beard. His eyes

127

filled with swollen tears which he tried hard to control. Mrs Mehta was heavily sedated, her eyes as lifeless as her daughter's, staring blankly into space as she sat on the kitchen chair that had been brought into the lounge for her. Mr Mehta, hands trembling, put his arm on her shoulder to comfort her.

She stared up at him. An empty and desolate look in her brown eyes.

Who knew where her mind was?

A black limousine drew up outside, the South Asian undertaker, immaculately dressed in top hat and tails, walked slowly in front. I could see the wooden coffin with its glittering brass handles, surrounded by bouquets: white and yellow carnations, white lilies, pink roses, and bright yellow marigolds. On top was a single flower in full bloom, a bird of paradise, shaped like the head of an exotic bird with a long beak and a dancing crest, vivid orange, red, blue and violet. The stalk was wrapped in a saffron silk scarf. The colours of the flowers contrasted with the grey, overcast morning.

On the grass in the front garden stood a floral wreath in the shape of a white swan, another which said *Princess* and another in pink and white carnations and chrysanthemums spelling out *Geeta*. Mr Mehta, his two younger brothers and three nephews, walked down barefoot in the cold and freezing morning, past the wreaths on the front lawn and towards the hearse. The undertaker opened the back door and pulled out the coffin smoothly, along silver metal tracks. Three men on each side bent down as the coffin was transferred onto each shoulder and carried up the drive and into the house. They called out the names of Hindu gods as they walked and chanted holy invocations. Past hundreds of shoes belonging to the mourners.

'*Om Shanti Om*

Om Shanti Om
Om Shanti Om…'

The coffin was brought in feet first through the front door. The mournful dirge started by the women got louder and louder, now everybody joining in, chanting louder and louder.

'*Hari Rama, Hari Rama,*
Rama, Rama, Hari Hari,
Hari Rama, Hari Rama,
Rama, Rama,
Hari Hari…'

People started weeping, some crying out aloud, others silent, letting the tears run down. The singing and the chanting overwhelmed the whole house.

'*Om Namah Shivaya*
Om Namah Shivaya
Om Namah Shivaya…'

The undertaker unfolded the supporting steel frame and placed it in the middle of the lounge. He adjusted it so the coffin would rest waist high. After it had been placed on the metal frame, he unscrewed the six brass screws with a brass butterfly clip, carefully removed the lid and placed it against one of the walls.

Geeta Mehta lay silent in her white satin-lined coffin. Some of the mourners gasped. The weeping and wailing grew deeper and louder.

The priest, in a white loincloth and dark waistcoat, shaved head with a small ponytail at the back, lit a *diva*. He placed it on the floor under Geeta's head. Her hair had been combed back highlighting the soft and beautiful face. Serene and peaceful. There was a hint of make-up on her face. Her eyes were now closed, not how I remembered them, wide open and staring at the sky, when I first saw her in the field on that cold morning.

The pale brown mascara and black eyeliner were understated, and a hint of lipstick brought to life the natural colour of her lips. Not the hideous black lipstick I remembered in the field. Around her neck was a garland of jasmine. She was dressed in a white *shalwar kameez*, its edges embroidered in golden thread, a pale blue silk scarf around her neck. The toenails on her small brown feet were painted red, the feet pointing up at the mourners.

I tried not to think of her smashed elbows and knees beneath her clothes. Or the other gruesome injuries.

As the mourners wept, the priest dabbed the third finger of his right hand in a red paste in a small brass bowl and marked her forehead with it. He pressed a few grains of rice on this and sprinkled drops of holy water onto her body. While doing this he recited passages from the *Bhagavad Gita*. Under her tongue he placed a small pearl which would guarantee Geeta's soul a safe passage to the afterlife. He put four packets of butter at each end of the coffin and a fresh coconut by Geeta's right side. Four rice balls were also placed at each corner of the coffin. Her father handed him a packet of chocolate-covered raisins, Geeta's favourite, and a compilation CD by classical violinists. Both were placed to Geeta's left.

Geeta's father was given a small brass spoon which the priest filled with holy water from the River Ganges, and Mr Mehta poured this between the lips of his dead daughter. His hands shook and some of the water dribbled down Geeta's chin and onto her neck. He wiped it with his hand, the tears flowing freely, and kissed her on the forehead. He sprinkled rose, carnation and chrysanthemum petals onto Geeta's body and circled the coffin. Standing at Geeta's feet he looked at his daughter, pressed his palms together, touched her bare feet and bowed his head to her. He was helped away by his two younger brothers.

Geeta's mother sobbed as she undertook the same rituals as her husband. But she couldn't finish them. She started shrieking and shaking her dead daughter.

'Come on, darling, wake up. Please wake up…'

She was led away into the room next door by the other women.

Each of the mourners circled the coffin and sprinkled petals on the body, prayed to Geeta, and wandered off to make way for the others. The mournful chanting filled the room.

'Hari Rama, Hari Rama,
Rama, Rama, Hari Hari,
Hari Rama, Hari Rama,
Rama, Rama,
Hari, Hari…'

Geeta's body was finally covered in flower petals. The priest continued to recite prayers and holy verses, only some of which I understood. The singing of hymns and dirges grew louder and louder.

I was annoyed at the unmistakable sound of somebody's mobile phone. The theme from James Bond of all things. People stared at each other. The priest fiddled with the pocket of his waistcoat while he chanted further verses from the *Gita*. He switched off his mobile. Not even the dead could have peace from a ringing mobile phone.

Suddenly, I felt mine vibrate in my breast pocket. I pressed myself against one of the walls, surreptitiously pulled it out and looked at the text message: *The ANPR cameras aren't picking up any suspicious cars, Sir. All the mourners seem to be bona fide. Nothing coming up from HOLMES.*

I had asked Shep and two other officers to use the Automatic Number Plate Recognition system in a van stationed close by and to scan all the cars that came to, or were parked anywhere near, the Mehtas' house. I was wondering whether the killer may have come around to gain gratification from his handiwork. Two officers were also stationed in the top room of the house opposite, to take photographs of all who entered and left.

The mourners filed past the coffin, sprinkled petals on the body and made way for the next person. It was almost time to close the coffin lid. The priest placed a white shroud on Geeta from the neck down. On top, he placed a bright reddish-orange shawl, the colour of death, the colour which transported the soul from one life, ready to be reincarnated into the next.

Geeta's father and mother, who had been helped back to the coffin, placed single red roses with long stems on their daughter's body. The final prayers were said. Geeta's father broke down and cried uncontrollably. Her mother continued to wail, desperately placing her hands on Geeta's forehead and cheeks. She was led away by her husband and her two brothers-in-law. The lid was placed on top by the undertaker and the brass screws tightened with butterfly clips.

It's so strange that the placing of the coffin lid on top of the coffin one last time marks the end of the person. Not the actual death itself or seeing the lifeless body. But the actual act of covering up the dead. Never to be seen again by family, loved ones, friends. And then the final immolation. On gas burners in Britain, on a pyre of sandalwood doused in oil and butter on the banks of the River Ganges in India.

Shep and I drove in an unmarked car to the crematorium, five miles away. We were following the hearse at a discreet distance, while two officers in the van behind us used the ANPR camera. The journey didn't show up anything unusual and the officers didn't radio in anything. The service lasted about thirty minutes; a few people choked back tears as they spoke about the Geeta they knew. The priest continued to recite holy verses and offered Geeta's soul for reincarnation, the red curtains glided electronically on their rails to hide the coffin, which was then transported to the ovens. The mourners filed out, lining up outside to pay their respects to the family.

The family went down to the ovens to look through the peephole and watch the coffin burning. This was a tradition which had grown in popularity over the last twenty years or so. A tradition which arose because rumours were once rampant that the staff who placed the coffins in the ovens opened the lids and stole the magnificent gold and diamond jewellery which they believed the Hindu dead, especially the women and girls, were adorned with.

Nobody had ever proved or disproved this.

Joy, Shep and I mingled with the crowds. I had asked Joy to go through some paperwork at the incident room earlier and she had joined us at the crematorium. I noticed Mrs Garland and some of the staff, including Miss Palmer, and students from Geeta's college. The local media, both newspaper and television, were also there. The van with the ANPR camera remained at a discreet distance.

As I looked around the three hundred or so mourners, I noticed Nasreen Khan outside the doors of the main chapel. I didn't realise she was here.

'Hello, Nasreen,' I said and looked at the man standing next to her. He was tall, in his late thirties, with well-groomed thick hair, wearing a dark and expensive woollen suit and tie.

'Hello, Inspector Sharma. This is Yusuf, my husband. A doctor too, I'm afraid.'

I smiled at Yusuf Khan and shook his hand.

There was a glimmer of a quick smile as he looked at me. Nasreen said Yusuf had not been to a Hindu funeral before and found the rites of passage very interesting. She turned to him and said, 'Would you mind waiting for me at the car? I just want to have a quick word with Inspector Sharma about the case.'

He stared at her, then at me, said, 'Oh, okay, how long will you...?' stopped himself, turned round and walked away. No goodbye to me, I noticed.

Nasreen shrugged and tried to smile. 'I've managed to examine the lining of Ayan Suleiman's lungs. Yes, definite traces of sandstone and coal dust. I also heard from the London School of Hygiene and Tropical Medicine about an hour ago. I asked them to get the results back to me before Christmas and I had to cash in a lot of favours. You owe me, Inspector. The tissue samples from Ayan's pulmonary aorta, and heart and liver, indicate the presence of cobra venom. Definitely the same killer. I will get the official reports to you when they arrive.'

I thanked her.

'You're welcome,' she replied, turned and walked away.

Sad as it was, the funeral was unremarkable. We didn't see anybody or anything suspicious. All the mourners and their cars seemed to be there legitimately.

It was only later when I was driving home in my car I realised how odd the meeting with Nasreen was. I was pleased she had taken time out to come to the funeral and was really glad about the update on Ayan. But found it odd that her husband was there. Maybe he did want to attend a Hindu funeral but I thought it perplexing that a busy doctor didn't have better things to do with his time on Christmas Eve. Yet Ben Carter, who should have been there to represent the forensics team, wasn't there.

CHAPTER 24

'Three Indian sisters have recently arrived from Tanzania, Rohan,' said my father. 'Do you want to meet the eldest? She's thirty-two, a good looker.'

'I'm sorry, *Bapuji*, I'm just too busy to meet women I don't even know.'

'Well, how about one of the younger ones then? Both are pretty.'

I shook my head and carried on savouring the chicken meatballs which my mother had prepared.

'Oh, leave the boy alone, Anil,' my mother said. 'Can't you see he's busy and getting famous on television? Now, what can you tell us about the case, son? The funeral was yesterday, wasn't it? Said so on the TV. Your father and I caught a quick glimpse of you among the mourners, didn't we, Anil?'

My father nodded between the mouthfuls of minced chicken which he was chewing with his dentures. I said I couldn't really say anything as the situation was changing all the time.

'Didn't the reporter want to interview you, *Beta*?' asked my mother.

'No, Mum, it was a funeral,' I replied.

My mother started deep frying lamb samosas. The scent of fresh coriander, chillies, cumin, cayenne pepper and roasted fennel seeds hung in the air.

I had arrived about an hour earlier, having delivered the presents to my children and Faye. I gave two Christmas cards, each containing one hundred pounds, to my parents.

'If you like,' my father eventually said, 'we can get you a country girl from a small village in India. Won't go around running with boys, wearing make-up and short skirts. Not like the ones born here.'

I carried on eating and didn't say anything. I knew this conversation, like a boomerang, would come back eventually.

As we sat at the table eating the main course, my mother looked at her watch and said we mustn't be late to hear the Queen's Christmas broadcast. Even in Kenya as a child I remember we did this because my mother always said we were British and should listen to what our Queen was saying.

Thinking about Kenya brought back thoughts of Maya, my sister, which I tried hard to dispel.

The Queen's unremarkable broadcast, like the other sixty odd before, came and went as we finished the *kulfi* in the dining room. After that, my father and I dozed off in front of the television.

By early evening, my father seemed to have a bit more energy, put on his jacket and coat, and said he was going out for some fresh air.

'Off to one of your drinking clubs, more like,' said my mother, as he walked out.

I suspected she was right but I didn't blame him for wanting to escape for a couple of hours.

My mother and I went to the kitchen and loaded the dishwasher. She washed the cut-glass whiskey tumblers, liqueur glasses and champagne flutes by hand and, after drying them with a tea towel, she asked me to return them to the corner unit in the front room.

I walked into the room, which was hardly used because it looked out onto the busy and noisy road. There was a stool near the bay window with a small Christmas tree in a brown clay pot. Fairy lights, white, gold and silver, blinked among the tinsel. The wall above the fireplace was covered with Christmas cards sent by relatives and friends. I noticed one each from Yasmin and Karan, they took pride of place and I felt glad about that. Their school photographs, framed in silver, stood at each corner of the mantelpiece. I also noticed a card from Faye but that was lost among all the others.

The fairy lights in the Christmas tree danced and jumped, the colours bouncing on the walls and reflected in the bay window. They outshone the light of the *diva* burning in a brass holder in the shrine. The shrine contained framed pictures of Hindu gods. The scent of sandalwood wafted into my nostrils and I breathed in deeply. My mother, a devout Hindu, had always prayed to the gods every day, even on Christmas Day, and she'd become even more religious after we lost Maya.

I carefully placed the glasses on the mantelpiece, unlocked the glass door to the corner unit, and turned to pick up the glasses again.

My eyes caught the dying flames from the oil-soaked cotton wick in the brass holder. The flame flickering and almost burning out.

Then I spotted it!

I rushed to the shrine, picked up the flower and saw the image. I stared at it for a long time. The room was very quiet. I could feel my heart banging against my ribcage. I rushed out of the room and ran along the corridor to the kitchen where my mother was. I held up the flower and said, 'Mum, what's this?'

'Oh, *Beta*, you shouldn't touch that. It's an offering to the Lord Shankar. The benevolent one. I know I shouldn't have the flower but I grew it in a pot in the utility room. They are very poisonous.'

'Mum, where did you get it from?'

'You know Mrs Patel who lives five doors down? She went to India seven months ago and hid some of the seeds in her luggage. I asked her for a few. I started growing it a while ago. It's a *datura* flower, has magical properties. But its seeds can kill you. Lord Shankar uses its power for many things.'

I held the flower between my forefinger and thumb and stared at the pale pink trumpet-shaped petals and the long green base in which they nestled.

'Rohan, you must return it to where I placed it. It's Lord Shankar's and not yours. It's a sin to take it back from the Lord… I'm not going to get in trouble with the immigration authorities, am I? The police won't arrest me, will they?'

'Mum, I *am* the police. Who is Lord Shankar exactly?'

'Didn't you see his picture in the shrine? The one with the *Naag*? The serpent?'

Jesus Christ, I thought. It seemed appropriate for Christmas Day.

I asked her many more questions. She spoke to me for more than two hours about the different Hindu gods and their significance.

I rushed home and went online to do more research. My heart was racing, beads of sweat on my forehead and upper lip.

I couldn't believe what I'd stumbled upon.

CHAPTER 25

I worked well into the night on the progress report for the team.

PROGRESS REPORT

Status: *Highly confidential.* **FOR YOUR EYES ONLY**
Author: *Detective Inspector Rohan Sharma*
Circulation: *Detective Sergeant Jack Shepherd, Detective Constable Joy Wheatley, Dr Nasreen Khan, Pathologist, Mr Ben Carter, Manager, Forensics Service*
Copy to: *Superintendent Breedon*
Date/time: *Christmas Day, 11.47pm*

INTRODUCTION

Given the difficulties in getting all of us together during the festive season, I thought I would bring you up to date about recent developments and identify further lines of enquiry. You know the profile of the two female victims. We also have a reasonable profile of the killer, based on their skills, behaviours and the signatures left on the bodies, especially of the two female victims. Please consider carefully what follows and if you have any comments, please get back to me asap. Many thanks.

THE SIGNATURE UNRAVELLED

Most people associate Hinduism with a multitude of gods. Hinduism is fundamentally dominated by three gods at the top of the pyramid and they are responsible for the creation, upkeep and destruction of the universe.

The other gods represent different aspects of the above. Brahma is the creator of the universe and it is Vishnu's task to preserve it. The final one in the triumvirate is Shiva, the Destroyer.

Shiva destroys and recreates the illusions and imperfections of this world and is seen as a source of both good and evil. He is known by hundreds of names including Lord Shankar, when he is being peaceful and an ascetic. Contradictory forces within him are constantly at war and these lead to extremes of behaviour. He is often seen retreating to the mountain tops, meditating and praying for long periods of time. On other occasions, he indulges in extreme hedonistic behaviour, including smoking cannabis and enjoying lengthy periods of unbridled sexual activity with his wife. This aspect of one of the main Hindu gods led many Western hippies to travel to India in the 1960s and 1970s to indulge in what they perceived to be the lifestyle of a free spirit. They still go searching for this kind of lifestyle in places like Goa.

Shiva's extremes of behaviour are tempered to a large extent by his intimate relationship with his wife Parvati who is known by many other names, including Uma. She holds his personality together and allows him to be both an ascetic and a virile lover. As a result, half of Shiva's body is sometimes shown as male and the other half as Parvati.

Shiva the Destroyer is represented by many features and our killer has decided to adopt some of these as his signatures. The following are especially relevant:

-   Both the bodies of Ayan and Geeta were drawn with a human eye. This third eye represents the wisdom and deep knowledge that Shiva possesses. It is believed to be the source of his wild and untamed energy and is an eye of cosmic fire. If he ever opens this eye the universe will be destroyed. This could represent our killer's narcissism.

- *Images of Shiva usually show him sitting cross-legged and looking serene, with a cobra around his neck. This demonstrates Shiva's power over the most dangerous creatures of the world and also demonstrates that he could use this power when he so desires. Hence the method of killing the two young women.*

- *The trident is, as the name implies, a three-pronged spear. This represents the three gods, Brahma, Vishnu and Shiva, and the latter is often seen in representations holding a trident. I am not aware that this has been used as a signature on, or near, any of the bodies. But it could happen so we need to be aware of it. For example, the killer could use it as a weapon, or a body could be mutilated with three deep points.*

- *The* vibuthi *are the three lines found on the forehead of Shiva. They are drawn horizontally in white ash and they represent Shiva's power and wealth over everything he surveys. The three lines of ash also cover up his third eye, the source of cosmic fire. Herein lies the conundrum for us. The killer crossed out the word 'ram' with four deep cuts at the site of the ashram where Ayan's body was found. Why four cuts and not three? Why not deface the whole word? Is it a reference to evil triumphing over good (the Hindu god Ram)?*

- *Shiva is worshipped for the power of his phallus, the* lingam. *The lingam is usually depicted as a cylindrical, polished stone image that is placed on a flat stone receptacle, the female equivalent, the yoni. The lingam is the symbol of everything that will ever be created and which will die. It is a further symbol of having the power of life and death.*

- *Leaves from the wood apple tree are placed when worshipping the lingam. They are used to cool down the heat of the lingam. Maybe the killer regrets his actions once he has committed them and places the leaves in the vagina of the dead women to indicate his regret?*

- *When a Hindu dies, the name of Shiva is chanted over and over again by the mourners when the body is brought into the house* (Om Nam-ah Shiva-ya). *The killer will derive intense satisfaction that so many people are calling out his name. He will feel a sense of absolute power.*

- *One of Shiva's alternative names is Bhangeri Baba. He is the lord of herbs and other mind-altering drugs. Cannabis and thorn apple (the* datura *plant) are his favourites. The seeds from the pods of thorn apples are mixed with cannabis leaves and smoked in a clay pipe. They lead to different ideas of reality and different levels of consciousness. Some believe that the dead, and even animals, are talking to them while others think they can fly like birds. Smoking this mixture can also lead to extreme forms of behaviour, including aggression and violence. Psychosis is not unusual in regular smokers of this mixture. When Shiva is depicted in this state his body is almost naked, he is untidy and unkempt, looks unclean and has long dreadlocks. His body is usually smeared in ash.*

- *Finally, Shiva the Destroyer is also known as the Lord of the Dance. He is often depicted in brass statues as Nataraja, the cosmic dancer, because he is responsible for the rhythm and balance of the cosmic world. He performs his most important dance, the* Tandav, *the cosmic dance of death at the end of an age in order to destroy the universe. The bodies may be posed in the shape of a swastika. However, it's also possible that they have been posed in the shape of Shiva performing his cosmic dance.*

QUESTIONS TO CONSIDER

I am not sure about the four cuts at the ashram where Ayan's body was found or the significance of the four cuts on Geeta's body. They do not fit the rest of the killer's signature. Has anybody any ideas?

Although the killer has adopted the signatures of Shiva the Destroyer it does not mean he is a Hindu, Indian or white. We just cannot be sure of his ethnic background.

I am assuming there is one killer. But we also have to consider the possibility that there are two. And what about the role of his wife or girlfriend, if he has one? Is she an active participant in these deeds?

The killer will strike again soon. The festival celebrating Shiva (known as Shivratri) where Hindus stay up all night, go to the temples, chant devotional songs, play music, worship the Shiva lingam and generally have a good time will be upon us in a few weeks' time. The killer may well strike at this time, if not before. We need to be highly organised and well-prepared for this.

<u>Under no circumstances should the information contained in this report be discussed with anybody else, even your partners or parents. As I state at the top, it is on a 'For Your Eyes Only' basis.</u>

I read the report on my computer screen and was quietly confident about its contents. It brought the others up to speed and I had covered my back with Superintendent Breedon. I clicked on the encrypted email service, attached my report, stifled a yawn, and hit the '*Send*' button.

CHAPTER 26

The next day, Boxing Day, I was working late, sifting through all the evidence and witness statements once more, wondering whether there was something I'd overlooked. The fluorescent lights buzzed and hummed, and the flickering gave me a dull headache. I was pleased at unravelling the killer's signature, or most of it, but wasn't sure how far this would lead us. At least it gave us a glimpse into the mind of the killer. What worried me most was that he would strike again. And soon.

I picked up the phone and called Ben.

'I'm really sorry to bother you so late, Ben,' I said. We then discussed aspects of my report and I pressed him on the urgency to identify where the coal dust and sandstone dust in the victims' windpipes and lungs could have come from.

'Well, we could use small amounts of tissue from the windpipes and lungs of both women,' Ben suggested. 'Put them through further tests at the regional forensics centre, use a scanning electron microscope which is linked to an X-ray dispersive unit. We can also use a gas chromatograph. These will break down any sample, liquid, gas, solid or tissue, into the millions of component parts that form it. Mass photospectrometry uses light to identify each microscopic particle. The results can then be compared with a known database of all particles.'

'If we use these bits of kit, we need to destroy the tissue samples to discover what they contained?' I asked.

'Yup.'

'Do it, Ben. We'll have enough left over for further research. And enough to present as evidence in court when we nail this bastard. Can you liaise with Dr Khan and get going on this please? ASAP.'

'Will do my best, Sir. But it's the holiday season and many of the technicians and scientists are off work till after New Year's Day. It may take some time.'

It made me wonder why he hadn't suggested this course of action before.

'You know it's Shiva, don't you?' said Joy, on the phone. The late evening news was on the TV in the background.

'I know it's Shiva,' I said. 'It's in my report to all of you.'

'No, I mean the four cuts. They stand for Shiva,' she replied.

'Shiva has three horizontal lines of ash on the forehead, one on top of the other, not four lines. I'm not sure what you're talking about Joy, I don't see the connection.'

'Okay, let me start again because you seem to be acting thick today, Inspector Sharma,' she said.

I smarted at that because I felt she was taking the informality a bit too far. Still, I let her continue.

'He etched the word "ash" on an oak tree where Geeta's body was found. She had four deep cuts to her middle. And he'd crossed out the suffix "ram" from the word "ashram" leaving the word "ash",' she continued.

'You don't say, Joy,' I said.

'Don't be sarcastic,' she replied. 'How many different ways can you write the number "four"?'

'Well, we can write it as a number or as a word…' I said.

'Yes … and we can write it as a Roman numeral. As in IV,' said Joy. 'So put IV into the word "ash" and what have we got? Voila, Shiva! It's an anagram.'

'Jesus Christ, Joy! You're brilliant. Well done! I could kiss you.'

'Promises, promises,' she replied.

I ignored the comment, my attention distracted by a TV news bulletin.

'*...and the police are searching for a serial killer they've named "Shiva the Destroyer". He's believed to have killed the two young women in Leicester and the police also think he killed a middle-aged Irish man in Liverpool. They called him "Shiva the Destroyer" after the Hindu god because he uses a deadly tropical snake, a cobra, to kill his victims...*'

I stared at the television set as Wendy Weaver read the news, the bottom of the screen running a ticker tape stating, 'Breaking News.' An iron fist rammed into my stomach. I wanted to throw up.

Fuck, fuck, fuck.

'Joy, I'm sorry, I've got to go. If you're near a TV, watch the local news.'

Somebody had leaked my report to the media. It had to be Shep. But why? Because I knew his secret? Surely he wouldn't have been that stupid? It could also have been Superintendent Breedon, or any of the other senior officers who must have seen the report.

Although late, I rang the superintendent. I had to cover my back with him, even if he was involved in some way. Maybe ask him to remove Shep from the case.

But there was no reply on either his mobile or his landline.

I couldn't sleep during the night. My anger was rising and then subsiding and then rising again. Who the hell had leaked the details of the investigation and why? I came downstairs and tried watching television but I couldn't concentrate. I sat on the settee and stared mindlessly at the screen. I felt myself nodding off now and again.

The clanking of the central heating pipes woke me up at about six in the morning. My body was stiff and my neck ached from lying at an awkward angle. I got up from the settee, had a quick shower, fed Fernando and left him some extra melon and pumpkin seeds and slices of pear, and made tea. I surfed TV channels as I ate my cereal and was horrified to see that some of the national stations had picked up on the story, adding that the police were appealing for witnesses or any information that could help them catch 'Shiva the Destroyer.'

The most important person I needed to speak to was Superintendent Breedon. I tried his mobile at seven, not too early for a senior officer, I thought. Straight to voicemail. Tried again after thirty minutes. No reply. Then tried again at about ten to eight.

'Ah, Rohan, been expecting to hear from you. Sorry, been busy and didn't have time to get back to you. Festive season, with lots of formal engagements and family occasions to attend.'

Lucky him. I wouldn't have minded attending some myself.

'I also had to engage in damage limitation on your behalf,' he continued. 'The media liaison team alerted me of what was being reported last night —'

'Why the hell didn't they come to me? Sir? Why haven't I seen anybody from that team?'

'I'm not sure about that, Rohan. We can sort that out later. Let's just say that the proverbial has hit the fan, even at this early hour. The leaders of the Hindu community — I'm sure being one yourself you know these people — have already complained about the police blaspheming one of their venerable gods by equating the Lord Shiva with a serial killer. The leader of the Council for Mosques said that something like this would never happen with his faith, which is based on Allah the Merciful One, that some Hindu gods promote lechery, drunkenness, drug-taking and unbridled sex. They're also worried about copycat killings, since one of the victims was a Somali Muslim. And the leader of the English Defence League has tweeted to say this is a Christian country and the practices of heathens have no place in our civilised society. They're talking about holding a demonstration on the streets here. If they do, policing resources will be side-tracked into that and will obviously impact on your investigation.'

'Jesus Christ,' I said.

'There's no need to blaspheme against Christianity.'

I paused, unsure whether he was a devout Christian.

'Just joking, Rohan. See how easy it is to offend somebody?'

I didn't need a lesson on blasphemy from him but decided to let him play the superior.

'What I don't understand, Sir, is how my report reached the media. I sent it to four colleagues I thought I could trust, copied you into it. I assume you sent it to the Assistant Chief Constable —'

'Yes, and copied in the Chief Constable. Given the sensitive nature of this case, he's got to be in the loop.'

'Where's the leak then, Sir? Assuming it wasn't you, the Assistant Chief Constable or the Chief Constable.'

'Be careful. I'll assume that was a tongue-in-cheek comment.'

I wasn't sure it was but I didn't say anything.

'Your inner team is Shep, Joy, Ben and Dr Khan. One of them's not got it in for you, have they?'

'No idea, Sir. Shouldn't have. I found out Shep's having an affair with somebody who works at the regional office of the local TV station. I saw them together in a wine bar and Shep hasn't been the same with me since.'

'His personal life's his personal life. Sergeant Shepherd's been in the force a long time, a hard worker and a good copper. Salt of the earth, as they say. Will make detective, I'm sure. Don't assume he's guilty until you have the evidence.'

'Or I could assume they're all guilty until I'm convinced of their innocence,' I replied.

'As you wish. But we need to find out who the mole is. I'll start looking into it myself as well. I'll have to go. Got to appear in front of the TV cameras so I can dampen down some of the hysteria... I'll tell the media they're not to report any further details about the case unless they get prior approval from us. The material they've got has obviously come from ... shall we say ... "unofficial" sources. I'll say they're obstructing a murder investigation and we could have them for that. But Rohan —'

'Yes, Sir?'

'We need the media on our side, especially if we want witnesses to come forward. Can't muzzle them for long otherwise they'll bite us in the backside. They have to report the news, especially regional TV stations and small provincial newspapers competing with national and international new channels, online newspapers, and social media. We can manage some of the flow of information. But not all.'

'Okay, Sir. Thank you for your time. But who's the "we" that's managing this flow of information?'

He had already broken the connection and I wasn't sure whether he heard my question. The answer was obvious but I had to ask it.

I really wasn't sure whether I could rely on him for any support. But to be fair to him, there wasn't a lot more he could have said at this stage. Let him deal with the media. I could do without the hassle anyway.

CHAPTER 27

I was going to stay at home on New Year's Eve but Hugh Armstrong and his wife Phoebe, mutual friends from my time with Faye, had pressurised me into going to their house. Phoebe knew some of the story behind the abduction of my sister Maya on New Year's Eve all those years ago in Kenya and thought I might get depressed thinking about it. She didn't understand that I thought about my sister every single day. Having had a pleasant evening and a few drinks, they insisted I stay the night because I could not drive home. I eventually relented.

I pulled up outside my house late morning on New Year's Day and the patches of ice and frost crunched under my tyres. My head was muzzy because I'd mixed my drinks the previous night. I didn't switch off the engine immediately as the DJ on *Classic FM* was playing a selection of Western classical interpretations of music from Africa, Asia and the Middle East. My mobile vibrated in my pocket but I ignored it. I would return the call later. I wanted to listen to the last track till the end.

I got out of the warm car, felt the bitterly cold wind enter my lungs and rubbed my hands together. I got the key from my pocket and walked in through the front door. The cold and damp hit my face. *Shit*, I had forgotten to leave the central heating on. *Oh Christ, Fernando*. I rushed into the living room and found him on his perch. There was still some seed in his tray but he had eaten all the fresh fruit. A small amount of water rested in his water tray, two sunflower seeds floating on top. The room was very cold.

He stared at me through his cage, scratched the side of his head with his foot and said, 'Rohan's a bad boy. Rohan's a bad boy.'

'I know, Fernando. I'm really sorry, I didn't mean to be out all night.'

He squawked, lifted his tail and pooped on the dirty newspaper at the bottom of the cage.

'It's freezing in here, Fernando. We'll soon have the house warmed up. I'm shivering.'

'Shiver, my timber.'

'Yes, Fernando, shiver my timber. Shiver my timber.' Then I froze, and not through the cold. 'What did you say, Fernando?'

'Shiva my timber! Shiva my timber!'

I stared. He'd never said that before.

My heart started racing. I rushed over to the central heating controls. They'd been switched off. I never do that.

I switched them on. The red coasters on the coffee table with the sideways view of a dancing elephant on each were facing away from each other. Again, something I never do. I'd thought they'd been moved before, a few weeks ago. This time, there was no denying it.

Fuck, fuck, fuck.

It had to be the killer. What the hell had he been doing here? He must have taught Fernando the phrase. I went into my bedroom. It seemed okay. Nothing amiss.

I went into the bathroom. And there it was. Drawn with bright red lipstick. An open eye with a big iris and pupil. Smack in the middle of the square mirror above the wash basin.

I ran downstairs and looked into the kitchen. All seemed fine.

Staggering into the lounge, I sat down heavily on the settee near the front window, trying to calm down. Taking deep breaths and thinking about what to do next.

As I sat there my eyes focused on the CD player below the television set. I noticed it was switched on but the symbol on the display indicated that the 'pause' button had been pressed. One of my compilation CD cases was lying empty on the carpet. I picked up the remote control and pressed the 'play' button.

I recognised the bass guitar introduction immediately and Sting's voice singing, '*Every breath you take, every step you take, I'll be watching you.*'

No mistaking the message. I hit the stop button.

My eye caught something dark on the carpet. I blinked and focused.

A ball of dark fur, with flecks of dried blood. About two inches wide, slightly longer in length.

I stared at it. What was it?

I leaned back, wondering whether to pick it up. Something cold and damp tickled my neck. Something moving.

Then I heard an unmistakable hiss...

CHAPTER 28

I shot up and grabbed my mobile and car keys from the table.

I bolted to the front door and flung myself out, slamming the door shut. I leaned against the car, my breathing heavy and my chest heaving. I felt faint.

Finally, I unlocked the car, sat down and called Ben on my mobile, staring at my front door all the time.

'Ben, I know it's New Year's Day but this is an emergency. I need you and some SOCOs down here. The killer's been in my house. He's left the cobra in there. Almost got me. I heard it hiss.'

'You sure, Sir?'

'Of course I'm bloody sure... Sorry, Ben. It's a frightening experience, that's all. I'm sitting in the car outside the house now.'

'I'll come right now, Sir.'

'Thanks, Ben. Contact the zoo, please. We'll need somebody who can handle deadly snakes.'

Ben was with me within an hour and three scene of crime officers followed not long after. While they put on their white outfits in the back of the incident van, an expert on deadly snakes arrived from the local zoo. I shook his outstretched hand as he introduced himself as David Bloom. Apparently, Mr Beauchamp, the snake expert I'd met previously, was on leave and nobody knew where he was, or if he'd gone out of the country on holiday. His mobile went to voicemail and he hadn't left a contact number.

David Bloom entered the back of his white van, put on a pair of goggles, ensured that his trouser bottoms were firmly tucked into his brown suede boots and pulled out a six-foot-long metal pole with a crook at the end. He held a hessian sack, the opening of which was tightly wrapped around a grey plastic pipe about six inches in diameter and at least a foot long. Standard equipment for trapping cobras. The goggles would protect his eyes. Cobra venom can travel at high speed and hit targets accurately from two or three metres, he said, and the crook would enable the head to be pressed down but not injure it. Cobras liked quiet, dark holes and it would slide into the hessian sack through the plastic tube as long as it was not startled.

David Bloom went in first through my front door; Ben and the three SOCOs followed. I decided to stay outside. A small crowd of brown faces started gathering near my car and across the road. I said there was nothing of interest but they ignored me and carried on staring at my front door and window.

I didn't want to interfere with what was going on inside my house but I asked questions as officers entered and came out. Eventually, Ben beckoned me to follow him inside.

'We've collected as much evidence as we can, Sir, from all over the house, including the bathroom. Easy to get past the Yale lock in the door with a metal palette knife. The furry ball you saw next to the settee looks like the regurgitated remains of a mouse. But there's absolutely no sign of a snake anywhere. We've looked in all the places it could've hidden. Airing cupboard with the hot water tank, behind the gas heater, under the kitchen sink, in the loft, and so on. You name it and we've searched it. Also used infrared but nothing's showing up.'

'But Ben, I felt its flickering tongue on the back of my neck. And I heard it hiss. Did you check behind the settee and between the cushions?'

'Only you can say what you felt and heard, Sir. The only thing I can think of is that the hiss came from the air pressure valve at the top of the radiator. The one behind the settee is rusted and almost coming off. The steam rushing through the pipes after you turned on the central heating could've produced a hissing sound.'

'What about the sensation on my neck?'

'Could've been the curtains as you leaned back on the settee? Some cold water has seeped through and the curtain edges are damp. Or the steam from the radiators could've moved them. I'm not really sure, Sir. But definitely no sign of a snake here.'

I stared at him, not knowing what to say. The three SOCOs smiled at me, probably wondering whether I'd lost it, while David Bloom looked bemused and kept nodding at everything Ben said. My head could see the logic but I didn't want to be in that house on my own. There was a cobra lurking in there somewhere. They just hadn't looked hard enough.

But I was a detective inspector. I had to save face; couldn't admit I was afraid to be in my own home. Ben said he'd get the results of any evidence back to me as soon as he could, including fingerprint analysis. He didn't sound hopeful of finding anything significant and neither was I.

I waved them goodbye, told the last of the crowd outside to go home, and went inside. I didn't want to sit on the settee again, so I went over to Fernando put more food and water in his trays, brought over a wooden chair and sat in the corner of the lounge near the front door where I would see anything crawling towards me. I stared mindlessly at the TV screen but my thoughts were on all the potential hiding places for a six-foot-long cobra. I jumped up, turned on all the lights in the house, and poked and prodded with a stick in all nooks and crannies. Nothing.

Should I stay and risk a sleepless night? Or should I go somewhere else?

My phone vibrated in my pocket. A text message. Probably somebody wishing me a belated Happy New Year. I pressed the envelope icon and the first line wished me precisely that.

Saal Mubarak, Inspector Sahib,
Hope you enjoyed my clever poem
Taking you to homo paradise on Christmas Eve,
To see yet another bent copper (ha ha).
I enjoy regularly visiting your house,
Not very nice, is it?
Still, I hope the parrot gave you my message.
Nice bird full of life. Not like the Monty Python one.
By the way, speaking of pythons,
Naag, the serpent, will keep you company for a while.
No need to look for him,
He'll come and find you.

The killer was following me, knew my every movement and was sending me text messages.

And had literally placed a serpent in my Garden of Eden.

Fuck, fuck, fuck!

CHAPTER 29

It was mid-afternoon and I was sitting at the long desk in the incident room at HQ. The light was already fading, tolling the death knell of yet another day. I stared at the blank projector screen and at the piles of paper in front of me. I had reviewed all the evidence, wondering whether we had missed anything, a clue, a witness statement, the forensic evidence which could have told us more than we initially realised. I watched again the video of the grounds where Ayan's body had been found and the video from the automatic number plate recognition system. The text messages to me untraceable on pre-paid mobile phones.

I couldn't spot anything that we had missed.

I had spent the last three nights at a hotel, not far from the junction with the M1 motorway. I had asked David Bloom and his team to re-check my house for the cobra and asked him to take Fernando to the zoo since I couldn't bring him to the hotel. Hopefully, Bloom would keep quiet about me moving out because I didn't want to be the butt of canteen jokes at HQ. Word would eventually get out that I'd been made homeless by a snake but I tried not to let that worry me. I was wondering whether the zookeeper, Mr Beauchamp, was back when my mobile rang.

'Hello Inspector Sharma, David Bloom here. No news I'm afraid. The mice we left in traps in each room are all still alive. We checked everywhere again. After three days and three nights, there's no evidence that a cobra or any other reptile is in the house. I'm not sure what else we can do.'

I hesitated. 'Any chance of meeting me outside the house? And please bring Fernando with you. I'd be really grateful.'

'That's fine, Inspector. I'll be there in about forty-five minutes.'

'By the way,' I asked, 'is Mr Beauchamp back yet?'

'No, nobody's seen him. Not like him at all.'

I hit the disconnect button and dialled Ben's number. He picked up on the third ring.

'Hi, Ben. Any test results on the tissue from Ayan and Geeta?'

'Glad you rang, Sir. Was going to contact you. The chromatograph, electron microscope and the mass photospectrometry tests have all been done. And some more. We performed further tests on the dirt found behind the finger- and toenails of both women. The tissue and dirt samples show additional trace minerals and chemicals. Both were kept in the same hiding place before death. The test results show traces of calcium sulphate, the source material for gypsum and anhydrite, the building blocks for cement powder, plaster and plasterboard. There were also minute traces of copper and iron minerals, galena, which is a lead sulphide, and molybdenite, a lustrous crystalline mineral. This is in addition to the coal dust and sandstone dust we already know about. The academics in the geology department are pointing to specific parts of north-east Leicestershire. Even the northern parts of the city. Not the north-west and central areas of the county, as we originally thought.'

'Thanks for the good work,' I said. 'But it's still a vast area — '

'The geologist said their expert will be back soon. She knows everything there is to know about rocks, minerals, fossils, different types of dust for most, if not all, of the county. Will

159

let you know if I get any more news or find out anything more.'

I thanked him but he had something else to add.

'By the way, I'm sorry about the trouble you're having. Not being able to stay at home. You want the problem to crawl away, don't you?' Ben laughed.

The news hadn't stayed secret for long.

A tension headache was creeping from the top of my crown, lodging in my sinuses, between the eyes. The fluorescent lighting and lack of fresh air were making it worse. I rubbed my temples and shut my eyes for a while.

I opened them, picked up the internal telephone, dialled Superintendent Breedon. I told him I was worried about the safety of my children. The stakes were getting higher and I asked if it was possible for Yasmin and Karan to get police protection to and from school. He asked a few questions, said he empathised with me and he'd see if he could release extra officers.

I gathered up my papers, tidied up what I could, hoped I still had some paracetamol in the glove compartment of my car, switched off the lights and walked out.

I didn't really want to sleep in my house tonight but everybody had to know I wasn't afraid of being back. The extra locks on all external doors and windows helped.

I waited for David Bloom outside the house and he drove up in his van at the appointed time. He opened the back doors and pulled out Fernando's cage. Fernando squawked, complaining about being assaulted by the cold. We went into the house, David collected all the mice, still in their traps, poured the water out of the aluminium dishes into the sink, assured me yet again there was no snake in the house, bid me goodbye and left.

It felt good to be in my own home but I was still edgy as I warmed up chicken in a mushroom sauce and a few oven chips. I sat on the wooden chair in one corner of the lounge, still avoiding the settee and watched the television, not taking much in. And I wondered whether the killer was outside observing the house. I turned off the light in the lounge and peered through a gap in the curtains. All was quiet. Nobody about. No strange cars in the neighbourhood.

In the early hours of the morning, I switched off the downstairs lights, turned off the television, carried Fernando's cage upstairs and put him in my bedroom. I rolled up a bedsheet and covered the gap between the door and the floor so nothing could get in. I didn't cover Fernando's cage and left the light on. If a snake entered my bedroom Fernando would squawk like hell and wake me up.

Whoever heard of a parrot as a guard dog?

I nodded off now and again but for most of the night I was awake. I tried talking to Fernando, who was understandably upset with me for deserting him and wasn't very communicative.

At about five in the morning, I decided to get up. I leaned over the bed, looked under it, told Fernando I'd be back soon, removed the bedsheet covering the narrow gap between the door and the floor, and went downstairs. Padded gingerly into the kitchen, senses on heightened alert, made a mug of tea, switched on the television and sat on the chair in the corner, watching *Al Jazeera*.

I sipped the tea, had enough of watching people's inhumanity to other people and looked for the remote control to switch channels. As I did so, I heard the familiar 'ping' of a text message on my phone. Identity withheld. My heart raced. I opened the message.

A fist rammed into my stomach.

The message named the mole in my investigation. Not Shep or his lover Christine. A different snake in the grass. A person I liked and trusted.

Who the hell had sent the message?

Obviously, somebody who knew the investigation in detail.

CHAPTER 30

It was past four o'clock in the afternoon and I was in Superintendent Breedon's office, facing him across the expensive desk. I didn't want to be here, didn't want to talk about betrayal, but I knew I had no choice but to approach my superior. I had wanted to see him earlier but he'd been in meetings. He leaned back in his leather chair, immaculately dressed in his uniform, black tie, white shirt, glistening epaulettes on his shoulders. He pressed the palms of his hands together, looked at me with his deep blue eyes.

'Why did Nasreen Khan arouse your suspicions, Rohan?'

I had no idea whether he was the one who sent me the anonymous text message identifying her. If he had, why hadn't he just come out with it? It may not have been him but I had my doubts. I was beginning to wonder who the hell was telling the truth and who wasn't.

I focused on his moustache. 'There were some tell-tale signs. Not looking directly at me when I spoke to her, shifty body language, evasive answers. Don't get me wrong, her work is of a high standard but her behaviour made me suspicious.'

I tried not to believe any of these things as I said them. Trying not to think of the text blaming Nasreen for the leaks.

'I see,' he said, and I wondered whether he did.

'She invited her husband to the funeral of Geeta Mehta, the second murder victim. I can understand her being present. But her husband? Don't get that at all. A cold, distant man. I'm not sure what his role is in any of this. Maybe none at all, I just don't know.'

Superintendent Breedon drummed his fingers on his desk. 'Wendy Weaver rang not long before you arrived. Wanted to know whether we'd managed to find the snake in your house.'

I stared at him and didn't say anything. This place leaked like the colander I use to drain my spaghetti. 'What makes *you* think Nasreen Khan's the mole?' I eventually asked.

'I contacted the head of the IT unit at the hospital where Dr Khan is based. Asked him to trace all email communications from her desktop computer and any other devices she has access to. Transpired your progress report was sent from her office computer to the editor of the television station.'

'Do we know it's definitely her, Sir? Somebody else could've used her computer.'

'Oh, it's definitely her all right. Her computer is password protected.'

I sighed. 'So that settles that.'

'Yes, that settles that, I'm afraid.'

'What would you advise me to do next, Sir? Contact her or do you want to do that?'

'I think it's best if you do. Your investigation and all that. Find out what she's playing at. Hopefully, we won't need her services for a while.'

He was getting into the life raft and leaving me behind. I hoped the ship wasn't sinking. Why had Nasreen placed me in this situation?

He stood up, indicating that our meeting was over. I thanked him and turned towards the door but he put his hand on my shoulder.

'I looked at all the email traffic from her for the last few months. There were a few emails from her husband. Sometimes referred to her as "Uma". You don't know why that would be, do you?'

'No idea, Sir, though it's an Indian name and it's also one of the many names for Shiva's wife.'

The thick carpet on the corridor muffled my footsteps as I walked away from Superintendent Breedon's office. Officers and support staff nodded in my direction. It was no good. I had to contact Nasreen. Find out what the hell was going on. The damage had already been done. I dialled her number. No reply.

As I approached the door leading downstairs to the incident room, my mobile vibrated in my breast pocket.

'Sir, I think we've got a breakthrough,' said Shep, breathless and excited. 'Joy and I are at the local police station in the eastern part of the city, near the sixth form college. There's a man here claims to have seen the killer. Seems very plausible, though he's difficult to interview. Very disoriented and frightened and sometimes aggressive. But what he says fits in with the other evidence. We rushed here when the duty sergeant at the station contacted the incident room. We knew you were busy with the superintendent.'

'Great work, Shep. Well done! I'll be right there.'

CHAPTER 31

I rushed through the glass doors of the police station. Shep was waiting for me near the main reception desk.

'This way, Sir. He's in the pink room,' said Shep, leading the way down the long corridor.

'Pink room?'

'Yes, Sir. Where rape victims are interviewed. Or victims of domestic violence. Thought it the best place for our witness to feel relaxed, talk more freely.'

Shep and I walked quickly, hearing the rapid *clip*, *clip*, *clip* of our heels on the hard floor. We came to a door at the end of the corridor. Shep walked in without knocking and I followed.

The room was like a spacious lounge in a well-kept detached house. A large window, crimson curtains pulled back, looked out onto the green fields which bordered the back of the station. The carpet was thick. Two people sat on the settee, above which was an abstract oil painting splashed with bright colours, in the style of Jackson Pollock.

A coffee table in the centre supported a tall vase of fresh flowers. Ceiling spotlights bathed the room in a soft glow. Pink walls. The colour to soothe the soul. To quieten the restless spirit. To calm anger and frayed nerves. A colour to wrap around the heart. A colour to heal.

Joy stood up from an armchair. 'This is Neville, Sir. And this is Bridget, she's a voluntary worker with the homeless. Neville's a war veteran. He fought in Iraq and served in Afghanistan. He was discharged on medical grounds with post-traumatic stress.'

Neville sat at one end of the long settee. He looked in his early fifties with thick brown hair which hadn't seen a comb for the last twenty years. His curly dark beard couldn't hide the blotches and burst capillaries around his nose, a sure sign of an alcoholic. A black woollen hat, full of holes, sat next to him. He stared aimlessly at the carpet and didn't even look up as Shep and I stepped into the room.

I looked at Neville and then at Bridget, who hadn't been born when Neville went off fighting for his country. I said hello to both. She shook my hand. Neville did not. He continued staring at an imaginary pattern on the carpet.

'Are you all right, Neville?' asked Bridget.

He didn't say anything for a long time. I looked at Bridget who shrugged. We all waited. I could smell a thick aroma of mustiness and unwashed sweat coming from him. I tried not to look away.

'Neville, I'm Inspector Sharma,' I said after a while. 'I'd like to talk to you about what you saw.'

He looked at me through rheumy blue eyes, wiped his nose with the sleeve of his torn and dirty trench coat. A piece of fraying string served as a belt.

Bridget said, 'Neville, if you tell Inspector Sharma what you told me and the other policeman, you can have a drink from your hip flask.'

'Bloody wogs, I called to Dave, me best mate. Can hear 'em scurryin' in desert, like rats, just off road in Helmand, in Afghan... "Dave! Get down! Get down!" I shouted. The grenade whistled wheeeeeee, exploded near us, half Dave's face missin', brains hittin' side of me face. Killed me bes' mate.'

He stared at me. His mind and his life in a distant place in a distant time.

'Neville,' I said, 'I'm really sorry about Dave but can you please tell us what you told the duty sergeant.'

He continued to stare at me. His face expressionless. 'He were th'devil,' he said after a while. 'Half naked, long black snake twisted roun' his arm. Danced and danced, roun' and roun'. Like them wogs in desert in Iraq. Sliced off th'head of chicken with great big knife. While he were dancing, like. Rubbed oil an' ash on his body. I hid in corner so he couldn't see me in dark. Fuckin' devil from hell, he wer'. Had to keep meself quiet. Never seen nothing like it. Made me wet myself.'

I looked at Shep and then at Joy. I couldn't believe what I was hearing. My heart started racing. 'Where was this, Neville?'

'Where I sleep. When it's cold. When I need to get away like, to be by meself.'

'And where's this, Neville?' I repeated.

'Down big cemetery, in north of city. Where they also burn th'dead, like. Crypt in middle of cemetery. For big, rich family.'

I turned to Shep. 'Okay Shep, secure the area, get Ben's team there, see what we can find, even at this time in the evening. Do it pronto!'

'Already done,' said Shep, with what I thought was a hint of a smile. He stood up and left the room to make his way to the cemetery.

'Aren't you afraid to sleep in the cemetery by yourself, Neville?' I asked.

He shrugged. 'The dead can't hurt ya, can they? Not like th'livin',' he replied.

'What did this man look like, Neville?'

'Couldn't see much in dark. He burned lamps on grave… Could see shadows. Had muscles. Long thick hair. His face were dark like.'

'Dark like what, Neville?'

'Just dark,' he replied.

'Thanks very much, Neville,' I said after a while and asked him whether there was anything else he could remember.

He stared at me, the sorrow deep in his fading blue eyes. He shook his head. I got up, thanked both of them, asked Joy to take written statements and walked towards the door. As I did so, I heard Neville ask Bridget if he could now have a drink from his flask.

He did, said 'Aahhh', smacked his lips, and then said, 'Rum weather, rum weather.'

I stopped in my tracks. I turned around and looked at him.

I'd heard that phrase before. Where was it?

I walked out of the room and rushed down the corridor.

My Mercedes fishtailed as I swung it through the gates of the cemetery and followed the signs to the public car park. Cars and vans from the incident support unit were already parked up. About half a mile away, the darkness was pierced by a circle of arc lights shaded by canvas around the crypt, with men and women dressed from head to toe in scene-of-crime outfits. I grabbed a torch from the glove compartment and ran towards them, the icy wind cutting through my windpipe and lungs, my breathing getting heavier and heavier. I needed to go to the gym more often.

Ben stood next to one of the arc lights, directing the team. Shep was standing near him, both dressed in white forensic suits. I leaned against a gravestone, breathing hard, steamy breath spurting out of my mouth. My eyes watered and my chest hurt.

'What ... have ... we ... got?' I asked.

'The killer was definitely here, Sir,' replied Ben. 'Why don't you get suited and booted and we'll go down.'

Within minutes we were standing inside the crypt near the old wooden door. Two freestanding arc lights, powered by mobile generators on the ground above us, bathed the underground room in a bright white light. Two crime scene investigators dressed in white body suits stood near the stone sarcophagus, brushing every inch carefully, and gathering anything of interest in evidencecollecting jars. They removed some dust by placing Sellotape onto it. The lights gave out heat and I felt warmer standing near them.

'We've been working here a fair while, Sir. Ever since Sergeant Shepherd's phone call earlier in the evening. We've found bloodstains. Most probably from the dead bird over there.' He pointed to the headless white cockerel thrown into the corner. The head was still on the stone sarcophagus. 'There's also some grease, looks like oil, and if I'm not mistaken it has the smell of olive oil. There're small quantities of black ash, like the ash from burnt cotton wicks. The really interesting thing is this.' Ben held up a small cellophane bag with grey ash in it. 'Notice this ash has granules in it. If I'm not mistaken, they look like ashes from a crematorium. The ash is mixed in grease. May well be the oil. No idea.'

'He's one sick bastard, Sir,' said Shep. 'And in the corner, we have traces of urine. Can tell by the smell and by the stains. Could be Neville's, while he was trying to hide.'

'Oh, and there's one more thing,' said Ben. 'We found traces of congealed fluid, thick and grey, looks like gobs of spit. It's been squirted around the crypt in a circular motion. A few feet away from the sarcophagus.'

'Could it be cobra venom, Ben?' asked Shep. 'Neville said the killer was holding a snake while dancing round and round.'

'Could be,' said Ben.

170

'Jesus Christ,' I said, looking around me. The dead cockerel was undoubtedly Thumper, stolen from the farmhouse where Geeta Mehta's body had been found. I was desperately hoping for some DNA evidence. Any kind of breakthrough in the case.

Ben said his team would most probably work throughout the night and he would get the forensic results back to me as soon as possible. I told Shep to go to the crematorium the next morning and ask whether there had been a break-in, then told him to go home as there was nothing more to be done here.

I did the same.

It was late as I opened the front door. I tried not to think about whether there was a cobra in the house. I gave some seeds and dried apricots and pineapples to Fernando. He ate them quickly and put his beak in the tray of fresh water. I left him in my bedroom. I still wanted Fernando near me, he would squawk if anything was slithering about at night. It was illogical but it made me feel better.

I went downstairs and poured a large glass of Sauvignon Blanc, the first sip making my mouth water, then cooked frozen cod and oven chips. As I ate, I sent yet another text message to Nasreen, asking her to get in touch. It was late and I wasn't expecting a reply. What the hell had happened to her? She wasn't replying to my calls and messages. I knew she'd tried to ring me on New Year's Day because there was a missed call from her on my mobile. I had just pulled up in the car outside my home after having stayed at the Armstrongs' for New Year's Eve. The phone had vibrated in my pocket but I had carried on listening to the classical music on the radio. And now she'd vanished, leaving me in a terrible position, having leaked my report on the case to the media.

CHAPTER 32

Tring, tring. Tring, tring.

'Wake up, Rohan. Wake up, Rohan,' I heard Fernando say.

I picked up the receiver.

'Hello, Rohan, Superintendent Breedon here. I'm sorry to bother you at this time but we've got a real emergency. Your mobile's switched off.'

'What time is it?' I asked, stifling a yawn.

'Five-thirty. You awake enough to talk?'

'Yessir,' I replied, like I had a choice. I brushed back my hair with my fingers.

'We've got a report of a missing twelve-year-old Asian girl. Never came back from school yesterday. Her father, Mr Sandhu, is a multimillionaire and is well-connected politically. Knows all the local councillors, MPs, senior officers. Good friend of the Chief Constable. Does a lot for charity and is in line for a knighthood or peerage.'

'Ah,' I said.

Superintendent Breedon ignored my interjection and continued. 'His daughter Simran was being driven home from school late yesterday afternoon. They never made it. Mr Sandhu was in London, hurried back by train when his wife rang him, organised a search for his daughter, asking friends and family for help. They followed all the known routes to and from the school but couldn't find anything. It seems the daughter, driver and car have vanished. Into thin air. We need to find them quickly, Rohan.'

'I'll organise a search as soon as it gets daylight, Sir. We'll need the police helicopter and all available uniforms and cars.'

'Just do it. Don't worry about resources. We'll cover it.'

I thought of how little had been done to find Ayan when she disappeared. Money and power. When you haven't got either, there's not a lot going for you.

'By the way, there's something else you need to know. Simran's going blind because of congenital retinal problems. The capillaries in her retina keep bursting. She has some vision but it's sometimes blurred and sometimes ends up as tunnel vision. She'll be permanently blind before long. She also suffers from muscular dystrophy and has a mobility scooter. The muscles in her legs and upper body are wasted. She needs regular exercise and physiotherapy to keep them strong. We need to find her quickly.'

'Jesus Christ,' I said.

'Jesus Christ indeed, Rohan. The scooter's one of a kind and was in the car with them. The father had it specially made as a present for his daughter, cost thousands. State-of-the-art technology. I've seen a photograph of it, which I'll send to you. Looks like an expensive tricycle. No sign of that either. Just so's you know, the father's holding us personally responsible for the safe return of his daughter.'

I knew what 'us' meant. I could see my boss safely in his life raft waving back to me as I stood on the deck of the listing ship.

'Fuck,' I said, after I replaced the receiver onto the cradle.

'Fuck,' repeated Fernando. Then, 'Shiva my timba.'

'Yes, shiva my timba, Fernando,' I said.

Although Superintendent Breedon and I hadn't said anything, we both knew it was highly likely that Shiva the Destroyer had got Simran and her driver.

I jumped out of bed, showered, quickly downed some cereal, gulped hot tea and rushed to the incident room at HQ. I rang

Shep and Joy as I was driving, asked them to meet me, and when they did, I asked Shep to organise the available uniforms to undertake a detailed search of all known routes between Simran's school and her home. Each patrol car had two officers and they were allocated a geographical grid within which to search.

As the darkness started to lift and the grey gloom of a winter's morning started taking over, the patrol cars were dispatched with their instructions. Heavy cumulus clouds rolled slowly across the horizon as the helicopter, which we shared with other local police forces, lifted off with its thermal-imaging equipment and powerful magnifying scopes and cameras. A damp mist hung in the air, the threat of heavy rain ever present. I tried to push away the pervading sense of foreboding the clouds brought with them.

Joy and I went to Mr Sandhu's house, tried to comfort the bewildered, tired and inconsolable parents and members of the extended family, asked for recent photographs of Simran, asked questions about her likes, dislikes, the medication she needed and how often she needed to take it, her friends, whether she had reported anything suspicious, either online or offline, and so on. Mr Sandhu was adamant that the driver wouldn't have been involved in Simran's disappearance. Coleman, he said, had worked for him for many years and was a devoted and loyal employee.

As we drove away from the opulent house, the impression both Joy and I had was of a girl from a wealthy background, who was universally liked, intelligent and bubbly, had a good sense of humour and who tried her best to live with her chronic conditions. Not a spoilt brat.

'But how'd she come to the notice of the kidnapper?' asked Joy, looking out of the car window as we drove back along the route that Simran and her driver would have taken. 'I'm assuming our friend Shiva's kidnapped her,' she continued.

The route skirted the southern, eastern and northern perimeter of the city and was punctuated with built-up areas, ribbons of industrial units and linear settlements of houses. There were long stretches of isolated country lanes, with black snakes of tarmac, and one of these must have been where the kidnapper struck. But which one? And where?

'Just what I've been thinking, Joy. Simran attended a special school, was driven to and from school and didn't go out by herself. You could argue that both Geeta and Ayan came to the attention of the killer when they were out and about with friends, or shopping with their families. Not so Simran.'

'Yes, but her father's well known,' said Joy.

'He is. But not his family. Doesn't allow any publicity about his daughter. So, apart from the fact that Ayan, Geeta and Simran live in Leicester, there's not a lot in common between them. They're from different ethnic and socio-economic backgrounds. Ayan was Somali, Geeta was a Hindu and Simran's a Sikh. Both Ayan and Geeta were considerably older. Is there a common thread which links all three of them, Joy? Are we missing something?'

'I just don't know,' replied Joy. 'Could it be a teacher or a member of staff who has worked at all three educational institutions?'

'I thought of that when Geeta was found, tried to work out whether there was a connection between her and Ayan's academy. Nothing. No connection between the staff, including the admin staff, or with supply teachers. And since Simran was at a special school, it's unlikely there will be cross-pollination of staff. You need to be specially trained to work in a special school. Simran had — has — such complex needs. We'll check again, just to play safe.

'Then,' I continued, 'there's the case of Brian Flannery in Liverpool, a middle-aged white Irish guy. We need to identify what connection there is between him and our case, if any.'

Joy turned around and looked at me. She looked unbearably sad, her eyelids dark and puffy from lack of sleep. I so hoped we would find Simran alive.

We continued driving, the roads getting busier with the early morning traffic, and police cars, some marked some not, were travelling and searching in different directions. We drove towards HQ, the 'chop-chop-chop' sound of the helicopter receding in the distance above us.

Back in the incident room I rang Mrs Coleman, the wife of the driver, who'd been up all night and kept bursting into tears. I tried to comfort her by saying we were doing everything possible to find her husband, asked Joy to go round and take a statement, and set up family liaison services for her. I would visit her later. I asked one of the admin staff to ring the local media, asking them to come to HQ later in the morning for an important announcement. I still hadn't heard anything from the media liaison department, despite Superintendent Breedon saying he'd look into it. I rang them and asked them to post an appeal on all social media to find Simran Sandhu, or for any further information about her.

I prepared my statement and when members of the local press and television arrived, I explained the circumstances of Simran's disappearance and said that seventeen police cars and a helicopter were searching. Another hundred or so officers were looking for her and the driver, who was not being treated as a suspect in the case. Privately, I was still keeping an open mind about that. I handed out copies of photographs of

Simran and Coleman, asked them to circulate these to all their outlets, both local and national, took some questions about the kind of girl Simran was, how her parents desperately wanted her back, and so on.

I stressed this was a missing persons' enquiry at this stage and there was no evidence that Simran or the driver had been abducted. I wanted the local community to know the case was being dealt with properly and I also had to reassure Mr Sandhu and his family that all available resources were being deployed in the search. All the reporters, including Wendy Weaver, were reasonable and appreciated the gravity of the situation and said they would help in whatever way they could. I referred them to Superintendent Breedon if they had any queries and couldn't get through to me.

Nothing like covering your back from all angles, I reasoned.

CHAPTER 33

The wall-mounted television was switched on so we could monitor what was being reported on the local and national news. A small team of support staff were answering the telephones, taking calls from the public on anything to do with the case. Most of the calls from well-meaning people were a waste of time because the description of the car Simran was travelling in didn't match, or it was seen in the wrong area, but we had to follow through all the information, just in case.

I sat at the end of the conference table, staring at the interactive screen, and Joy was handling the remote control. We were on street view on Google Earth, following the routes that Simran and Coleman could have taken. We had covered all the major roads and were now looking at the country lanes, the white arrow Joy was clicking on moving in a north-easterly direction. The images gave us a good idea of the layout of the land, the farms, the fields, the waste ground, the areas with industrial units, residential areas, disused coal mines, and so on. I was particularly interested in looking for sites where a car could have been hidden because the kidnapper could not have driven two cars. It was highly unlikely he was on foot in such remote areas. Had to be in a car. Unless, of course, two people were involved. I couldn't discount any theory at the moment.

'Sir,' said Joy. 'There's a barn here … just off this B road, could hide a car, shall we ask one of the patrol cars to look at it?'

'Yes, please call them. See whether they've checked it out already.'

'Will do.'

It was almost midday and the work was painstakingly slow. Still, there was no other way and none of the people out in the field, including the crew in the helicopter, had reported anything of value yet. There had to be something soon. My mobile rang. It wasn't a number I knew but I instantly recognised the voice at the other end.

'Nasreen, where the hell are you? I've been trying to get hold of you for days.'

'I'm sorry, Inspector Sharma. Got a new mobile.'

'Nasreen, I need to see you. What have you been doing?'

'I haven't been doing anything, Inspector.'

'Precisely, you haven't been to work, you haven't been contactable while a major murder investigation's going on. There may well be other deaths, if you've been watching the news. I know you've been leaking information to the media.'

'What? Look… I, um, think it's probably best if you and I meet. I'll try to explain everything. But I'm scared of the consequences. I'm scared of what I've already done and what else may happen.'

'Where are you, Nasreen? Are you at home?'

'No, I'm not at home, Inspector. Can we meet later today?' She paused. I thought I could hear her breathing. Like somebody inhaling and exhaling cigarette smoke. I put the thought out of my mind because Nasreen was a doctor. Surely she wouldn't smoke.

'Tell me a time and place and I'll meet you there.'

It was early afternoon as I parked my car on the third floor of the multi-storey car park situated to the west of the city. I got out and the north-easterly winds from the Arctic hit my cheeks and the sides of my neck, sharp needles piercing my skin. I lifted the collar of my jacket, pulled on my leather gloves, and started walking, staring at the lines of cars.

The heavy smell of detergent, diesel and damp hung in the air despite the wind. Nasreen and I had agreed on which floor to meet but I wasn't expecting to agree anything else. I looked to the left and right, walking slowly, searching for her maroon BMW saloon. At the end of one side of the floor, I turned right, and walked towards the other. A white couple in their late twenties thunked the heavy metal door and came through, laden with plastic shopping bags. They ambled towards me and the woman smiled. I smiled back. The man ignored my gaze.

I carried on towards the grey breeze blocks of the wall in the distance, steel retaining joists crossing from left to right, holding up the concrete floor and about a hundred cars above my head. A white van had reversed into a parking space and I could see there was a space behind it. The bonnet of a dark car peeked out from behind the van and I could hear an engine running. I couldn't make out the model of the car in the afternoon gloom. It didn't look like a BMW though, more like a hatchback, a VW Polo or a Golf.

I was about to turn around when the headlights of the hatchback flashed. And again. The beam bouncing off the low brick wall facing it.

I quickened my pace, strode past the bonnet of the van, and saw Nasreen sitting in the driver's seat of the hatchback. I opened the passenger door and sat down, glad to feel the warmth of the fan heater on my face and on my legs.

The heavy, sweet smell of cigarette smoke hit me.

'I didn't know you smoked. Being a doctor and all. Tut, tut.'

She was wearing a pale pink *shalwar kameez* with gold embroidery at the edges of the neckline and cuffs. The gold stud in her left nostril glistened as the headlights of a passing car caught it. Her hair was untidy and she didn't have any make-up on. Her eyes were puffy and she looked as if she hadn't slept for days. Faint wrinkles stretched from the corner of her eye. It was a far cry from when I first met her running to the crime scene.

'I haven't smoked in many years, not since I was a medical student. I need it at the moment.'

She put the filter between her lips and inhaled deeply. I watched the embers getting brighter, then she took the cigarette out of her mouth and flicked the ash outside her window.

'Nasreen, d'you want to tell me what's going on? Why did you leak my report to the media?' I asked. 'Why haven't you turned up for work? Just when I needed you most? And what're you doing in this car? Where's your BMW?'

'I tried ringing you on New Year's Day but you didn't answer your mobile.'

'Why didn't you try again?'

'I couldn't ring you again. And I *didn't* leak your bloody report.' She flung the cigarette butt out of the window.

'What d'you mean? Who did then?'

A tear ran down her cheek. I lifted my hand, placed it on her chin and turned her face towards me.

'Nasreen, what happened? Who did this to you?'

There was heavy bruising around her right eye and on her swollen cheek. She lifted her hand to wipe away the tear and I noticed the bruising to the pale underside of her arm as the soft cream silk cuff slid down. I gently lifted her arm, pulled up the sleeve and saw the recent bruising. Hundreds of burst capillaries breaking through the light brown skin. Like a dark, intricate, spider's web.

I squeezed her hand and asked again, 'Nasreen, please tell me what happened? Who did this to you?'

'Who d'you think? He did this to me on New Year's Day when we were in London. We were staying at a hotel on Christmas Day, right through to the New Year's celebrations. He said he was going out to lunch with his friends on New Year's Day. He came back early and noticed I had the mobile in my hand and asked whether I was about to ring anybody. I said no. He grabbed it, scrolled down the log of calls I'd just made and saw your name.'

She began to sob, her chest and shoulders heaving. I didn't know whether to put my arms around her or not. The front of the car was too small to do that anyway. I reached inside my jacket pocket and gave her some tissues.

'Rohan, I'm scared. Really scared. His rages are getting worse and his jealousy's unbearable. I only have to look at another man and he loses it. He's going to kill me if I don't get out.'

'I thought you were really happy. That you had a great marriage.'

'That's what he wants the world to think. And that's what I thought at first. I loved him so much, I missed the warning signs. He'd criticise the way I dressed, saying my skirt was too short, or I was showing too much cleavage. I used to change just to please him. Sometimes my hair was not styled right, or it was the wrong colour. If I came home late after a long, hard day at work, he'd criticise the food I'd just cooked. Wouldn't eat it or would order a takeaway, or go out by himself. Things got worse and worse. I dreaded going home. But I desperately wanted things to work out between us. I did everything possible to please him... Things got slightly better when his father died and his mother moved in with us. But that didn't last long.'

Her shoulders slumped. 'The first time he hit me I didn't expect it. Nobody'd ever hit me before. It was over such a silly thing. He was working on his laptop on the dining table after our meal and I was clearing up. I didn't realise there was some wine in his glass and when I picked it up a small amount spilled. He called me a stupid bitch and before I knew it he'd slapped me, hard.'

Nasreen sat in the driver's seat and shivered, even though it was warm inside the car. The tears rolled down her cheeks. I wanted to hold her and say that everything would be all right.

'After the first time,' she continued, 'it became more frequent. Sometimes nothing would happen for a few weeks and then, without warning, he would slap me or punch me in the back. Always in a place where bruising wouldn't show. The slaps were mostly on Fridays. Sometimes, the bruising on my face would still be there on Monday and he would ring the hospital or my regional office to say I wasn't well, wouldn't be coming to work that morning. I was so worried people would think I was enjoying a long weekend.'

'Nasreen, you've got to get out. I'll send Shep — Sergeant Shepherd — and Constable Darlington to arrest him. Penny Darlington specialises in domestic violence. I take it he's at work?'

'No, Rohan, you mustn't do that. It'll bring shame and dishonour to the family. He and his relatives will never forgive me. You know about *izzat*, don't you? Family honour? My cards, and those of the rest of my family, will be marked forever. If not me, they'll come for my mother or sister or whoever. I just can't risk that.'

Her eyes, brimming with tears, looked longingly at me. I wanted to hug her. Not just for confiding in me but also for calling me by my first name.

'But you can't go back home. How about going to your mum? Or to a friend's house? Or your sister?'

'He'll find me. He'll come calling for me at those places. He said if I ever ran away he'd find me. And kill me. He meant it.'

'What about your BMW? Where is it?'

'It's at the second-hand car dealer, believe it or not. I bought this old car some time ago with a credit card. To get me out and about unnoticed.'

She dabbed her eyes and then blew her nose.

'Nasreen, you cannot go back home. How about going into a women's refuge until we sort this out? Penny can help you. We'll make sure he never comes near you again. If you go back, he's going to kill you. You know that and I know that. Maybe not today. Maybe not tomorrow. But some day soon.'

She bit her lip and didn't say anything for a long time. I didn't push it any further.

Eventually, she said, 'Okay, Rohan. But promise me one thing?'

'What?'

'Please don't say anything to anybody else. I will liaise with Penny Darlington if you have a word with her. That'll get me out of harm's way. I can then decide what to do.'

'I'm really pleased, Nasreen. It's for the best.'

She smiled and touched my hand. 'Sometimes he came home drunk and would rape me. He used to shout, "Fuck Uma, fuck Uma." Or maybe it was, "Fuck kuma, fuck kuma." D'you know what that might mean?'

'Did your husband ever live in East Africa, Nasreen?' I couldn't bring myself to call him by his name.

'Yes, he was born in Pakistan but as a teenager he went to live in Tanzania for two years. With one of his uncles. Then he returned home. Why d'you ask?'

'"Kuma" is a Swahili word. Chances are it's that particular word he was using. I don't know.'

184

'Oh,' she said, and paused for a while.

I rang Penny Darlington who spoke to Nasreen and they made the necessary arrangements. I said I'd come to see her before too long, and we said goodbye.

As I walked to my car, the cold wind cutting into my face, I could hear her engine idling behind me. I remembered I had not asked her about my report being leaked. It can't have been her though. She had no reason to do it. But something she said about being away in London between Christmas Eve and New Year kept bothering me. I wasn't sure why. Like a lingering itch between your toes that you can't scratch because you're wearing shoes. I also couldn't bring myself to tell her that the word 'kuma' is a derogatory term in Swahili for a vagina. Its use would make sense for a man who hated women. I couldn't bring myself to explain it to her.

I got into my car, was about to drive off when my mobile rang.

'Hello, Sir,' said Shep. 'We found a saloon with the driver's body. Not the estate belonging to Mr Sandhu. I've organised everything for when you get here.'

He told me the location.

'No sign of Simran I take it, Shep?'

'Oh sorry, Sir, thought you'd already seen the footage which was posted on YouTube.'

'What footage? What are you talking about?'

'Superintendent Breedon got YouTube to remove it. Sorry, I assumed he would've told you. We've saved it on the hard drive of our system if you haven't seen it.'

'Shep, for God's sake, just send it to me, will you? Please?'

A few moments later, I clicked on the attachment. And watched the few seconds of film with horror.

CHAPTER 34

The camera panned around what looked like a basement. The whitewashed walls had traces of damp and algae, with unevenly laid bricks and crudely applied mortar. The room was dimly lit by a single bulb dangling from some thick old grey wire protruding through the ceiling. Simran was lying on her back in a single bed. Her eyes were closed and her body lifeless. She didn't appear to be breathing but it wasn't possible to tell for certain. A dirty white sheet covered her from feet to chest, like a shroud. The old, rusted iron bed had a thin mattress. Like a bed in an old prison.

The camera zoomed in. I could see the bottom of the crinkled shroud moving up and down. Slowly, very slowly, the cobra's dark head emerged from under the sheet, between her feet. It flicked its thin forked tongue and licked the sides of its scaly mouth. Its round eyes glistened like black diamonds pressed into the sides of its head. It moved cautiously, tongue flicking, head moving from side to side. Its hood was pulled tight within its head because it didn't feel threatened.

The snake crawled up the shroud, hundreds of coiled muscles pushing the long body forward. The dark, scaly skin undulated. The cobra paused. Looked around. Paused again. And continued. The head slid upon Simran's chest. The snake stopped, stared at Simran's face, as if about to crawl towards her neck.

A loud noise, like the popping of a balloon, shattered the silence. The cobra's head erect in a flash, a foot or so above Simran's neck. Swaying. Left to right. Right to left. Muscles tense. On heightened alert. Ready to strike. The hood extended. The black spectacles visible on the back. The long, serrated fangs dripping venom.

I could almost hear its hiss.

The film ended.

The bastard, the bastard. Oh, God, no! Please, not Simran as well.

I turned on the car engine. My foot pressed down heavily on the accelerator.

The front tyres squealed as I swung the steering wheel around the concrete corners, the car travelling at high speed, round and round, down and around each floor of the car park.

Half an hour later, my foot slammed on the brake pedal, the car fishtailed and stopped at the side of a lonely country road. I cut the engine, banged shut the driver's door and ran along the single-track lane next to a fallow field on my left. At the far end of the field, there was a small copse of evergreen trees.

I could see the white forensic tent in the distance, covering part of the wide drainage ditch which bordered the ancient hedgerow around the field. Two vans from forensic services were parked in the field, a fair distance from the tent, so as not to contaminate the site. Ben Carter and several of his team, dressed in their white suits, were taking equipment to and from the vans. Shep was already there and he beckoned to me when he saw me running towards them. Joy Wheatley was there too, along with a few uniforms. I recognised Constable Angie Deacon, who had told me about the original investigation into Ayan's death.

My breathing was heavy as I approached. I nodded to all of them as I slowed down, tried to catch my breath, steam tumbling out of my mouth and nostrils in the cold air.

'Okay Shep, what have we got?' I asked.

'The farmer wanted some hay from that barn over there, to feed his cattle. Brought his tractor and trailer through that gate you've just come through. A silver four-door saloon had been pushed into the drainage ditch, next to that hedgerow. The car was mostly covered with dead branches and leaves. Quite a desolate area so the killer would've been able to take their time.'

Ben approached. 'We're still trying to get the results from the crypt to you. Now we get this.'

I thanked Shep for the information, and for organising and protecting the site.

'Got the body of a middle-aged man sprawled across the front seats,' Ben said to me. 'I assume it's the driver. Came to a nasty end. The jugular's been severed, deep knife wound in the throat, another in the lower back. There's a mobile too. Looks like the girl's. Pink case with flowers. The last call she made was to her mother. No sign of the girl. I gather the car they were travelling in was a four-by-four Lexus RX. Would've been easier to abduct the girl in that. This silver one must be the car the killer was originally in. False number plates. We're going through it with a fine toothcomb but there's not a lot to go on. Not much trace evidence, such as hairs and fibres. Must've covered the seats and then taken the sheets away. Was probably also wearing leather or cotton gloves. I think he'll have tried to keep this car scrupulously clean. Anyway, it's early days for me and my team. Let's see what we find.'

A man approached. 'Sorry to interrupt you, Inspector Sharma, I'm Dr Allan Rolleston, the pathologist,' he said. He was carrying a medical bag and dressed in a dark duffel coat with a hood.

'Dr Rolleston is covering for Dr Khan while she's ... absent,' Ben said.

'Will let you know what I can once we perform the post-mortem. The cause of death seems straightforward,' the pathologist said.

'Some of the uniforms are already out making enquiries at nearby farms and houses,' said Shep. 'Joy's spoken to the farmer's wife and their teenage daughter.'

'Nothing much to report, I'm afraid,' said Joy. 'They were both at the farmhouse, the daughter's been in bed with flu and her mum is looking after her.' She shivered, as she plunged her hands into her pockets.

'What about the uniforms here, Shep? What're they doing?'

'Helping Ben and his team gather evidence. A lot of ground to search from here to the main road. If you'll excuse me, I'll go help them.'

'Before you go, what about possible vantage points for the killer? Remember when we found Geeta's body, we thought the bastard might have been spying on us? He might be looking at us from those woods over there or from across the road?'

'I thought of that, Sir, but we're a bit stretched for staff. A lot of the uniforms were miles away on the other side of the county looking for Simran and the chauffeur. Ben needs help to search for evidence, so I decided to focus there. And it'll soon get dark so we don't have much time. If the uniforms go wandering off into the woods, the killer, if he's there, will only escape. We can't use the chopper either. It's been redirected to the Nottinghamshire force to chase down a joyrider who killed an elderly woman in a hit-and-run.'

I turned to walk towards the van to fetch a forensic suit. As I did so, I noticed a red kite flying high in the mid-afternoon gloom, using the power of the strong cold breeze to circle in the sky, looking for prey. The reddish-brown body, cutting the

189

air with angled wings and deeply forked tail, was a highly efficient killing machine. Like our killer, except the kite hunted to survive. Joy followed my gaze but said nothing.

As I walked towards the van, I dialled Jamie Shriver's number, the head of our IT unit. I asked him about the video footage of Simran and the cobra, whether it was possible to track down where it was posted.

There was an incoming call from Superintendent Breedon. I put Jamie on hold.

'Rohan, I'm sorry I should've contacted you earlier. You've seen the YouTube footage?'

I confirmed I had.

'The killer tweeted the link to our Twitter account, with the by-line "from Shiva the Destroyer". We contacted YouTube and Twitter and got them to remove the video and tweet. But it took a while. I didn't want Mr and Mrs Sandhu to see it. The accounts have been taken down. I'm hoping not too many people saw it or downloaded it.'

I thanked him, annoyed he hadn't contacted me immediately, but let it go. I put Jamie back on. Jamie gave me the answer I was expecting. The video footage had been bounced across servers in different parts of the world; they tried to trace it but lost it between South Korea and the Philippines. Same with the Twitter account, they could not trace the precise origin of the message. They were still working on it and hoping a signal could eventually be traced back to a provider, hopefully a communications mast, in the UK.

I paused and then asked Jamie to dig around some more in relation to the email systems, websites and servers used by the educational institutions attended by the victims. See if they had been compromised in any way.

I then thanked him and hit the disconnect button.

Angie and Joy were both laughing at something Angie had said.

'What's so funny, you two?' I asked as I approached them.

Angie turned towards me, a few feet away, smiled and said, 'Oh Joy was just —'

The bullet slammed into Joy's chest and turned her whole body round, like a ballerina, pirouetting on tiptoe. I held out my arms to catch her and, for a brief moment, we were doing the waltz. She stared at me wide-eyed, not knowing what had happened, then slumped. I grabbed her and we were in a bear hug. She was heavy. I couldn't hold on and I bent my knees and slowly took her down with me to the cold ground, supporting her neck in the crook of my elbow.

Joy gazed up at me. A patch of blood oozed through her pale-yellow woollen coat, the crimson shape like a map of Africa. It was getting bigger. I tore off her cashmere scarf and pulled open her coat.

'It was him, Rohan, wasn't it?'

'Joy, please don't talk,' I said.

I shouted to Angie, who stared back at us, wide-eyed and frozen, to get an ambulance. And to Shep to get officers into the woods to search for the perpetrator.

Joy was struggling to breathe and I could hear the gurgling of blood and air escaping from her chest, just below the breastbone. Her blouse was rapidly turning bright red. The map of Africa disappearing fast.

'Please don't talk, Joy. You'll be fine. An ambulance is on its way.'

Her face was ashen and her cheeks cold and clammy. She was going into shock. A tear ran down the side of her face and into my elbow. She closed her eyes.

'Joy, please don't close your eyes. Talk to me. I'm here. Don't fall asleep.'

'Okay... Okay, Rohan... You ... are ... always ... good to me.'

She opened her eyes. Lids heavy. Pupils dilated. The iris a watery blue. Her legs shuddered involuntarily.

A strand of golden hair blew across her face and I gently pushed it back and stroked her cheek. A robin sang in a nearby hedge.

'Rohan? I can't see you. Are my ... are my eyes ... still open?'

I looked at the shining blue eyes with the long lashes. Wide-eyed and looking straight up at me.

'No, Joy, they're closed.'

Her chest heaved. 'Is that a robin I can hear?' she asked.

A tear ran down my cheek. 'Yes, Joy. We'll soon get you to the hospital...'

'Not even ... not even ... a nightingale ... for me, Rohan... Ssstory of my life...'

She shuddered. I held her tight.

Her body tensed. I cradled her in my arms.

And she died. Her blue eyes open wide.

CHAPTER 35

The white van wasn't made for speed as I pushed the accelerator right down. It slid on the cold, damp grass. I could barely control it but I drove fast towards the woods where I thought the shot came from, Shep holding onto the handle of the passenger door next to me. The van bobbed up and down on the uneven field, my head hitting the roof. A figure on a motorbike came out of the woods, stopped, turned around and looked at us for a fleeting moment, and then sped away.

I told Shep to radio for a patrol car to chase him. I wasn't holding out much hope, though. We got to the woods, jumped out and looked around. Although daylight was rapidly fading, made worse by the thick foliage and the tall trees, it was obvious where the killer had been hiding from the crumpled grass at the bottom of the old tree and the scuff marks on the trunk. I told Shep to contact the forensics team so they could carry out a thorough search of the area.

I drove back to the others as the killer was now long gone. I wasn't sure what else we could do today in the gathering gloom and the dying light.

I was praying that what had just happened to Joy was a bad dream.

But God does not answer all prayers.

The following few days were the worst in my life. Worse even than the day of my sister Maya's disappearance and worse than finding out that Faye had been sleeping with Pierre. Poor Joy. I thought about her all the time, day and night, every single moment. I could not sleep or eat. Why her? I was near her, why did he not go for me? Or Angie Deacon, for that matter? Or one of the other officers? Was it a mistake on his part?

Unlikely. He must have had a scope on his rifle and must have had Joy in his sights. Was it because she was attractive and he wanted another trophy? Or did she and the killer have a connection of some kind? I had no idea.

Fernando sensed my unhappiness and was subdued too. I fed him regularly but we didn't have much to say to each other. Faye, the kids and my mum rang regularly to check up on me. Even Nasreen rang. I was happy to hear from her.

The image which haunted me day and night was Joy's head, blonde hair falling back, resting in the crook of my elbow. Blue eyes open wide. I was staring into those eyes while she died, my face reflected in the clear, moist irises. There was nothing I could do to save her. To change anything. The words of a Leonard Cohen song wouldn't leave me and I constantly heard them inside my head: *hey, that's no way to say goodbye.*

As each minute of each day dragged by, I tried to focus on the task at hand. Find the bastard who had killed Joy and who had killed Ayan and Geeta and Robert Coleman, the driver. And, yes, Brian Flannery as well. And who now had Simran Sandhu. My inner team on the investigation was disintegrating. Joy was dead. Nasreen Khan, for all intents and purposes, had gone. The media and other vested interests had also started putting heavy pressure on the investigation and hence on me.

The national newspapers, television news channels and online news websites were using Joy's photograph from when she joined the service. Joy, aged twenty-three, five years younger, blonde hair tucked under her constable's hat with its black and white diced band, blue eyes staring straight at the camera, cheeks glowing, lips smiling, a starched white blouse with epaulettes. Proud, a long and happy life stretching in front of her. Mown down in broad daylight in middle England.

I hoped the killer had not filmed Joy's killing but I wouldn't be surprised if he had. The thought of the video ending up on YouTube filled me with dread.

Meanwhile all commentators, politicians and journalists were saying that Joy's killer must be caught. And soon. That no effort should be spared to find Simran Sandhu alive. They were asking the usual questions. What progress was being made in hunting down the killer? Was the team experienced enough? Why was Joy Wheatley targeted? Was there a connection between Joy's death and the death of the driver? Was there a connection between these deaths and the earlier deaths of two young women, Ayan Suleiman and Geeta Mehta, as some sources inside the police service seemed to be indicating? Where was Simran Sandhu? Had a ransom demand been received? Thankfully, the editors were holding the line on not mentioning snakes and cobras.

Superintendent Breedon decided to go in front of the cameras and issued a statement. Simran Sandhu was missing but we should not assume she was dead. No ransom demand had been received but her father had offered a substantial reward for her safe return. He stressed that the public at large had nothing to fear and everything possible was being done to apprehend the killer or killers.

Superintendent Breedon had agreed to my request for more foot patrols on the streets, more officers in patrol cars, more images in the media of officers scouring the land around where Joy and Robert Coleman had been killed. All this so the public would not get too alarmed. Already there was talk about the streets not being safe and discussion in social media about setting up vigilante patrols. We quashed that with a reminder that such patrols were illegal.

'Was the team experienced enough?' was a recurring question in certain sections of the media. That was directed at me. My background and relative inexperience in leading homicide investigations had probably been leaked by one of my colleagues. *Well, screw the bastards*, I thought. But my reputation and my career would be damaged if I didn't find the killer quickly.

This was made quite clear to me by Superintendent Breedon when we met. He informed me that Mr Sandhu was holding me personally responsible for his daughter's safety and had been putting pressure on the Chief Constable to get more experienced detectives onto the case. Senior figures from the Home Office in London had also been making noises about whether another police force should review the handling of the investigation.

'You have my full support — for the time being, Rohan,' Superintendent Breedon said. 'But we need results soon. Otherwise, I may not have a choice in the matter.'

He sat behind his desk, immaculately dressed and groomed.

'Sir,' I replied, 'my team's working at full stretch, constantly reviewing the evidence and looking at new lines of enquiry. I'm sure we'll get a break soon.'

A distinct aroma of expensive aftershave floated between us. Cinnamon and clove, with just a hint of patchouli.

'Be that as it may,' he said, his thick salt and pepper moustache moving up and down, 'the killer or killers are getting more brazen. You said in your report he may be planning something spectacular at the time of *Shivratri*. Isn't that the night Hindus celebrate the power of Shiva? That's in a few weeks' time, isn't it? You'll know that better than I do. We can't afford to have that, Rohan. It'll be our careers down the drain and — I don't know about you — but I'm not going to let that happen to mine.'

'Sir, the team's suffered a major setback. Constable Wheatley's death has affected morale but it's also led to a renewed drive and energy to find the killer. Apart from you, I don't seem to be getting any support from anywhere else. It seems as if I'm being hung out to dry.'

His blue eyes pierced me. 'If you need more staffing and resources, let me know. I'm not promising anything but I'll see what I can do. For what it's worth, I know you can catch the killer. Your analysis of his MO and his signature was excellent. We need to nail the bastard, Rohan.'

'Thank you for your support so far, Sir.'

'Oh, don't be too hasty in thanking me. If I take you off the case, it'll look bad in the community and reflect on the force, including me. People will ask why one of the few detectives from the local community has been removed without being given proper support and a proper chance. If I place more senior detectives with you, that'll look bad too. The politically correct lobby will be up in arms, saying it reinforces stereotypes that only white officers can solve difficult cases. Either of these two options, which remain on the table, will damage your career. Results, we need results.'

I held his gaze and said I understood. The image of the life raft and the sinking ship came to my mind again.

He looked down at his desk, shuffled a few documents, looked up at me. 'One more thing, Rohan. Another reason I'd like to keep you on the case — for the time being — is that I know Dr Khan did *not* leak your report to the media. There are some vested interests, sad to say, here at HQ, which are working against you.'

'Sir?'

'Dr Khan's laboratory assistant is called Mrs Duffield.'

'That name doesn't mean anything to me, Sir.'

'No, I wouldn't necessarily expect you to know the name. Mrs Duffield is obviously her married name. Her maiden name was Genner — Tracey Genner.'

I remembered the chubby woman in her mid-thirties, with a snub nose and dark hair, who was assisting Nasreen Khan during Geeta Mehta's post-mortem. I stared at him, trying to work out the permutations of this information.

'Yes, Rohan, Detective Inspector Frank Genner's sister. Remember Frank, and your bust-up with him? He was, is, the SIO in the Ayan Suleiman murder. Well, his sister knew Dr Khan's password. She needed it to access and send post-mortem and other reports when Dr Khan was out in the field. Your report was forwarded to the editor of the local TV station two days after you sent it to Dr Khan. It was emailed from Dr Khan's workstation, not her tablet or mobile. Seems Tracey felt Frank should have been leading the case, not you, because it tied in with Ayan's case. When he solved both, it would've made him a celebrity.'

I now realised what was bugging me about what Nasreen had said to me when we met in the car park.

'Of course,' I said to Superintendent Breedon, 'Dr Khan was on leave at the time. She told me she was in London from Christmas Day until New Year's Day. I emailed the report to the team late on Christmas Day. So she couldn't have done it.'

'Precisely,' said Superintendent Breedon.

I felt an overwhelming sense of relief. 'What about Tracey Duffield, Sir? What's happened to her?'

'The hospital's suspended her for gross professional misconduct. She'll end up losing her job.'

'Shouldn't we arrest her for interfering in a murder investigation?'

'I thought about that but it's best not to. I found out she's been having an affair with DC Neil Wainwright, good friend of Frank Genner, and who's on your team, isn't he? He's probably been leaking inside information to her about the investigation. Pillow talk. I think it wise not to wash our dirty linen in public.'

He looked down at his desk, stared at the documents, indicating he had nothing more to say.

I quietly closed the heavy door behind me.

CHAPTER 36

Rays of pale vanilla winter sunlight fought their way through the frosted skylight panels in the incident room. The vents near the ceiling hummed, sending cascades of warm air through the large room. It was a couple of days since I'd had my meeting with Superintendent Breedon. I was pacing around the conference table, which was littered with arch lever files full of documents, the remote control in my hand, reviewing all the evidence on the interactive screen, plugged into a couple of computers, including HOLMES. Looking for any new leads, anything we may have missed, looking again at video footage, witness statements, forensic test results in the killing of Ayan Suleiman, Geeta Mehta, Brian Flannery, Robert Coleman, and now Joy Wheatley. I was hoping against hope that Simran Sandhu was still alive but each minute that ticked by made it less likely.

There was no common profile to the victims and that bothered me enormously. They were different ages, sexes, ethnicities; the two young women had been sexually assaulted, the men had not; they were killed in different ways, from cobra bite to knife wounds to a high-powered rifle with a telescopic sight. The golden thread linking the victims was missing. The means and opportunity to kill them were clear but the motive in all cases wasn't. Some people are born bad and mad. But I had to have more than that. Not just the nature versus nurture argument.

Shep and Angie Deacon, whom I had requested should be formally seconded to the investigation team, were organising further roadblocks and the team was taking statements from motorists who may have seen anything when Simran Sandhu and her driver were ambushed. Disused mines were regularly inspected and a central database of such visits created. The shared helicopter was used over large parts of the south and east of the county to see which route the motorbike rider may have taken. Again, witness statements were taken, any relevant information was uploaded onto HOLMES and we looked for a breakthrough in the cases. Appeals were constantly run on social media for further information, with regular reminders of the reward offered by Simran Sandhu's father, which was now being matched by the constabulary to reflect the seriousness of the crimes. And, I suspected, as a damage limitation exercise.

I was anxious about the length of time it was taking for Ben to get back to me with further test results from the crypt, from the silver saloon, or anything from the woods where the killer was hiding when he killed Joy.

The door opened and Jamie Shriver walked in.

'Good afternoon, Sir,' said the IT man. 'You were right about the email systems, websites and servers in the three educational establishments the victims attended. All hacked prior to the disappearance of each one. Personal records of many students were trawled including, obviously, our three victims. Records with names, home addresses, phone numbers, parents' names, parents' workplace numbers, doctor's names and addresses, hobbies, interests and so on of each student.' Jamie looked as if he hadn't slept for several days. 'You won't be surprised to hear, Sir, we couldn't trace where the hacker was. Signal bounced around the world.'

I sat down at the conference table and asked Jamie to do the same.

'Have you heard about Joy's funeral?' I asked.

The coroner had released Joy's body because the cause of death was clear. The inquest would be held later. Her parents had the body transported for a cremation in Dorset in a couple of days and it was going to be a private affair. I understood the family's need for privacy. Superintendent Breedon had said we would arrange a local memorial service for Joy where anybody could attend and there were also plans to create a permanent memorial for Joy sometime soon.

We reminisced about Joy and then Jamie stood up and smiled a sad smile.

I thanked him as he was about to close the door but he didn't turn around. My eyes were drawn to the white envelope which rested on the desk near my elbow. It contained a sympathy card with a glossy photograph of a pale-yellow magnolia flower, flecks of pink and red on the inside of the petals. Inside I had written the words of Rumi, the Persian poet:

'Out beyond ideas of wrongdoing and rightdoing,
There is a field.
I'll meet you there.'

I would send it tomorrow, along with a long-stemmed single red rose and a note asking Joy's parents to place both in her coffin.

After Jamie Shriver had gone, Ben rang. He updated me on his findings and informed me that the geologist from the university was still working on the samples recovered from the crime scene, especially from the silver saloon. I thanked him and drew up a more up-to-date profile summing up the investigation so far.

I re-read the report, sure that nothing significant had been omitted. I hit send and circulated it to all the relevant people.

CHAPTER 37

Mid-morning, and I was driving back with Angie Deacon from a difficult meeting with Simran's parents. Mr Sandhu was holding me personally responsible for his daughter's safety and as each day went by without finding Simran, I was becoming more pessimistic of finding her alive. The first forty-eight hours are crucial in any investigation where a victim has been kidnapped and it was a few days past this marker.

As I drove along the outer ring road towards headquarters, my mobile rang.

'Sir, we found him,' shouted Shep, breathless. 'We've got an image.'

'Shep, slow down, please. What are you talking about? What image?' I glanced at Angie.

'CCTV image. A bit grainy in parts. Got it from a dealer in exotic animals and pets. Near Cambridge. He's here at HQ, brought the hard drive with him.'

My heart started racing. I pressed my foot down on the accelerator.

I slammed the door open against the wall as I rushed into the interview room where the witness was, Angie behind me. The hard drive of the CCTV camera was connected to a laptop. My breathing was laboured and my chest hurt as I sat down on the edge of the table in the corner.

The interview room didn't have any natural light. It smelled musty and had not been thoroughly cleaned for a long time. A middle-aged white man sat on one side. Shep put the laptop on the desk in front of me. I stared at the screen.

The image lasted only a few seconds. I watched it; Angie craned to see.

I watched it again. And froze it. Ran it slowly, frame by frame.

The image against a grey background was the profile of a man's face and shoulders as he walked past the camera. Probably mid-thirties, he had long dark hair parted on the left, the side facing the camera. A hand reached up to push back a few strands of hair. The hand looked feminine but strong, the Adam's apple pronounced. A brief glimpse and then the face disappeared.

'This here is Andrew Houghton,' Shep indicated. 'Owns a warehouse and pet shop near Cambridge. Deals in exotic animals and reptiles.'

Andrew Houghton leaned forward, rubbing his hands, eyes shifting from me to Angie to Shep. Obviously nervous.

'I'm Inspector Sharma, Mr Houghton. Can you please explain what exactly we're looking at? Where the images were taken and why you've brought them to us.'

'Yes, of course. I own a warehouse near where the A14 meets the M11 motorway. I specialise in reptiles, iguanas, snakes, frogs from the Amazon, tortoises from Madagascar, and the like. They come by ship to Felixstowe and are then transported by lorry. The market for exotic pets is enormous and growing, I hope I'm not going to get into trouble, Inspector. I've been struggling with my conscience for a long time about this…'

He stopped. His eyes darted between me and Angie. Then flickered to Shep.

'I can't say anything until I know what you're talking about, Mr Houghton,' I said, trying to make him look at me.

'The market for deadly snakes like cobras and black mambas and kraits has been growing,' he said. 'There're customers who want something more adventurous than harmless rock snakes, grass snakes and adders. And they're fed up of pythons and boa constrictors that're cute when young but then grow to more than ten feet. Not exactly a pet you can keep in a council flat.'

'That explains,' interrupted Shep, 'why some are abandoned in country parks and country lanes.'

'Precisely, Sergeant Shepherd. Cobras and kraits don't grow that long or that thick. The people who buy 'em sometimes ask that the sacs containing the venom are removed first. I get that done in the country of origin. Wouldn't get me putting my fingers into the buggers' mouths.' Houghton stopped and rubbed his hands together before continuing. 'The bureaucracy surrounding the importation of poisonous snakes is constricting, if you pardon the pun. I sometimes bend the rules. Don't declare everything. A bit of *baksheesh* here and there. You'd be amazed how many're prepared to turn a blind eye. Or papers are sometimes forged in the country of origin. In India, for instance, you can get it done for five or ten pounds.'

'So,' said Angie Deacon, 'you had a cobra or two in your warehouse. Imported illegally.'

'Oh, just the one, officer…'

'And what about this man? D'you know him?' I asked, indicating the figure on the screen.

'No, I'm sorry. No idea. I stared and stared at the image for weeks. Never come across him before.'

It then dawned on me how old the video was. It dated back to November last year. The time of day in the bottom corner of the screen was 6.39pm.

'The date and time, Mr Houghton. Anything significant about them?' I asked.

'The only thing I remember happening that day was a serious accident on the A14. The traffic on the M11 heading towards the Midlands was diverted around Cambridge and the surrounding country lanes. Our warehouse is signposted on the road leading into the city. Maybe this was one of the diverted drivers.'

'So, you're saying this man stole the cobra from your warehouse, Mr Houghton? One which had not been declared. Why's it taken you so long to come to us? It's a case of perverting justice.'

'I know, Inspector. As I said before, I've been struggling with this for a long time. I knew you were interested in any poisonous snakes missing from pet shops around Leicester. It's a small world. One of the shopkeepers in Loughborough mentioned during a phone call that the police had been round. Asking him whether anything was missing and so on. I had a lot to lose, my whole livelihood if I lost my trading licence, so I didn't say anything.'

Shep's enquiries would not have covered Cambridge because it was more than thirty miles from Leicester. I remembered asking him to stick to that radius. A mistake as it turns out but I'd had to make the best use of scarce police time.

'What changed your mind, Mr Houghton?' asked Shep.

'It was hearing on the news about the disabled girl disappearing. The fact that a young woman had been killed earlier. A mention of deadly snakes. Wanted to say something before it all died a death. Oh, sorry, I didn't mean...' He looked at the pale green carpet, frayed in parts, the crumbling underlay showing through. 'After the girl went missing, I decided I didn't have a choice. I couldn't have her death on my conscience.'

'Didn't you have a burglar alarm for the warehouse?' I asked.

'Oh, yes. But it was deactivated by the intruder. Used a screwdriver to break through the locks. Removed the main battery and the back-up battery in the control box. The alarm would've gone off for a minute or so at most. The warehouse is among industrial units, no residential area nearby. I doubt if anybody passing by would've paid much attention.'

'Thank you very much, Mr Houghton, for coming forward. It'll help us a lot. However, we have to report you to Customs and Excise for importing dangerous animals —'

'What? Even though I came forward with the information?'

'If I make a special case on your behalf, they may well be lenient.'

Andrew Houghton looked resigned to his fate.

I asked Shep to take him to another room and sort out all the paperwork. I rang Ben and asked his team to go to the warehouse, see if they could pick up any evidence, but I wasn't too optimistic after all this time.

I stared at the image on the laptop screen again.

'Are you thinking what I'm thinking, Sir?' said Angie.

'I doubt it, Angie. What were you thinking?'

'That the killer may be a Cambridge graduate who works in a research laboratory. Maybe for one of the pharmaceutical companies that have sprung up there. And the killer visits Leicester regularly.'

'You're right, Angie.'

'Really?'

'No, I wasn't thinking that at all. I was thinking the killer may have graduated from Leicester University and visits Cambridge regularly.'

We smiled.

Angie and I went with a hard copy of the man's screenshot to Mrs Suleiman, Mrs Mehta, Mrs Coleman and the Sandhus.

After staring at it for a long time, they all said they didn't recognise him.

Later that evening, I was sitting in front of the television, tray on my lap, the remnants of another microwaved macaroni cheese, the dregs of Sauvignon at the bottom of the glass. The TV screen showed Shane, the ageing gunslinger trying to change, to lead a more worthy life, ending up defending the farmers against a cattle baron, cantering towards the town, the starry-eyed little boy running a long way behind, calling out his name, wanting to be with him, the loud beat of the kettledrums in sync with the horse's hooves, while the moody, hired killer, dressed in black, waits for Shane in the dark saloon. The final showdown. We all knew how it would end. If only I could say the same for this case.

It was 10.23pm and I was tired. My phone vibrated in my breast pocket. I didn't want to answer it.

I stared at the screen as it flashed a link to YouTube. No message. I moved the cursor to the link and pressed. And waited. The progress bar on the screen ran its course and the image sprang to life. Joy and Angie walking towards the camera. A distant view. The camera zooming in, obviously an integral part of the rifle scope. Both laughing. Me walking next to them. Joy turning around, the red dot appearing on her chest, her body spinning around, the red dot getting bigger and bigger, me grabbing her, trying to steady both of us, going round and round, and then falling to the ground. All in slow motion. To prolong the agony and the pain.

The screen went black. I felt sick.

It flickered back to life. A tunnel appeared, carved out of roughly hewn rocks, the roof high, dimly lit. The person holding the camera walked slowly. They stopped. A portable flashlight was switched on and dark shadows danced. The image showed a normal light bulb with a faint glow, dangling from a length of wire which ran along the roof of the tunnel. The torchlight pointed to a fork in the tunnel. Then focused on the tunnel to the right. Its mouth full of rubble. Old wooden cross-beams cracked and broken. Huge grey boulders in front of the tunnel entrance. The camera panned onto a round metal sign which had fallen to the ground, 'Extreme danger. Tunnel roof unstable'.

I tried to control my rising panic.

There was loud laughter and an electronically modified voice shouted, 'The blind bitch doesn't need a room with a view anymore. She's got her own tomb! Her own Taj Mahal!'

The image went black.

My stomach punched by an iron fist.

Simran Sandhu was dead.

A message pinged again on my phone, *D'you think I'm so fucking shallow Sharma? D'you think I'd strike on Shiva's night? On Shivratri? How fucking predictable, you thick bastard.* It ended with an emoji of a winking face. Then another ping. *And I can see you. Peek-a-boo! See, it rhymes. Been here a few times.*

My screen flickered and was replaced by a real time image of me sitting on the settee in my lounge, tray on lap.

I gasped and leapt up. I spun round. There! A tiny spy camera painted white was pinned in the corner of the door frame. I rushed to it, eating knife in hand, and carved it out, damaging the frame, but I didn't care. There would be other electronic equipment hidden in the house to enhance the signal.

I hit my contact list, heart thumping, got Jamie Shriver, who wasn't happy to be disturbed at this time, told him to get his team down and do a thorough scan of my house.

I hit the disconnect button and almost immediately my phone pinged. I hit the green icon on my mobile. Video footage was being streamed straight to my phone, not even through YouTube.

CHAPTER 38

I sat rigid on my settee, gripping my phone with both hands as I watched a grey metal door opening. Bright light from two arc lamps standing in the corners flooded the underground basement. The camera focused on the wall to the right which had been crudely bricked up. Some mirror tiles clung to the side, a few had come off and dropped to the floor. The wall looked damp and clumps of bright green algae and moss had forced themselves through the gaps between the bricks. The ground was bare, dusty and uneven as the camera panned to the left and focused on an old wooden chair with armrests. Each of the armrests had plastic ties at the end, the sort anyone could buy at a garden centre. Not far away was a single metal bed frame, with a stained mattress propped against one side. A mouse crawled near it, sniffing one of the bed posts, and then the edge of the mattress. It wandered off. A glass rectangular storage box stood on the floor, not far from the mouse. The box had straw matting on the bottom and the dark plastic lid had small holes drilled through it at regular intervals. It was empty.

The camera turned towards the ceiling. The screen went black for a second and then the image returned. I could hear a whimper. Then a sob. The camera zoomed down and focused on the side view of a head with shoulder-length black hair. The head turned up and towards the camera. It was wearing a cardboard face mask of 'Shiva the Destroyer', the muscular male face painted pale blue as all Hindu gods are, with long hair tied up in a bun, a cobra round the neck. The camera moved down, past a dirty, creased white blouse and dark skirt, to the legs, the knees grazed.

There was a muffled sound around the microphone and the killer must have shouted out something. The girl, her hands tied behind her back with plastic ties, turned. I caught a quick glimpse of a dog lead around her neck stretching tight above her head.

The camera panned down past the grazed knees and then focused on the bare feet. And zoomed out.

The full horror of what I was seeing hit me. The girl stood on a block of ice. It looked as if it had been made in a large plastic storage box placed in a chest freezer. The girl's feet looked numb and frozen.

It was only a matter of time before the ice melted and she would be strangled. A broad, gleaming sharp knife filled the screen. Its point held up a string with the message on white cardboard, 'Ice with a slice?' and a smiley face at the end.

The knife disappeared. The camera moved up to the girl's head. The killer ripped away the mask.

Yasmin!

NO!

I slammed my fist on the table. The banging sound drowned out the killer's distant laughter, the fading roar taking a large part of my heart with it.

I took in a few deep breaths. *Mustn't lose control. Had to save my daughter.* A few more deep breaths. *In. Out. In. Out. In. Out. Compose yourself, compose yourself.*

I rang HQ and asked for the team dealing with police escorts. They informed me that one of the officers had reported ill in the morning. All other available officers were deployed on other cases. PC Myers had said it was only a question of escorting a schoolgirl home after rehearsals at school and what could possibly go wrong with that? He had volunteered to pick her up by himself. They tried to radio him while I stayed on the line. No response.

I hit the disconnect button. Rang Ben and explained what was happening and asked for the phone number of the geologist from the university.

It was almost midnight. Fiona Lightfoot said in a sleepy voice that she was still undertaking soil sample tests and it was a slow process and she was analysing the trace elements found at the previous crime scenes and could not be sure yet about the precise location.

'Dr Lightfoot, please, please, what's your best guess about the location?' I implored her.

'Well, the tissue samples from Ayan Suleiman and Geeta Mehta had traces of gypsum and anhydrite, the building blocks for cement and plasterboard and the like. There were also minute traces of copper and iron, galena and molybdenite. In addition, their windpipes and lungs had minute quantities of coal dust and sandstone dust. This could mean the location could be in large parts of north-east Leicestershire, could be a coal mine or tunnel or cave —'

'*Please*, Dr Lightfoot. What's your best guess about where it could be?'

'Well, what was confusing me was the iron and steel filings…'

Jesus, I thought. And realised how badly I needed him.

'…these were evident in minute quantities under the womens' fingernails. And on the brake pedal of the car where the driver was murdered. It means the soles of the killer's shoes were linked to the two women. An old coal mine wouldn't necessarily have these filings because they look fairly fresh. Not all the iron filings had signs of rust, though some did.'

'So?'

'The only place I can think of which may — and I stress *may* — fit this evidence profile is a disused tunnel just a few miles north of the city. An old railway tunnel. It was renovated, its structures and girders strengthened by the city council a few years ago. That could explain some of the fairly new steel filings and possibly some of the iron ones too.'

She explained to me where the tunnel was and about its historical significance.

A few moments later I was on the phone to Shep. 'Get all members of the team to the incident room at HQ. Quickly, we don't have much time.'

Next up was Superintendent Breedon, who stifled a yawn as I told him I needed two firearms teams. Urgently. He ummed and aahed and said it wasn't that easy, think of the consequences of using them and what if some officers and innocent civilians got killed or injured and I had to remind him my daughter's life was at stake, that the killer had already killed a police officer, maybe two. He reluctantly agreed to release two armed units of four officers each but insisted on being the gold commander as I was not senior enough for such deployment. I asked for the teams to be sent to the briefing at HQ as soon as possible.

'Rohan,' he continued, 'there's a conflict of interest in you continuing to lead this investigation because your daughter's now involved —'

I hit the disconnect button. Fuck his conflict of interest.

A large part of me wanted to rush straight to the tunnel with a handful of officers and rescue Yasmin. But this was out of the question. I needed to plan this properly and with enough officers to provide proper back-up. I just hoped we had enough time, that we'd got the right location, that the ice wouldn't melt yet because it was a big block.

The call I was dreading came through. I hit the green icon and before I could say anything, Faye screamed, 'You bastard, what've you done? What've you done to us?' She was sobbing and gasping for breath. Her anguished and broken voice explained how they had been looking for Yasmin for hours, had rung all her friends, had rung HQ for information about the escort car which nobody could provide, didn't want to disturb me because she knew I'd be busy, and then had been sent ... had been sent ... and she broke down. In the background I could hear Karan crying, saying, 'No Mum, please don't, please don't cry, no Mum, please ... please ... don't'. I said I'd get to Yasmin as soon as I could, said I'd get her safely back, she kept repeating, 'You bastard, you bastard,' and 'Without your work, this wouldn't have happened.'

The killer must have sent her the video footage as well. There was no other way she could have known.

CHAPTER 39

'This is the entrance to the disused tunnel, or what's left of it. Located not far from the hospital, the cemetery and crematorium,' I said, as the image of the tunnel was projected using Google Earth. The officers assigned to the case looked silently and intently at the screen, all wide awake, even though it was almost one o'clock in the morning.

The mouth of the tunnel, running under roads and houses, stood there, the tall arch and top half bricked up, while two large wooden black doors denied entry to sightseers, casual visitors, bored children and adventurous teenagers.

'The tunnel was built in 1830,' I continued. 'It's slightly less than two miles long and is now disused. The top part with these doors is at the northern end and the rest of it runs below houses and other properties. So that's a fair amount of hiding space. The other end has a house on top of it, so there's no exit. But the length of the tunnel is dotted with thirteen or so ventilation shafts on top, such as these.'

The images they saw were of large cylindrical shapes, standing tall in the urban landscape, made out of brown bricks with a wire-netted dome at the top for ventilation. One or two were along roadsides or grass verges, others were in people's back gardens.

I speculated that the killer may have a hideout somewhere in the tunnel. It was also possible he lived nearby to make it easier to go unnoticed into and out of the tunnel. The killer would thus have a ready supply of electricity, food, and other essential items. The geographical profiling also fits, I explained, given the tunnel's proximity to Ayan Suleiman's flat, the crematorium and the cemetery.

I flashed the image of Yasmin's feet on the large block of ice and said we would have to act quickly. Each ventilation shaft had to be guarded so the killer couldn't escape. The killer had a high-powered rifle.

'This girl,' I said, my voice choking, 'is my daughter.'

There was some shuffling of feet. Some throats being cleared. Then silence.

Sadly, I carried on, we would have to recover Simran Sandhu's body from a collapsed side tunnel. There may be other side tunnels too. We had to be ready for all possibilities. The tunnel was only a few miles from HQ and we could be at the entrance in fifteen or twenty minutes. The block of ice could take a few hours to melt, depending on the humidity in the tunnel and the temperature.

I outlined a plan, took questions and made sure the various teams knew what they were doing and that we were all wired-up with radios. All officers were issued with body armour and helmets. The eight officers from the two armed units sat in the briefing room, didn't say much, already dressed for action. I tried to hide the panic that was tearing me apart.

I dismissed the team. Shep and I got kitted up. We ran to my car and I pressed the accelerator hard as we shot down the outer ring road, the traffic thinning as the night grew longer.

'I really am sorry, Sir,' said Shep, and he placed his hand on my elbow. The first genuine and friendly gesture from him for a long time. I welcomed it. 'We'll get the bastard,' he said, as the long white bonnet of my car reflected the lights flashing by on either side of the dual carriageway.

My mobile rang. 'Mr Sharma, I know it's very, very late. We didn't know if we should wait until the morning to ring.' It was

Mrs Mehta, Geeta's mother. 'We know who's in the picture. The one you left with us. The CCTV image.'

I stared at Shep. The neon lights flashed by. At an angle. The car swerved to the left and almost hit a crash barrier.

'Really, Mrs Mehta?' I said, pulling the car back towards the middle of the road.

'Yes, Inspector. My husband scanned the photograph into his computer and used some software to play around with it. Lightened the face because it was a bit dark, made the features sharper… Anyway, he now looks a bit like the locum doctor at our surgery. Where I work as a receptionist. I couldn't be sure before.'

Christ, I should've got the IT team to do that. But in my hurry to get to the witnesses I didn't. Mistake on my part.

'Are you sure it's him, Mrs Mehta?'

'Such a nice man. I can't believe it's him but it looks like him. He even lived in East Africa I think… He came to our house on the day of Geeta's funeral. To pay his respects.'

She didn't know where he lived or how to contact him but the senior partner at the surgery would know. Mrs Mehta gave me her mobile number.

I rang the number, even though it was so late. Dr Stella Fitzpatrick was not best pleased to be woken up in the early hours and wouldn't give me any information because she didn't know who I was. She relented when I threatened to send a patrol car with two officers to interview her more formally.

She rang back a few minutes later, said she had accessed the GP's personnel file from the surgery's management information system. He lived in the northern part of the city and she gave me the address, along with a contact phone number. A mobile number, not a landline.

As she spoke, Shep was looking up the address on his iPad. He gave me a thumbs up, turning the screen towards me. The street and house were directly on top of the tunnel.

Dr Fitzpatrick said there was nothing remarkable about the GP. He was a medical student at Birmingham University, became a hospital doctor but the long hours didn't suit him, spent time training as a general practitioner, worked in Derbyshire and then came to Leicester. Was supposed to be married but didn't talk much about his wife. Didn't want a permanent position, wanted the flexibility to choose his own hours and was generally a good doctor. He spoke Hindi, which helped 'because of the kind of patients we have'. He should be at home because he'd been at work in the morning. She described him as a nice and polite man, thirty-seven years old, physically fit, strong muscular body, and enjoyed long walks in the countryside. I asked her to send me a screenshot of his photograph, which she did.

The engine purred as I pressed down on the accelerator. My mobile rang again.

'Sir, we have news about PC Myers who was escorting your daughter,' said the leader of the team dealing in police escorts. 'One of the patrol cars came across him in a ditch along a narrow country lane. To the south of the city. His body was found trussed up in the boot. Jugular sliced through. The officers at the scene have called in homicide and the forensics team. Dan was a lovely lad, had a young family.'

I didn't want to appear heartless but there was nothing I could do for PC Dan Myers.

My mind was focused on keeping my daughter alive.

CHAPTER 40

It was past two-thirty in the morning. I sat in my parked car in a residential side street at the far end of the tunnel entrance. Shep had joined one of the other teams. Andy Johnson was in the passenger seat. He was an expert marksman in full body armour and he wore a black shirt and trousers. A standard Heckler and Koch MP5 carbine, a semi-automatic machine gun, rested across his legs. Around his hip a wide polymer belt held a holster with a Glock 17, a semi-automatic pistol.

The ends of his trousers were tucked inside his black leather boots which ended just below his calf muscles. Strands of curly blonde hair stuck out from under his dark and tightly fitting ballistic helmet. Infrared goggles dangled from an elasticated leather strap around his neck. I could only just make out his deep blue-grey eyes as they looked at me. I wasn't a trained firearms officer so I couldn't carry a weapon. I decided not to wear a ballistic helmet and opted for a standard black peaked cap instead. Andy asked me to reconsider. I ignored his advice.

The area was mostly dark, although alternate streetlights were switched on, casting a pale ghostly glow. The inside of the car was cold. Needles of pain shot through my knees and I rubbed each in turn. My bulletproof vest restricted my movements. I stared at the January night sky as cumulus clouds drifted in front of a large and silvery full moon nestling low on the horizon. Orion burned bright, the stars of the sword twinkling against the black velvet sky. The windscreen had a haze of condensation. I wound the window down slightly to clear it. The cold breeze shot down my windpipe and into my lungs. I rubbed my hands, trying to warm them up through the thick leather gloves.

The armed assault teams had arrived in two black BMW estate cars and, as instructed, one team of four officers was positioned in a quiet, dark alley across the road. The other team, plus Shep, was huddled in some undergrowth at the end of a quiet cul-de-sac, detached and semi-detached houses on either side, half a mile away. A few yards in front of them was a chain-link fence, about eight feet high, beyond which was some waste ground strewn with boulders, rubble and debris, thick bushes and trees. At the end of the waste ground stood the imposing wide Victorian brick-built arch, the middle of which housed the two giant wooden doors, pulled shut and bolted with heavy-duty, wrought-iron metalwork and locks. My radio crackled as both armed teams, Trojan 363 and Trojan 365, reported they were in place. All known exits and entrances to the tunnel were now covered.

'Roger, maintain positions, await further orders, Alpha One Zero out,' I replied. All teams were on the same encrypted frequency. 'Okay, Andy, let's go,' I said. I turned off the switch to the interior light of the car so it wouldn't shine when the doors opened.

We got out of the Mercedes, gently pushed shut the car doors, crouched and ran silently towards the first ventilator shaft, on the wide grass verge at the side of the road and on top of the tunnel beneath us. A van equipped with a mobile transmitter was positioned about a third of a mile along the route of the tunnel, while another was positioned a mile further away. The specialists back at HQ were not sure whether radio communications could be maintained from within the tunnel, despite the ventilation shafts, and advised us to bounce signals from the mobile transmitters if necessary. Just in case.

Andy Johnson and I leaned against the ventilation shaft, our breathing heavy, and I stared up at its top as it towered five or six feet above me, a cylinder of brown brick, at least six feet in diameter, iron bolts and thick wire netting at the top. I cast the rope ladder with its curved metal grappling hooks to the top, they lodged among the metalwork, I tugged at the ladder to make sure it was secure. A pair of heavy-duty metal cutters and another rope ladder hung across my shoulders.

I radioed the others. 'Trojan 363 and Trojan 365, this is Alpha One Zero. We're going in. We're going in. And for God's sake, don't shoot us by mistake in the tunnel.'

'Yes, Sir,' replied the leader of Trojan 363.

'Roger, Alpha One Zero,' came the reply from the commander of Trojan 365.

I scampered up to the top of the shaft, cut the wire mesh and metal bolts, beckoned Andy up, threw the other rope ladder down into the tunnel. We descended quickly and jumped off the last few rungs, landing softly on the dusty and undulating hard ground. A chill breeze hit my cheeks.

It took a few moments to get used to the light inside the tunnel. It was dark and my infrared camerapicked out glistening eyes, scurrying in different directions. High-pitched screeches. Rats. I released the thermal-imaging camera from the belt around my waist and pointed it forward. It looked like a speed gun used by traffic officers.

'Nothing, Sir. Just rats,' crackled Jamie Shriver's voice through my earpiece. Jamie was in one of the vans above ground, analysing the laptop images my thermal imaging camera was producing. 'There seems to be a cat moving some fifty or sixty yards in front of you, don't know whether you can see it. Must be an entrance somewhere for it to have come through.'

'Roger, Jamie,' I whispered. 'Hold positions Trojan 363 and Trojan 365.' The confirmations came through from both teams.

I turned to Andy and gestured for him to follow the tunnel wall to the left and I would do the same with the right. He nodded. Both of us paced slowly, walking into blackness, tightly hugging the side of each wall as we moved. Occasionally, faint chequered light outlined a metal grate through the ventilation shafts. Andy pointed the semi-automatic carbine in front of him, safety catch off, while I pointed the thermal-imaging camera in front of me. We moved forward. I was ahead and could sense Andy's footsteps a few yards behind me and to the left.

We carried on, slowly, carefully, quietly.

I could hear my breathing. Adrenalin was coursing through my body. I pointed the camera forward. The kaleidoscope of swirling bright colours on the small screen didn't mean much to me. They swirled around at random, like the map of a hurricane on the TV weather forecast.

I shivered. A dank smell was all around, the smell of rotting vegetables. The cold pushed into my nostrils, making them run. I wiped my nose with my sleeve. A sudden screech. The flap of wings. I ducked. Hundreds of bats flew through the air towards us, over our heads. Swiftly gone. I looked back. Andy gave me a thumbs-up sign from his crouching position. My breathing slowing, becoming more normal. We set off again. The centre of the tunnel was littered with large stones, the occasional granite boulder, and old and rotting railway sleepers. As we moved forward there was a faint glow in the distance as the tunnel turned to the right.

'Alpha One Zero. Halt! Halt!' came through my earpiece.

'What is it, Jamie?' I whispered.

'On your left further down, maybe seventy or eighty yards in front of you, there're two heat sources. Human in shape. One's moving slowly. Very slowly. Maybe crawling on the ground. The other is laying still, not far from the moving figure.'

I stared at the screen on the thermal imaging camera. I could see the reddish orange. 'Roger, Jamie. Trojan units, stand by to go in. Repeat, stand by to go in.'

'Roger Alpha One Zero,' came the response.

'Jamie, can you pinpoint the ice block?'

'Negative. No ice. No blue on screen. Could be in an anteroom where the thermal camera can't penetrate.'

'Roger.'

What to do? What to do? Yasmin was in front of me. Couldn't be anybody else. She had to be alive because of the temperature readings. But she could be badly injured. Who was the other person? Where the hell was the killer? Was he waiting to ambush us? Anything could've given us away, including the rats or the disturbance of the colony of bats. He could be waiting to pick us off with his high-powered rifle.

I gestured to Andy to slowly move forward. One step at a time. Andy with his semi- automatic pointing forward, me with the infrared camera. It had gone very quiet. I could hear my breathing. My hands were cold, even through the gloves. My earpiece came back to life.

'Alpha One Zero, d'you copy?'

'Yeah, Jamie. What is it?' I replied.

'I'm sorry, Sir. But one of the bodies is rapidly losing heat. Must have died. Not long ago. I'm really ... really very ... sorry, Sir.'

My heart shattered into a thousand pieces. *The bastard, the bastard. Why did he have to do that? I'll kill him. I'll kill him. But maybe it wasn't Yasmin? I must keep in control. Must. Must. Keep in control.*

I hissed into the microphone pinned to my lapel, 'Trojan units. Trojan units. Hostage down. Hostage down. Go in. Repeat. Go in. GO, GO, GO!'

'Alpha One Zero. This is Trojan 363,' I heard a voice say in my earpiece. 'Suspect has escaped into tunnel. Repeat, suspect has escaped into tunnel.'

'Alpha One Zero. This is Trojan 365,' came the team leader's voice. 'Suspect is near mouth of tunnel. Is now coming through gap between the door and tunnel wall. He's crouching. Now running … after him. After him!'

'365. Take alive. Take alive! Do *not* kill! Repeat, do *not* kill,' I shouted into my microphone.

I ran as fast as I could. Towards the mouth of the tunnel. Towards my daughter. Faint lights hung from the tunnel roof, the sockets dangling along a black wire. Andy ran next to me, breathing heavily, machine gun ready. I glanced at him. He glanced back through his goggles.

I almost didn't see the dirty grey metal door on the left as I shot past it. I turned back. Pushed it open two to three inches. Bright light poured out. My heart raced even more. Yasmin could be in here. In the cell. Had to get to her.

I opened the door. An enormous explosion reverberated throughout the tunnel. The sound deafening. I instinctively covered my face and head with my hands. Stones and broken lumps of wood flying everywhere.

I was knocked off my feet as a chunk of an old railway sleeper smashed into the side of my head. Why the hell hadn't I followed Andy Johnson's advice and worn a ballistic helmet?

CHAPTER 41

'Sir, Sir, wake up. Wake up.' Shep's voice. Excited. Breathless. 'She's alive! She's still alive!'

I had a piercing headache. My vision blurred. What was going on? I was still on the cold hard ground. Shep and Andy were kneeling down and peering at me.

I blinked. 'Oh ... thank God, Shep. Thank ... God.'

He stared at me for a moment and shook his head.

'You've been out cold for a few minutes. I'm sorry, Sir. I didn't mean Yasmin. I meant Simran Sandhu. She's dehydrated but otherwise fine. She's been trying to speak to us.'

I touched the side of my head and winced at the pain. My hair was matted.

'What about the body? Is it a body? Who's that?' I asked, not really wanting to know.

'It's a woman,' said Shep. 'Looks in her early thirties. Could be the killer's wife. Multiple stab wounds. A frenzied attack. Poor woman, died a slow painful death.'

'Yasmin, Shep. Yasmin, where is she?'

'Sorry, Sir. No sign of her.'

'But she was here, Shep. The video footage was from here. What's he said? You've got him, haven't you?'

Shep shook his head. 'It wasn't him running from the tunnel. It was a homeless person. He was sleeping behind the tunnel doors. Heard the commotion. Decided to run, not knowing what was going on.'

'Shit!' I wobbled on my feet, helped up by Shep and Andy. As I did so, I looked down at the ground and noticed

226

something glinting in the dust. I bent down, picked it up, looked at it and asked Shep to put it in an evidence bag.

'Where the fuck is he, Shep? Where the fuck is *she*? Where's Yasmin? And what caused that fucking explosion? Do we know?'

'Not sure, Sir.'

'Okay, let's have a look at this dungeon,' I said.

I pushed back the door. The bright lights were on. We looked around, the mirror tiles coming off the walls, the algae and mould, the damp, the single bed with the mattress against its side, the chair with the arms. It was definitely the basement cellar where Yasmin had been kept, the one in the video footage. But there was no sign of her, or the block of ice.

I could hear Shep's breathing over my left shoulder as we stared at the video footage on my phone. Andy stood in front and remained quiet.

'Sir, can you pause the image of Yasmin on the ice block please?'

I did as Shep asked. We both stared at the image. I couldn't see why he wanted it pausing.

'See, Sir, the shadows don't match. The lights here are on the left. Yasmin's shadow on the wall and of the ice block should be on the right. In the video, they're on the left.'

'The bastard's superimposed Yasmin and the ice block onto the image of this room.' My thinking powers were returning, despite the swarm of bees buzzing inside my head.

'Shep, stand down all the teams, get Ben Carter and his forensics team here, get Simran Sandhu to hospital and get a private ambulance for the dead woman.'

Shep explained that the explosion seemed to have come from behind the rubble from the other side of the tunnel. In his view, if the killer wanted me dead then he would have booby-trapped parts of the tunnel or the dungeon in which he'd held my daughter. What he was saying seemed to make sense. So, what then had caused the explosion? I had no idea.

Shep and I sat in my car on the road above the tunnel. The teams had been stood down for the time being and the forensics team were on their way. We were both quiet. It was well after three o'clock in the morning. The steady drone of the bees in my head was receding, the bleeding from the side of my head had stopped some time ago, and I was at a loss at what to do next. *Think. Think. Yasmin wasn't here. The killer wasn't here. Where on earth could they be?* Had to be a place the killer knew well. Where he felt secure and was familiar with the area.

I rang Dr Fitzpatrick again, apologised, and asked whether she could remember the location of the surgery in Derbyshire. She told me it was on the edge of Bakewell, just off the main road running from Matlock and Buxton. It was a small rural surgery, he'd told her he had applied to work there because it reminded him of his rural upbringing. She looked up the address and gave it to me.

I rang the senior duty officer of the homicide team of Derbyshire police, a force we worked with closely. I apologised for ringing in the early hours, explained who I was, why I was ringing and I asked whether there were any caves in the Bakewell and Buxton areas. Chief Inspector Pemberton laughed. She said there were hundreds. The area was predominantly limestone, and rainwater draining down had created underground caverns. There was no immediate way to identify where the killer might be without any other clues. I said I was not an expert but the wall I could see in the dungeon looked like some sort of granite, not a soft chalk-like material like limestone.

I asked if she could check the records for our suspect GP. She did. No record, not even points on his driving licence.

I thanked Chief Inspector Pemberton and switched off my mobile.

It pinged almost immediately. A text message: *Still wondering where I am? And your darling?* followed by a yellow emoticon of a laughing face jumping up and down.

Fuck, fuck, fuck. What to do? What to do? Think, think.

Shep was about to say something but I stopped him and showed him the message.

'Power up your iPad and bring up the ordnance survey maps for the Bakewell area please.'

'Already on, Sir.'

A thought occurred to me. 'Hang on a minute. We know Yasmin's mobile is switched off. But I wonder … maybe she has her eReader with her. If it's switched on, we may be able to locate it.'

Shep stared at me. 'No idea, Sir. Never heard anything like that. But worth a try. Why don't we ring the company that you bought it from to find out?'

He looked up the helpline support number of the online retailer. I rang their call centre in the Philippines, where it was already late morning. The customer adviser informed me that their IT team was not available because of the time of night in the UK. I explained again who I was, that I needed to talk to somebody urgently, pleaded with her to find somebody, anybody, anybody who could help me. She said she'd try and put me on hold.

Come on, come on. I drummed my fingers on the dashboard. Trying to be patient. Reminding myself what time it was.

Eventually, a man came online. He said eReaders use the mobile telephony network, through the 4G wireless connection. If my daughter's eReader was switched on, and I knew the unique code for it, the mobile phone company may be able to track it down. I gave him my details, name, address and told him I'd bought it just before Christmas. He looked up my account, asked me to confirm my credit card number (*Jesus!*) and then gave me the unique code of the device, which Shep noted on his mobile as I repeated it aloud. The man gave me the names and numbers of the technical teams of the mobile companies which covered the Peak District area.

I rang the first one. Explained to the senior manager on duty I needed to confirm whether an eReader was switched on in the Bakewell area and gave him the unique serial code. No record of that number. Tried the second company, and hallelujah, yes, they had a record of Yasmin's device. He told me to hang on, eventually came back online and said yes, my daughter's device was switched on, the electronic transmitter mast near Bakewell had picked up the signal and it was about three miles north-east from there.

I slammed the dashboard and said thank you, thank you over and over.

'Shep,' I said, looking at the map, 'tell the Trojan units and the other teams to meet us at the county showground. Edge of Bakewell.'

I pulled the gear paddle down, pressed the accelerator and we sped along the A46 towards the M1, at a hundred miles per hour.

I rang Chief Inspector Pemberton on the hands-free, updated her and asked for a team of officers who were experienced in local caving and potholing to meet us at the county showground in an hour or so. She said she'd get that organised. Then an idea occurred to me. 'Have you got any drones fitted with cameras, preferably infrared?'

'You're really pushing it, Inspector Sharma. We're trialling two at the moment. No more because of budget cuts. And our staff aren't properly trained in handling them yet.'

I thanked her and hit the disconnect button. There was no way we could use the helicopter; it would be too noisy.

'How about trying the local TV station, Sir?' Shep said. 'They have plenty of equipment for aerial shots, nature documentaries and so on. There may even be some fitted with infrared cameras. The station owes us one for using unauthorised information about the case.'

'Shep, that's a brilliant idea. Get me the editor's number or the managing director. Or whoever's in charge.'

'Inspector Sharma, d'you know what time it is? This'd better be good,' said Tim Curtley, the senior manager of the local TV station. I explained that we were engaged in a manhunt and I needed as many drones fitted with cameras as possible, ideally some with infrared, and also needed the personnel who were skilled at flying them. I didn't give him any more details but said the TV company owed me one. I also asked him to keep this request confidential.

He informed me the station had six drones fitted with cameras, wide-angle and zoom lenses, including two that had infrared. He would keep one of the drones in reserve at the studio for any breaking news story but I could have the other five. The drones were fitted with solar panels and high-powered lithium batteries with a long charge, which made them very quiet to enable the filming of wildlife. Ordinary drones sounded like a swarm of hornets, he said. The cameras and their operatives were based in their studios in Nottingham and he would ensure they were on their way to Bakewell as soon as possible. They'd arrive at about the same time as us. I ended the call.

The phone rang almost immediately and Ben's voice boomed through the car's speakers.

'Just to let you know, Sir,' he said, as we sped northwards on the M1 past the Nottingham and Derby junction, 'we've found the body of a cobra among the rubble in the tunnel. It's well preserved. Looks as if it died fairly recently. No more poisonous snakes to worry about, Inspector.'

No sooner had he disconnected then my multi-media screen on the dashboard showed another caller. 'Private Caller' it said as the phone rang through the car. My fingers trembled as I pressed the icon for playing video footage.

I swerved the car onto the hard shoulder of the motorway and slammed on the brakes. Travelling at more than a hundred miles an hour Shep was thrown forward, jerked hard against the seatbelt. The car fishtailed. As I tried to control the steering wheel, I could smell burning rubber.

Colourful pixels flashed and danced and sparkled as the image came to life on the screen. Yasmin's face in profile, her once beautifully groomed hair dusty and matted. Her hands tied behind her. Struggling to free themselves. A leather dog-lead with silver studs buckled around her bruised neck. The lead stretched tight above her head, out of camera shot.

I clenched my fists.

The camera moved further out. It looked as if she was in a deep cave. Bright lights shone on her body so it was difficult to tell what kind of stone was behind her. Limestone maybe. An image of a long and broad steel knife, point curving up, filled the screen. The blood gutter ran all the way down the side of the finely tempered blade. The knife held in a surgical glove, twirling around, the blade glinting and flashing in the bright light.

As the image filled the screen, an electronically disguised voice said, 'I knew you'd find the dead bitch. Fucking Uma! Got what she deserved. Wanted all this to end. Was going to betray me. Didn't want to spend the rest of her life in prison. Selfish bitch! Got a bit of the Crocodile Dundee treatment. Enjoyed her slice of life.' Loud laughter filled my car.

The screen went black. The pixels danced again and came back to life.

The camera had moved further away from Yasmin. We could see her standing on the block of ice. Her feet were black and blue. She was trying to lift one leg and then the other.

The camera panned slightly to the right, focusing on the ground, away from her feet. A portable gas heater had been placed a few feet away from the block of ice. There was a patch of water below the ice and the length of the trickle was getting longer. The area getting wider and wetter.

'Jesus Christ!' whispered Shep.

It was only a matter of time before the ice would crack with Yasmin's weight. Strangling her.

I said nothing. I gripped the steering wheel harder, put the gear paddle into drive and pressed hard on the accelerator. Over the horizon, daylight was breaking, although the stars still shone bright.

As the car touched one hundred and twenty miles an hour, the screen came to life again. An image of the twirling steel blade and the melting block of ice. The words 'Ice and a slice?' superimposed over the latest image of Yasmin.

I could hear the roar of distant laughter as it faded into the depths of my car dashboard.

CHAPTER 42

As the sun rose above the leaden, grey horizon most of the residents of the market town of Bakewell were still asleep. Only the farmers were up, feeding their cattle and scattering broken bales of hay for their ponies. The town itself was quintessentially English. A main road cut through it, past stone-built houses and shops for the locals and for the tourists, and the stone bridge stretching over the River Wye. All Saints' Church stood majestically on the hill, overlooking the town, its eroding stones remembering the passage of more than a thousand years. The cemetery in its grounds hid the skeletons and dust of people who had lived and died over the centuries. The dust of countless dreams not realised, lives unfulfilled.

I rang Superintendent Breedon and informed him what was going on. He was concerned about me leading the case now but I told him my team and I were the only ones who could do anything about Yasmin. As far as I was concerned, I'd covered my back and ended the call quickly.

The Trojan units gathered in a semicircle in front of me at the showground near the edge of town. I briefed them about what we knew, what we didn't know, what we could do and what we couldn't. There was a stunned silence as I explained to them about the block of ice, the portable gas heater and the limited time to save my daughter. I had a feeling that the killer would prolong my agony for as long as possible. Maybe I was clutching at straws, desperately hoping for more time.

As I finished the briefing, the team from the TV station with the drones arrived in three white Range Rovers and two Land Rover Defenders, all four by fours made for crossing rugged terrain, mounted with a satellite antenna on each roof. Good to see that the TV company was treating my request for help seriously. I explained we were actively searching for the Lexus estate car that Simran Sandhu was in when she was captured. There'd still been no sign of it and, as the killer had abandoned his silver saloon with Robert Coleman's body inside, it was possible he was driving the Lexus.

The local officers with expert knowledge of caving and potholing hadn't arrived. Typical. The ones with the shortest distance to travel are always the last. I tried to hide my irritation and asked Shep to wait for them.

I jumped into one of the two unmarked red BMW X5 estate cars carrying the four officers from Trojan 363 and instructed the other armed officers and the drone crews to follow us. We drove along a country lane leading south-west from Bakewell and then pushed due north-west and then north, heading in the general direction that the signal from the eReader was coming from. It was still a vast area to cover. The signal would be coming from below ground if Yasmin's belongings were with her. But how was the signal escaping? I wasn't sure. Neither was anybody else.

After a few moments, I asked the officer driving our car to stop near the gate to a field. The other cars pulled up behind us. To our left the frost-covered Lathkill Dale looked majestic, with its undulating hills and vales and a dense covering of winter grass and hardy bushes, thick hedges and the occasional tree. We could hear sheep bleating but couldn't see them in the still grey light. To our right were more hills and I could hear the scurrying of small animals. The frost on the hills and on the hard ground shimmered against the growing warmth of the late winter sun.

I tried not to think of the frost forming into a trickle. Like a trickle of water from a block of melting ice. Not much time left.

Hang on, Yasmin. Please hang on…

Within moments, three drones, codenamed *Amanda*, *Belinda* and *Caroline* flew in the sky, gaining altitude, not too close to alert anybody to their presence. One of them was equipped with an infrared camera and it flew north-west, one went due north and the third due west, a Range Rover with a driver and a pilot following each, images relayed to a laptop-sized screen fixed to the dashboard. The two Land Rovers were ordered to travel another two miles further along the road and the remaining two drones, *Debbie* and *Evelyn*, took off, one heading north and the other north-east. All drivers following, the drone pilots flying their machines and scanning images on their screens, the vehicles driving along usually inaccessible country lanes, and through farmers' fields and narrow gateways.

The rest of us stayed where we were. Waiting. Hoping for a positive sighting of the stolen Lexus. Maybe activity near a cave or the opening of a pothole. Who knew what they would come across?

A cold morning wind brought tears to my eyes as I paced up and down. I looked at Andy Johnson, the expert marksman. He looked back at me, the concern etched deep into his eyes. I got into the BMW to warm up. One of the other armed officers got out and went behind some bushes to relieve himself. Steam rose from his urine.

I looked at my watch. Another half an hour had gone. I got out and started pacing in the field. Went back to the car. The others stared at me. The clock on the dashboard told me another twenty-five minutes had passed.

My mobile came alive. It was Fred Bevan, affectionately known as the 'Squadron Leader' by his team of drone pilots.

'Inspector Sharma, we have a possible hit on the Lexus. Repeat, possible hit on the Lexus.'

My heart started racing, pounding against my chest, its beat thumping on my eardrums. 'Where?'

'I flew *Evelyn* through a large open-air barn. Most of the hay in the middle's been cleared. A red Lexus estate is parked in the space. The infrared camera picked up the car because the engine block's still warm, must've been used in the last hour or two. No sign of any occupants.'

He gave me the GPS location.

'Shep,' I said into my microphone, 'when the local cavalry gets here, tell them to identify any caves or large potholes or whatever in this area. Anything at all which could be used as a hiding place. Where the hell are they? Should be here by now.' I gave him the location.

I had to get to Yasmin before the ice melted. I just had to.

I was travelling with Trojan 363 and both teams arrived at their rendezvous points in under twenty minutes. We stopped behind a hedge, about a hundred yards from the barn.

I instructed Trojan 365 to skirt behind the barn and approach it from the furthest end, while 363 and I would approach from the front. We ran behind hedges and drystone walls to give us cover, the armed officers wearing their ballistic helmets, releasing the safety catches on their firearms. We moved swiftly and got to the main opening of the barn a few yards in front of us. We crouched and waited a few moments. No sign of life. I saw the four members of Trojan 365 squeezing past bales of hay, one by one, moving quickly, silently, eyes alert, machine guns ready.

The team leader and I approached the front of the Lexus, the engine block still cooling, faint crackling sounds audible. Bales of hay were packed tightly against all sides of the car and on the bonnet. I peeked through a gap and into the rear window. A sleeping bag, rolled up, a pair of walking boots, a rolled-up tent with a mallet and pegs, half a dozen bottles of water still wrapped together in plastic, an anorak and a bulging rucksack. It looked as if he was ready to escape and had stocked up with provisions.

He and Yasmin had to be somewhere not far away. There were no houses or farms or lock-up barns nearby so we decided to look for entrances to caves or potholes. I paired up again with Andy Johnson.

In pairs and threes, the teams moved out in all directions, machine guns pointing forward, eyes peeled to the front and to the ground. Andy and I walked uphill in a north-easterly direction, staring at miles and miles of fields.

We carried on walking, carried on looking, becoming breathless as the land rose and became more hilly. Wearing body armour didn't help.

Where the hell could the killer be? Where was Yasmin? No sign of caves here. No potholes. We stopped. I breathed in the cold air. Andy scoured the horizon with a small but powerful pair of binoculars. Neither of us said anything.

In the stillness of daybreak, birds flew through the air: blackbirds, crows, rooks, the occasional robin. Cattle mooed in the distant fields. Hungry sheep carried on bleating. I stood perfectly still. My senses at heightened alert. My hearing acute. I turned to Andy. His moist eyes stared back at me. Quizzical. Wondering. There was no question about it, through the noise of nature, I could hear a low humming. A whirring sound. Like a quiet lift in a tall office block. Andy could hear it too.

We ran towards some gorse bushes and heather. Hidden by them was a rectangular concrete cover, about three feet long and two feet wide. It was raised a few inches above the ground and covered in wire netting.

The whirring sound was coming from below ground.

CHAPTER 43

The concrete block was too low to house an electricity substation and it didn't look like an exchange for telephone cables, or anything else that I was familiar with. I crouched down, lay flat on my stomach and peered through the fine wire mesh. It was awkward with my bulletproof vest on. A dull red light cast a strange hue. Probably infrared lighting.

I pushed myself up and mimed to Andy to look for a trapdoor. We bent down, staring at the turf, looking for any signs of disturbance to the ground. Before long, Andy noticed a square patch of artificial grass not far from the concrete cover.

He removed the artificial grass to reveal a dirty grey metal door, fitting tightly into a metal frame. His Heckler and Koch machine gun, safety catch off, was at the ready under his right arm, a Glock 17 pistol in his left. As Andy did this, I whispered this latest information into my microphone for the rest of the team.

I pulled up the heavy metal door, silently, and saw an old wooden staircase of about twelve steps. Since Andy was armed, he went in first and I followed. I could hear the whirring sound more clearly now. We were careful to walk at the extreme edge of the staircase, a step, and then stop, a step and then stop. The dry wooden steps must not creak. All senses alert. At the bottom, we looked around.

The small room had walls which were once pale yellow. The paint was now peeling, revealing a dull grey metal lining. Perfect soundproofing. An infrared tube light was fixed to the ceiling, obviously powered by an electric generator, hence the whirring sound. In the middle of the room a small wooden table and to the right a folding camp bed. A high-powered rifle with a telescopic sight stood in the corner. The rifle that had killed Joy.

I felt the anger rising in my chest. On the bed was Yasmin's rucksack. The killer had rummaged through it and her mobile phone lay crushed on the floor. Peeping out of the rucksack and directly below the concrete-covered ventilator was her eReader in its soft brown leather cover. The signal transmitted through the ventilator.

My heart was racing. Thudding against my chest. Blood rushing to my eardrums. Praying to God we could reach her in time. Hoping the block of ice had not cracked yet. *Please hang on, Yasmin. Please hang on.*

On the left, another narrow staircase went down a level below this room. I heard the sound of a metal spoon stirring inside a cup. The killer was whistling 'What A Wonderful World', by Louis Armstrong.

I looked back at Andy, pointed to the other staircase going down, and indicated for him to follow me. As I moved, the step creaked loudly. The whistling stopped. The tinkling of the teaspoon died.

We stood at the top of the staircase. My chest was heaving. Adrenaline rushing. Heart pounding. 'Armed police!' I shouted. 'Come out with your hands up!'

No response. Just a deathly whirring silence.

Andy looked at me from under his ballistic helmet. I looked back at him. Yasmin was in a cave. Not here. I gave him the thumbs up.

He lifted his machine gun and opened fire.

A hail of bullets hit the bottom of the stairs and the wall opposite.

We dived to take cover as hot molten lead flew towards us. It bounced back from the metal lining and a piece hit me in the chest forcing me to slump backwards. The armour saving me. I steadied myself, grabbing the corner of the wall where the staircase went down.

The firing stopped. I looked at Andy and jumped down the stairs.

We rushed into the tiny room which was just high enough to stand up in. Nobody was there. A low watt electric bulb hung from the ceiling. It was the kitchen area. An electric Baby Belling stove stood on a wooden table leaning against the wall with a kettle next to it. A mug of tea rested on the table with steam rising from it. There was a low wooden door to the right. I kicked it down. It was just a small petrol generator, flywheel spinning.

No killer. Absolutely no sign of him.

Where the fuck was he?

I started kicking the wall next to the cooker. Then flung the table to one side. The Baby Belling stove and mug of tea went flying towards Andy who ducked. A small area where the table had stood sounded hollow. I kicked the metal-lined wall again. The metal dented. The hidden trapdoor flew back. It clanged against the outside.

I rushed through it headfirst. Andy followed.

I tumbled out and rolled forward as the momentum carried me down a steep slope. The ground was cold and hard. I had no control as I plunged down. The skin on the side of my face tore against the stones and boulders, my hands were grazed and bleeding. I came to a stop at the bottom. The cold breeze hit my face. Everywhere was damp.

I staggered up. My eyes darted.

Then I spotted him. He was a fair distance in front of me. Running in a zig-zag pattern through the enormous limestone cave. Dodging between the stalagmites. Jumping over small boulders. Trying not to slip on the freezing, wet ground. He had a long flashing steel blade in his right hand and a blue duffel bag in his left.

I ran after him and Andy was close behind me.

And then... There she was! Yasmin — further ahead. My daughter. My baby. Still alive! Teetering on the block of ice.

The killer was fast approaching her. Ten, twelve yards away.

'Die, you bitch. Die!'

I turned round. Shouted, 'Andy, shoot him, for God's sake. Shoot!'

Everything happened in slow motion.

The killer was almost upon Yasmin. Shots cracked through the air. The gleaming sharp steel blade was in his hand. He plunged the knife towards her chest. She screamed. Blood spurted. Bright red drops hitting the cave wall. Thick red droplets running down. Yasmin fell to the ground. Both hands still tied behind her back.

Oh God, no, no, no.

CHAPTER 44

I ran over to Yasmin and loosened the dog-lead round her neck. Her face and chest were smeared in thick blood but she was alive. I asked if she was all right. She whimpered, in shock. I clutched her to my chest. Her body convulsed with uncontrolled shivering. Her teeth chattering. She clung tightly around my neck. I twisted my head to look around.

Two shots had hit the killer and a further two cut the dog-lead pulling at Yasmin's neck. The final shot had shattered the block of ice into a thousand pieces. Ice crystals and water everywhere around us. Yasmin had fallen as he plunged the knife, missing her by centimetres.

I disentangled myself and went to the killer lying a few yards away near a cold, flowing stream.

Dr Stephen Merriweather's face, which I recognised from the screenshot sent by Dr Fitzpatrick, was ashen. His eyes blinked rapidly as he stared at the stalactites high above his head. Blood oozed from his right shoulder and his right buttock area. His body shivered.

I kicked him hard in the midriff. 'This's for my daughter.' Kicked him again. 'And this is for Joy. And for Geeta and Ayan and —'

'Sir, stop.' It was Shep, who grabbed me by my shoulders.

He and the rest of the team had arrived through the far entrance of the cave, the local caving and potholing officers having guided them down. He eased me aside and cuffed Merriweather's hands.

I went back to Yasmin, removed my body armour and jacket and covered her. We huddled together, with me holding and cuddling her. Yasmin whimpered, trembled, looked at me, looked at the ground, stared into space, tears rolling down her cheeks. She was deep in shock.

Shep arrived back with blankets. I wrapped a couple around Yasmin. I stood up and asked one of the female officers from the local team to comfort her.

One of the caving team climbed up the hill which Andy and I had tumbled down, used a grappling hook and rope, went through the metal trapdoor and arrived back after a few minutes.

'It's a disused nuclear bunker. The Peak District's full of 'em. Built in the 1950s and 1960s during the Cold War. So important politicians and people from London could hide here. Must confess, didn't know about this one. Someone's then made a trapdoor into this cave.'

Merriweather lay on his back on the ground. Eyes closed now. The duffel bag lay next to him. The top was loose. I scrambled over to him, peered in at the contents. A clay pipe, a small plastic bag with what looked like marijuana leaves. Another plastic bag with datura seeds. A plastic food container. The long gleaming steel blade lay on the cold, hard ground next to him.

Shep stood next to me. I followed his gaze into the distance. 'Strange,' he said. 'Thought I saw something whip into the crevice in the corner over there.' His gaze lingered. 'Might just be shadows playing tricks,' he eventually said.

One of the team kicked Merriweather gently as he lay on the ground. And then again.

'Inspector Sharma, I think he's dead.'

The next few days were a maelstrom. I was carried along by events, desperate to rest, to reflect on what had happened but had no chance to do so. Up and down. Up. And down. Things happening which I understood. Things happening which I did not. Ecstatic. Broken. Furious. How can life be so cruel?

The newspapers carried headlines: *Hero Asian Cop Destined For The Top*; *Snakes Alive: Asian Cop Rescues Daughter From Cobra Killer*; *Jeepers Creepers: Asian Cop Saves Daughter From Drug-Crazed Killer* and *Hero Asian Cop Should Get Bravery Award*. All the stories carried snippets of truth mixed with gossip and rumour. They were accompanied by pictures of me when I joined the Leicestershire constabulary and of when I was a rookie in the Metropolitan Police in London. The television reporting was saturated for a while and, because the killer had been given the moniker of a Hindu deity, the case was reported on Indian satellite news channels. There was also coverage by *CNN* and *Al Jazeera*.

The media liaison team from police headquarters had suddenly come alive and there were repetitive shots on television screens of a smiling Chief Constable and his deputy, shaking hands with officers, including Andy Johnson, the expert marksman, who had saved my daughter's life. Neither the Chief Constable nor the deputy had contacted me yet. The Chief Constable was full of praises for the 'team effort' under the 'excellent leadership and management' of Superintendent Breedon that 'had finally led to the apprehension of the killer.' As in the case of all deaths involving police officers, he said, the matter had been referred to the Independent Office for Police Conduct. There were other pictures in newspapers and on TV screens, the Chief Constable and deputy shaking the hands of Mr and Mrs Sandhu, all faces beaming, their wide smiles straight to camera. Mr Sandhu was quoted as saying how grateful he was that the Chief Constable's team had been relentless in its efforts to rescue his daughter.

Simran Sandhu had become a national and international sensation. From her hospital bed she recounted to television news channels, the press and social media sites, of how she had escaped from the killer on her brand-new mobility scooter. But the killer had chased her, cornered her and entombed her. She was alive but trapped. Fortunately, her mother had packed chocolates, biscuits and other treats in the luggage space under the scooter seat, along with cartons of orange juice and two small bottles of water. There was a spare cylinder containing oxygen to help her breathe in an emergency, and a pencil torch. Not knowing how long she would be trapped down there, she ate and drank sparingly. There was no problem with air as there was a steady breeze coming through various crevices in the tunnel. There was no way she could lift the stones and boulders that had entombed her. They kept her safe from the killer but how long could she stay down there?

Finally, she came up with the plan. She stripped the brake cables running the length of the scooter and formed a long electric wire by joining them together. She then created a simple circuit, learned in science lessons. At one end, and far away from the wall of rubble that had trapped her, she placed the battery of the electric scooter. The two cables ran from the positive and negative terminals of the battery to the opening of the oxygen cylinder which she had pushed deep into the rubble. She twisted and twisted one of the cables until it broke and she now had a circuit breaker. She turned on the oxygen, crawled back and touched the two ends of the cable. The sparks caused an explosion which sent the rubble flying through the air. The explosion that knocked me out had created an escape route for her. Incredible ingenuity. I saw her in hospital and said so to her.

I went to see Ayan Suleiman's mother. The item I'd found in the dungeon was the gold bar that Ayan used to wear in her belly button. I gave it to her and told her I'd referred her case to the Criminal Compensation Board and to the local council housing department. She would be given financial compensation as a crime victim. She and her two sons would be rehoused in much better accommodation soon. As we said goodbye, she hugged me, saying '*Asante sana, Bwana, asante sana, Bwana.*' Thank you, Sir, thank you, Sir.

Yasmin was back home after staying in hospital for two nights. I went to see her when Pierre wasn't around and both she and Karan clung to me for a long time. It tore me apart. I wanted so much to be with them every day and to say goodnight to them every evening but it was not to be.

After exhaustive research and interviews with relevant contemporaries, we found out the following about Stephen Merriweather. He had been abandoned outside a convent in Belfast, his birth parents unknown, and the Merriweathers adopted him as a baby. His father worked for an international aid agency based in Oxfordshire and his mother was a maths teacher.

From an early age, he was identified as highly intelligent but showed signs of problematic behaviour. As he grew older, he became violent, not only towards his parents, but also towards animals. Some were found with broken legs, broken wings, eyes pierced by screwdrivers. The parents didn't know what to do when Stephen was expelled from his boarding school in Buckinghamshire, a place secured through a scholarship. He set fire to the dormitory in the middle of the night, endangering lives.

His parents decided to take him with them, to wherever his humanitarian father was posted, in case his worrying behaviour was linked to their absence. As a result, Stephen Merriweather lived in different countries, attended many different schools and had a very unsettled existence. He found it difficult to relate to people and to make friends. He was a loner.

When his father worked on a long-term placement with the rural poor in Tamil Nadu in India, his mother became fascinated by Hinduism. She read the religious texts and mixed with other Europeans in search of spiritual fulfilment. Stephen knew his mother slept with other men, because he burst into her love-making session in the guest bedroom one afternoon when he came home early from school. His mother was horrified, he was angry at the betrayal. The same betrayal he felt when, on his fifteenth birthday, his parents told him he was adopted with no warning.

Stephen became more and more withdrawn. He didn't communicate much and used this as a lever with his parents. He hated them and felt more relaxed with, and loved by, the voices coming to life inside his head.

His mother introduced him to the group singing of devotional Hindu songs, encouraging him to socialise more. To make friends. Maybe even find a girlfriend. He became genuinely interested in Hinduism, Islam and Christianity. He preferred Hinduism the best because the gods were human, they had human frailties, they seduced nubile girls, they killed each other and they killed others with abandon. They made love with women for ten thousand years, followers worshipped the penis in stone form, the *lingam*, which sat on the *yoni*, the vagina. Which other religion gives you that?

He loved Shiva the best. Shiva the Destroyer but also Shiva the Merciful One. The one with the power of life and death over others. Just like him. Shiva, who liked to smoke marijuana, who made love for aeons, who loved the dead, and who drank poison but still lived. Shiva with a cobra around his neck, who could be summoned by smoking the seeds of jimsonweed, or by boiling its leaves and drinking the mixture. He obsessed about the times when he wanted to kill somebody, or some animal, and had decided at the last minute he wanted them to live.

While they were in India, his father was the first to die. He went to lie down after lunch, complaining of feeling unwell. They found him dead in bed. He lay on his back, eyes wide open, the pupils dilated, staring at the aluminium ceiling fan moving jerkily above the bed. The bed was soiled with urine and faeces. Toxicology reports were completed within ten days and the cause of death was the ingestion of crushed seeds and leaves from jimsonweed, and traces of yellow oleander.

The pathologist's report stated the poisons were probably mixed with the curried king prawns which would have made it difficult for the victim to taste the poison. No trace of the poisons was found in the house. There wasn't an apparent motive for anybody to kill Mr Merriweather because he was perceived to be a decent human being. In the absence of other evidence, the police couldn't arrest any suspects. Stephen and his mother returned with the body to England where it was cremated and, several months later, the coroner returned an open verdict.

Stephen worked hard, studied hard, knowing this was his escape route. He could live life as the awesome one. Fellow students reported that he claimed to have a girlfriend back at home but she never visited. He studied the sciences and became particularly interested in information technology and the use of computers. He got very good grades in his subjects and went to study medicine at the University of Birmingham. After graduation, he started work as a trainee doctor in the East Midlands, registered on an online dating service, met and married a lonely Indian-born, Hindu biochemist working at the local university. They set up home in the north of the city.

She loved him. Was devoted to him. Worshipped him. Would do anything for him.

He acted normal. Was charming.

For most of the time...

CHAPTER 45

When things had quietened down, Superintendent Breedon asked to see me in his office first thing.

'Well done again, Rohan, for bringing the case to a conclusion. Just to let you know we found an abandoned white transit van just outside the city boundary a few days' ago. It had DNA traces of the killer and his victims.'

I smiled. He looked down, cleared his throat and then said, 'I hope your daughter's recovering well.'

'Thank you, Sir. Yes, she is. Are you putting me in for a commendation or a George Medal? Is that why we're meeting so early?' I said, half-joking.

'I'll explain more in a minute.' He shuffled a few papers on his desk. The soft aroma of cloves and cinnamon floated in the air between us. I wasn't sure what was going on. 'But first, just to confirm the cause of death for Merriweather or Shiva or whatever the hell he wanted to be known as, was a heart attack. Probably went into cardiac arrest due to the shock of being shot.' He stared down at his desk and cleared his throat. 'This is not easy for me. But I ... I have to suspend you from all duties with immediate effect.'

'What? You have got to be joking...'

'I wish I were. Orders from on high.'

'What orders? Why? By whom?'

'The Chief Constable. He's furious about unauthorised civilians being used in police operations. The TV crew flying the drones.'

'They helped save my daughter's life!'

'And apparently, you assaulted the suspect after he'd been shot. He had rights,' Superintendent Breedon continued.

'What about Geeta Mehta's rights, or Ayan Suleiman's or Joy Wheatley's or Robert Coleman's? Didn't they have rights?'

'I'm deadly serious. Sorry, Rohan. Got to follow orders.'

'The Eichmann defence, is it? Just following orders from on high.'

'*Inspector Sharma!* Don't compare me to Adolf Eichmann. I'm not a Nazi on trial for war crimes.' He was angry. But so was I.

He stared at me.

'What's become of you, Sir? I thought you supported me.'

'I tried to protect you as much as I could. I think you're a bloody good detective. But there're some things I can't protect you from. Although Mr Sandhu's been supporting us in public, privately he said to the Chief Constable the investigation was incompetently handled. We should have found his daughter long before. In any event, he maintains his daughter escaped without the help of the police.'

I stared at him. His deep blue eyes stared back.

'Please hand in your badge, mobile phone and any other official equipment you have, both here and at home, to HR. No communications with any other staff. And definitely not the media. Your suspension will remain confidential for the time being. If anybody asks, you're on extended leave to recover from the case. Please remain at home until further notice. The IOPC and the force will conduct an investigation into your handling of the case. I can't anticipate what their recommendations will be. Maybe a reprimand. But I have to warn you, dismissal is possible.'

I leapt to my feet and stormed out, banging the door hard.

The life raft had sailed with the superintendent on board, leaving me behind to drown.

I couldn't believe it. The euphoria of a few days ago had turned into one long nightmare. I went home and tried to eat but could not. Tried to sleep but could not. There was nobody I could talk to, except Fernando.

My life was in suspended animation. I stayed at home, getting up late, having long showers, coming downstairs, looking out of the lounge window as the world carried on, went for walks now and again but I didn't want to meet anybody I knew, didn't want to explain anything to anybody. The phone rang occasionally. I told my mum everything was fine at work, and I rang Yasmin most days to make sure she was doing okay. Spoke to Karan regularly too. Not much chat with Faye, who was still holding me responsible for what happened to Yasmin.

I kept going over and over the charges against me. Round and round it went in my head.

'Rohan's been a bad boy, Rohan's been a bad boy,' squawked Fernando.

I sat in the lounge, staring mindlessly at the TV, another long day, another lonely evening, a plate of untouched food on the tray on my lap.

'If I had been, Fernando, I could understand it. Why're some people such shits? Mmm?'

He looked at me and bobbed his grey head then lifted his tail and pooped on the newspaper covering the bottom of his tray.

I understood the sentiment.

My mobile rang on the third day of my isolation. It was seven thirty in the evening. A withheld number.

'Hello Inspector Sharma. This is Tanya Garrison, I'm the PA for the Police and Crime Commissioner. Sorry to ring so late but the Commissioner would like to see you in his office. One o'clock tomorrow lunchtime. Can you be here, please.'

Like I had a choice.

The Police and Crime Commissioner was an elected post and the Commissioner would be well connected, not only to local and national politicians but also with prominent business and so-called community leaders, including Mr Sandhu.

The heavy brigade had been called out. I wasn't sure if I'd survive this. They were all after me.

CHAPTER 46

'Would you like some tea, Inspector Sharma? I have proper Indian tea with masala, ground cardamom, cloves and cinnamon. Or you could have ordinary teabag tea. Or coffee, if you prefer.'

I looked up at Navin Patel as I sat in one of the soft chairs in his office, a round glass table between us. He sat opposite, his cluttered desk behind him.

'No thank you, Commissioner.' My posture was passive aggressive. Arms folded, legs crossed, looking straight at him.

'Something to eat? I've had Tanya order food. Samosas, pakoras, aloo chaat, and so on.'

'I'm not hungry, Sir. Can we get this over and done with, please? I'm not sure why you've asked to see me. Presumably to put pressure on me to resign or some such thing. I wondered whether to bring a representative of the Police Federation with me.'

He smiled, showing even white teeth. 'We'll get to the purpose of the meeting in due time, Inspector. But first, tell me a bit about yourself. Your personal life and so on.'

'You can look that up in my personnel file.'

'Please, Inspector Sharma. It would be good if you co-operated. The lead investigating officer from the Independent Office for Police Conduct is going to ring me about your case later. I wanted to meet you before I spoke to him.'

I stared at him for a moment. 'I'm not sure where this is going. Very well, if you want...' I told him where I was born, who my parents are, where I went to school, university, my time in the Met, when I came back to Leicester and so on.

'Any siblings?'

I hesitated. 'No.'

He raised one eyebrow. 'What about this case? Tell me about your involvement in it. Until the point where you rescued your daughter and the death of the suspect. You involved civilians in a police operation. They could've been injured or killed and the force would've been liable.'

'I asked for civilian help to protect my daughter. We don't have the necessary equipment because of budget cuts. Without the help of the TV station we wouldn't have located the car. We wouldn't have found the nuclear bunker and the cave beneath it. Yes, I did kick the bastard when he was down and it felt good. I will accept punishment for that, if you so wish.'

He smiled at me. 'Inspector Sharma, I would probably have done the same. But that doesn't make it right.' I was beginning to warm to him. 'I'll say what I have to say to the IOPC but they'll be more interested in policy matters from me. They'll speak to the Chief Constable and others about operational matters.'

That didn't sound good.

He looked at his watch. 'Thank you for your time, Inspector.'

'Where does this leave me, Commissioner?'

'We'll have to let things take their course. See what actions the Chief Constable and his deputy propose to take,' he said, getting up from his chair. 'For what it's worth, I do know what it's like for people like you and me. The constant battles for recognition, needing to be twice as good as any white person, being denied promotion…'

I stood, not sure what this meeting had been all about. As he offered me his hand, I noticed what looked like a tiny microphone on his desk. He saw me stare at it and said, 'No, I didn't record our meeting. But it comes in handy when you want to bug the offices of people who may be undermining you.'

I shook his hand and walked out.

As I drove home, I had no real idea what was going on. Maybe the Commissioner would put forward my case and support me. Or maybe he was a stickler for procedure. He had only been in post for a short while, not long before Geeta Mehta's body had been found.

Later in the evening, I poured a glass of cold Sauvignon Blanc, as a ready meal was heating in the microwave. I switched on the television because it was too quiet in the house and sat down.

My mobile pinged. I looked at it. A news story was breaking.

The Chief Constable of Leicestershire, Keith Francis Clayton, has unexpectedly decided to take early retirement with immediate effect. His deputy, Adam Brabourne, has announced a change in career and is also leaving the force with immediate effect. Navin Patel, the Police and Crime Commissioner, said that he accepted the request for early retirement and the resignation with great regret but fully understands the reasons behind them. He wished them well for the future.

What the hell was going on? There was nobody I could ring for further information. My mobile pinged. A text from a withheld number. *Who do you think sent you the anonymous text to protect your back during the investigation?*

I stared at the message for a long, long time.

I recalled the anonymous text message I received what felt like a lifetime ago, telling me that my report had been leaked by Nasreen Khan's office. I had approached Superintendent Breedon with the information and he had supposedly undertaken further investigations. Given his connections, the Commissioner must have known what was going on with Nasreen, her assistant Tracey Duffield, the fact that Frank Genner was her brother and her relationship with a member of my team, Neil Wainwright.

My recent experiences had such an unpleasant whiff. God knows what the senior officers in the force were up to, or what they said in the privacy of their offices.

Was I surprised at what had happened to me? Yes, I suppose I was. Still, some of those responsible for my predicament had been removed. But how many more were left behind? No, I mustn't think like that. I was sure Superintendent Breedon would ring before too long and tell me I'd been reinstated. All would be well again. Hallelujah! And I wasn't thinking of the Leonard Cohen song either.

I waited for the phone to ring. And waited some more.

Nothing.

It took two days before the phone rang late in the evening. It was one of the HR officers informing me I had been reinstated and would I return to work the following morning.

I switched off the mobile and stared at it for a long time. Not even a call from one of my superior officers.

'Look Ma! Top of the world!' I heard Fernando say.

'Yes, Fernando. Top of the world. Again.'

I looked at him in his cage. His big, round eyes stared back from under the fine grey and white gossamer feathers.

'Just you and me again, Fernando. Fancy a game of snakes and ladders?'

EPILOGUE

About three weeks after I had been reinstated, the days were getting longer and brighter, the weather milder and restless hearts much calmer. I was driving in the northwest of the county and heading back to base after interviewing a witness to a recent armed robbery. I was thinking about the case and admiring the rugged beauty of the Leicestershire countryside when my mobile rang.

After the usual pleasantries, David Bloom, the expert on snakes from the local zoo, who had tried to trap the cobra which I believed to be inside my house an eternity ago, asked me to visit him as soon as I could. His voice sounded urgent and because I was not too far away, I said I would be at the zoo soon.

He didn't say very much when I arrived and asked me to follow him to the Reptile House.

'What do you think of this, Inspector Sharma?' he asked, as we walked towards one of the big, glass cages.

The long, black body of the cobra glided down from the branches of the small, pruned tropical bushes and crawled among the lush, green leaves on the floor. The thick, glistening concentric muscles pushed the body forward, the dead black eyes and flickering tongue moving past the furry remains of an unfortunate small mammal, and then towards the glass panel.

I stared at it, mesmerised, and after a few moments, I said, 'I've seen this cobra before, David. Saw it when I came here early on in the case and spoke to Mr Beauchamp.'

'You saw a cobra, Inspector. But not this one.'

'You brought me here to show me a cobra?'

Within an arm's distance in front of us, the cobra stopped then raised its head. The black eyes bored into me. The hood expanded. The fangs bared. Venom dripped down. It suddenly lunged at me and I jumped back. Globules of venom slid down the reinforced glass.

'She really doesn't like you,' said David Bloom. 'This baby, I think, is the one we were searching for in your house.'

'What? It can't be.'

'Believe it or not, a park ranger in the Peak District spotted this one in the Monsal Dale area, not far from Bakewell. It was basking in the warmer weather and darted into a rabbit burrow when the ranger approached. She caught a glimpse of it and knew it wasn't an adder or a common grass snake. She had the good sense to get the fishing net from her four-by-four, placed it around the entrance to the burrow and then rang us. When I realised what it was and examined it here, we obviously wondered how and why it was wandering around in the open. And you, Inspector Sharma, are the common denominator.'

My heartbeat was still trying to settle down to a more regular beat. I didn't say anything as he continued.

'You, the killer, the cobra, the area. One of you could've brought it into Monsal Dale.'

'Well, it wasn't me. It just doesn't make sense, David. We found a dead cobra in the railway tunnel.'

He shrugged. 'Believe it or not, she's pregnant. If she'd not been caught, she could've laid about twenty eggs and we could've had... Well, doesn't bear thinking about. With global warming and climate change, many of them would have survived.'

'Bloody hell,' I replied. 'David, please don't say anything to anybody about how you acquired this snake. I don't want to cause a panic among walkers and ramblers.'

As I drove away, I was deeply troubled by this latest development. I thought and thought about the case. The snake was definitely dead. It couldn't be this one. Where the hell did this one come from then? A collector of exotic pets? Who'd discarded it near Bakewell? The coincidences that David Bloom had suggested were just too great.

I approached the outer ring road of the city after about half an hour, thoughts going round and round in my head.

Jesus Christ! That's it!

The killer must have used two cobras. Ayan Suleiman, the first victim, was killed by a cobra bite more than a year before Geeta Mehta. Stephen Merriweather was caught on CCTV in the Cambridgeshire warehouse after Flannery, the Irishman, and Ayan had both been killed. Why did he need another cobra? The first one must have died and its perfectly preserved body was found in the railway tunnel. The second one, which killed Geeta Mehta, this one at the zoo, must have been in the rucksack with him, along with his other gear. His death was due to a heart attack and we assumed that was the result of the trauma suffered from the gunshot wounds. No toxicology tests were undertaken, his body was quickly cremated and the ashes scattered. But it always bothered me that a supremely fit and healthy individual like him would succumb like that. The cobra must have bitten him as it became startled when the rucksack fell to the ground.

I remember Shep saying at the time he thought he saw something diving into a crevice in the corner of the large cave, but he wasn't too sure if the shadows were playing tricks with his sight.

I swung the Mercedes into a parking space and stared at the red brick wall in front of me. A steady drizzle on the windscreen activated the wipers, while soft classical music played on the radio. I remembered the desperate days during the height of the investigation when the killer had sent me a crude poem, stating he had placed the cobra inside my house and how it was going to get me. Well, there was poetic justice after all. The killer killed by his own snake! I turned off the engine, locked the car and walked towards the entrance of police headquarters.

A NOTE TO THE READER

Dear Reader,

Thank you taking the time to read the first DI Rohan Sharma thriller and I sincerely hope you enjoyed reading it. I grew up in Leicester and I still visit friends and family regularly from my current home not too far away. I am proud to call it my home city and, like with the story of many other communities there, my father moved to Leicester from Kenya. My mother and the rest of my siblings followed him several years later. As many of you will know, it is a vibrant and thriving city and an important part of its history and changing nature are reflected in the area of The Golden Mile to the north.

This is an exciting world and I wanted DI Rohan Sharma to be located there because it is his spiritual and cultural home, despite having lived in other parts and in other cities.

As regular readers in the genre will know, there are not many protagonists who are from Rohan Sharma's background. I wanted to write about an ordinary detective of South Asian origin who is trying to make a positive difference within his home city. But he also faces particular challenges because of his background and which he tries to overcome. I have not been a police officer but the professional life experienced by Rohan Sharma is similar to that experienced by others of a similar background. I also wanted to develop a complex character who straddles a multi-dimensional world and this is evident in many aspects of his life.

I undertake an enormous amount of research for each book, for example on history, geography, forensics and, in the case of *The Dance of Death*, the geological make-up of Leicestershire. I try to ensure that procedures for homicide investigations are accurate. If you find any factual errors, and if I am in a position to correct them without compromising the narrative, then I will do my best to respond to them.

Finally, if you enjoyed reading *The Dance of Death* could you please spare a few moments and post a positive review on **Amazon** and **Goodreads**.

Many thanks.

C V Chauhan

Sapere Books is an exciting new publisher of brilliant fiction and popular history.

To find out more about our latest releases and our monthly bargain books visit our website: **saperebooks.com**

Printed in Great Britain
by Amazon